THE EDGE OF VIOLENCE

THE EDGE OF VIOLENCE

WILLIAM W. JOHNSTONE
with
J.A. JOHNSTONE

KENSINGTON BOOKS
http://www.kensingtonbooks.com

KENSINGTON BOOKS are published by

Kensington Publishing Corp.
119 West 40th Street
New York, NY 10018

All Kensington titles, imprints, and distributed lines are available at special quantity discounts for bulk purchases for sales promotion, premiums, fund-raising, educational, or institutional use.

Special book excerpts or customized printings can also be created to fit specific needs. For details, write or phone the office of the Kensington Special Sales Manager: Attn. Special Sales Department. Kensington Publishing Corp, 119 West 40th Street, New York, NY 10018. Phone: 1-800-221-2647.

Kensington and the K logo Reg. U.S. Pat. & TM Off.

Library of Congress Card Catalogue Number: 2016945055

ISBN-13: 978-1-4967-0638-6
ISBN-10: 1-4967-0638-2
First Kensington Hardcover Edition: October 2016

10 9 8 7 6 5 4 3 2 1

Printed in the United States of America

CHAPTER 1

Decades ago—by Jupiter, a lifetime, an eternity—Jed Reno had laughed at Jim Bridger. When the old (by mountain-man standards) fur trapper, scout, and guide had teamed up with Louis Vasquez to build a trading post on the Blacks Fork of the Green River, Jed Reno had jokingly told Bridger that Bridger's nerves had finally frayed. That Bridger was selling out. That he was calling it quits. That, pushing forty years old, he was too long in the tooth to be traipsing over the Rocky Mountains, trapping beaver and fighting the weather, the wilds, and the Indians. While sharing a jug of Taos Lightning or some other forty-rod whiskey seasoned with snakeheads, tobacco, and strychnine, Reno had slapped Bridger on the back, and told him, "Well, you just enjoy your life of leisure. I'm sure you'll be richer than a St. Louis whiskey drummer with this here venture of yours."

"Runnin' a store, ol' hoss," Bridger had told him, "ain't as easy as you think it is."

"Balderdash," Reno had said.

Damnation, if Jim Bridger wasn't right.

As a bullet blew apart the copper-lined tin corn boiler, Reno ducked beneath the somersaulting axe handle that smashed the shelves behind him, sending metal-backed mirrors, salt and pepper shakers, scissors, axe blades, lanterns, baskets, jugs, matches, soaps, knives, forks, beads, containers of linseed oil, pine tar, and tins of tobacco flying every which way. He landed on the pile of pillow-ticking fabric and the woolen blankets he had not gotten around to stacking on the shelves, and he had to be thankful for that. At seventy years old, or something like that (Reno kept bragging that he had stopped counting after fifty), the onetime fur trapper wasn't as game as he used to be.

Which is why he had followed in Bridger's footsteps, and set up his own trading post about a dozen or so years ago on Clear Creek.

"You done a smart thing," Bridger had told him. "Make some money. Watch people go by. Drink whiskey. Smoke yer pipe. Easy livin'."

A hatchet fell with the axe handle, and the blade almost cut off Reno's left ear. A brass percussion capper bounced off his eyebrow. His good eye. An inch lower, and Jed Reno figured he might be wearing leather patches over both eyes.

Easy livin'? A body could get killed running a store.

He heard boots thudding across the packed earthen floor. His left hand reached up, found the handle to the hatchet that had almost split his head open, and jerked it free from the blankets and bolts of pillow ticking just as the bearded figure appeared on the other side of the counter.

A big man, bigger than even Reno, wearing fringed buckskin britches, black boots like those a dragoon or horse soldier might be wearing, collarless shirt of hunter green poplin, garnet waistcoat, and a battered black hat, flat-brimmed and flat-crowned. He also wore a brace of flintlock pistols in a yellow sash around his belly. One of those pistols was in his right hand.

Reno saw the hammer strike forward just as he flung the hatchet. Powder flashed in the pistol's pan, the barrel belched flame and smoke, and a .54-caliber lead ball embedded itself in the brown trade blanket rolled up on Reno's right.

"Horatio!" a voice yelled. Reno could just make out the voice as he sprang up, fell forward, and crawled toward the soon-to-be-dead Horatio, whose only replies were gurgles as he lay on his back as blood spurted from his neck like water from an artesian well.

The voice swore, and then barked at the third man who had entered Reno's trading post: "Sam, he's goin' fer Horatio's pistols. Get'm. Quick."

This time, Jed Reno heard clearly. The ringing from Horatio's pistol shot had died in Reno's ears. He dived the last couple of feet, ignoring the lake of blood that was ruining toothbrushes and staining wrapped bars of soap and the beads a Shoshone woman kept bringing him to trade for pork and flour, which, in turn, Reno sold to wayfarers from New York and Pennsylvania and Ohio and even Massachusetts who had been traveling so far that many of the ladies thought those beads from Prussia or someplace were prettier than rubies and garnets.

Reno jerked the second pistol from the dead man's sash. Horatio, Reno knew, was dead now because the blood no longer pulsed, but merely coagulated. Footsteps pounded, but not only coming from Sam's direction. The Voice was charging, too, and Jed Reno had only one shot in the flintlock he had jerked from Horatio's body. His left hand gripped the butt of the .54 Horatio had fired just moments before.

Sam appeared on the other side of the counter, where Reno had been refilling a barrel with pickled pig's feet when the three men entered his store.

Sam was the oldest of the rogues, with silver hair, a coonskin cap, and dark-colored, drop-front broadfall britches—which must have gone out of fashion back when Reno was a boy in Bowling Green, Kentucky—muslin shirt, red stockings, and ugly shoes. A man would have guessed him to be a schoolmaster or some dandy if not for the double-barrel shotgun he held at his hips.

The flintlock bucked in Reno's right hand, and just before the eruption of white smoke obscured Reno's vision, he saw the shocked look on Sam's face as the bullet hit him plumb center, just below his rib cage. With a gasp, Sam instantly pitched backward as if his feet had slipped on one of the bar-pullers, tompions, nuts, bolts, and vent and nipple picks that lay scattered on the floor. He touched off both barrels of the shotgun.

One barrel had been loaded with buckshot, the other with birdshot—as if he had been going out hunting for either deer or quail—and the blast blew a hole through the sod roof, and dirt and grass and at least one mouse began pouring through the opening, dirtying and eventually covering the ugly city shoes the now-dead Sam wore on his feet.

Reno rolled over, just as The Voice leaped onto the top of the counter. The pistol in Reno's left hand—the one he had jerked off the floor near the blood-soaked corpse of Horatio—sailed and struck The Voice in his nose. Reno caught only a glimpse of the revolving pistol The Voice held, because as soon as the flintlock crashed against the bandit's face, blood was spurting, The Voice was cursing, and then he was disappearing, crashing against the floor on the other side of the counter. Reno came up, hurdled the counter, and caught an axe handle on his ankles.

This time, Reno cursed, hit the floor hard, and rolled over, but not fast enough, for The Voice jumped on top of him and locked both hands around Jed Reno's throat.

Now that he had a close look at the gent, The Voice had more than just a rich baritone.

He had the look of a man-killer. Scars pockmarked his

bronzed face, clean-shaven except for long Dundreary whiskers, and his eyes were a pale, lifeless blue. Those eyes bulged, and the man ground his tobacco-stained teeth. The nose had been busted two or three times, including just seconds ago by Horatio's empty .54-caliber pistol. Blood poured from both nostrils and the gash on the nose's bridge. One of The Voice's earlobes was missing—as if it had been bitten off in a fight. He seemed a wiry man, all sinew, no fat, and his hands were rock-hard, the fingers like iron, clasping, pushing down against his throat, and cutting off any air.

He wore short moccasins, high-waisted britches of blue canvas with pewter buttons for suspenders that he did not don; a red-checked flannel shirt that was mostly covered by the double-breasted sailor's jacket with two rows of brass buttons on the front and three on the cuffs. The black top hat The Voice had worn had fallen off at some point during the scuffle.

But he was a little man, no taller than five-two, and a stiff wind—which was predictably normal in this country—would likely blow him over.

Jed Reno figured he was forty years older than The Voice, but he had more than a foot on the murdering cuss, and probably seventy pounds. Jed kept rolling over, and The Voice rolled with him. They rolled like the pickle barrel Sam had knocked over with his right arm as he fell to the floor in a heap and ruined the store's roof. Rolled against an overturned keg of nails and knocked over the brooms until they hit the spare wagon wheels leaning against the wall.

The Voice came up, pushing off one wagon wheel, then flinging another at Reno, who blocked it with his forearm, and sat up, slid over, and leaped to his feet.

Staggering back toward the sacks of flour, beans, and

coffee, The Voice wiped his mouth. The lower lip had been split. Reno tasted blood on his lips, but he didn't know if it belonged to him, The Voice, or the late Horatio.

"You one-eyed bastard." The Voice had lost much of its musical tone. More of a wheeze. But the little man was game.

He jerked a Bowie knife that must have been sheathed behind his back. The blade slashed out, but Reno leaped back. Again. The Voice was driving him, until Reno found himself against another counter.

The Voice's lips stretched into a gruesome, bloody smile.

The knife's massive, razor-sharp blade ripped through the flannel shirt; and had Reno not sucked in his stomach, he would be bleeding more than The Voice about this time. The blade began slashing back, but Reno had found the chains—those he sold to emigrants for their wagon boxes—and slashed one like a blacksnake whip. Somehow, it caught The Voice's arm between wrist and elbow, and The Voice wailed as the bones in the arm snapped, and the big knife thudded on the floor.

As The Voice staggered back, Reno felt the chain slip from his hand. He was tuckered out, too, and, well, it had been several moons since he had engaged in a tussle like this one.

The chain rattled as it fell to the floor, and The Voice turned and ran for the door.

Sucking in air, Reno charged, lowered his head and shoulder, and slammed into the thin man's side. They went through the open doorway, over what passed as a porch, and smashed through the pole where the bandits had tied their horses. Those geldings whinnied, reared, whined, and pounded at the two men's bodies. One, a black gelding, pulled loose the rest of the smashed piece of pine and galloped toward the creek. One fell in the dirt, rolled over, came up—and ran north, leaving its reins in the dirt and wrapped around the broken pole. The other backed up, reared, fell over, and came up. Reno couldn't tell which way he ran.

He was on his knees, spitting out dirt and blood, while wiping his eyes. He tried to stand, to find The Voice, when he tasted dirt and leather and sinew and felt his head snap back. Down he went, realizing that The Voice had kicked him. He landed, rolled, was trying to come up, when The Voice turned his body into a missile. His head caught Reno right in the stomach. Breath left his lungs. He caught a glimpse of the cabin he called a store flash past him as he was driven into the column that held up the covering over the porch.

The railing snapped. The covering collapsed, spilling more earth, debris, two rats, and a bird's nest. The two men kept moving. Past the cabin. Over dried horse apples. A fist caught Reno in the jaw. Then another. The Voice packed a wallop. Reno brought up his arms in a defensive maneuver, leaving his midsection open. A fist—it had to be The Voice's left, for his right arm was busted—hit twice. Three times. Reno fell against the woodpile, rolled over, hit the chopping block, and wondered if he had just busted a couple of ribs.

"Son of a bitch!" The Voice roared.

Reno blinked away sweat, blood, dirt, and dust. He saw the bandit standing next to the pile of firewood. He had a sizable chunk of wood in his left hand. Stepped forward, raising the club over his head.

Reno found the axe buried in the chopping block. Jerking it free, he flung it as he dived out of the way of the descending piece of wood.

He lay there, panting, played out, wondering why the devil The Voice didn't just finish him off. But that instant of defeatism vanished quickly. Reno rolled over, came up, and spit. He looked left, and then right, and saw his cabin, saw the woodpile, and finally his eyes focused on the moccasins and the ends of the blue pants on the dirt.

Neither the feet nor the legs were moving.

Wiping the blood and grime from his face, Reno limped to the pile. He had to lean against the wood for support, and breathing heavily, he looked down at The Voice, and the axe, and the blood.

"You . . . horse's . . . arse . . ." Jed Reno wheezed, and made a painful gesture at what remained of his trading post. "All three . . . of you . . . curs . . . dead . . . burnin' in . . . Hell. . . . Means . . . I gotta . . . clean this . . . mess . . . up . . . myself."

CHAPTER 2

Jed Reno salvaged what he could from the three dead men. The guns he could resell, even the two flintlock pistols, a matched set of A. Waters with walnut grips—antiquated as they were. Reno also found a nice key-wind watch, and wondered who the dead man stole that from, but decided that the odds highly unfavored the victim—if the victim hadn't been murdered—coming into Reno's store and seeing his watch for sale. The boots and shoes might bring a bit of a profit, or he could trade them to the Shoshone woman for some more beads, along with the hats. Not much use with the clothes, especially now that they were all pretty much hardened and stained with dried blood. Reno was lucky. He even found a few gold coins and some silver in the outlaws' pockets. He was alive, and figured he had made a pretty good trade with the three dead men.

It was shaping up to be one passable, profitable day. But Reno certainly didn't look forward to cleaning up the mess.

He loaded the corpses onto his pack mule, saddled his bay gelding, and led his cargo away from the post, crossing the tracks of the iron horse. He looked east at the town, still mostly tents, although a few sod houses and frame buildings had been put up. Then he looked west, following the iron rails and wooden crossties laid by the Irishmen working for the Union Pacific Railway. He could see black smoke puffing out of the stacks of a locomotive down the line. Back east, he heard the screeching and ugly hissing and saw more black smoke as another train made its way through the settlement, hauling more spikes, rails, crossties, fishplates, sledgehammers, and maybe even a few more workers.

It was a big undertaking, the transcontinental railroad, and as much as Jed Reno despised the damned thing, he had to admit it was progress. And had made him fairly wealthy.

He rode about five miles north, decided that was good enough, and dumped the bodies into an arroyo. Buzzards had to eat. So did coyotes. And one thing Jed Reno did not like about that railroad was the fact that since they had started laying track across this part of the territory, most of the game had left the country.

Reno could remember talking with Jim Bridger, Kit Carson, and other trappers. It hadn't been at one of the rendezvous because, the best Reno recalled things, those gatherings had ended by then. Maybe it had been at Fort Bridger. Talk had reached Bridger's trading post about a railroad being planned, one that would stretch across the country. Carson had shrugged. Bridger had allowed it was true. Reno had laughed and called it a fool's folly.

"How you gonna get one of them trains across these Rockies?"

"Don't underestimate man's ingenuity," Bridger had said.

"Where, by thunder," Carson had said, "did you pick up that 'in-gen-yoo-ah-tee' word?"

"And in winter?" Reno had said. "Can't be done."

Of course, a few years earlier, Reno would never have thought he would be seeing prairie schooners by the hundreds crossing the Great Plains and then across the mountains, bringing settlers from New York and Pennsylvania and other places foreign to a man like Reno, bound for the Oregon country and later California. Farmers. Merchants. Women and children and even milch cows and dogs. One gent had been hauling sapling fruit trees to start some orchards in the Willamette Valley.

Born in 1796 in what was now Bowling Green, Kentucky, Jed Reno had seen much in his day. His father then apprenticed Reno to a wheelwright up in Louisville, and Reno took that for longer than he had any right to before he stowed away on a steamboat and went down the Ohio and Mississippi rivers. New Madrid. Then St. Louis. And then he signed up with William Henry Ashley and set out up the Missouri River and became a fur trapper. That had been the life, maybe the best years Reno would ever live to see, but . . . well . . . nothing lasts forever. Beavers went out of fashion. Silk became favorable for hats. Now fur felt had become popular. By Jupiter, Reno had a hat of fur felt on his head now, too.

So when Reno happened upon some men who said they were surveyors, and when they paid him gold to do their hunting and scouting for them, Reno decided that Jim Bridger was a pretty wise gent after all.

Reno had only one eye, but few things escaped his vision, and he had two good ears. And to live in the wilds of the Rockies and Plains since 1822, you had to see, and you had to hear. Reno listened to the surveyors. And he watched.

Apparently, there were a number of surveys going on. A couple were down south, which made a lot of sense to Reno. Weather would be warmer, less hostile, across Texas and that desert country the United States had claimed after that set-to with Mexico. Another up north, somewhere between the forty-seventh and forty-ninth parallels north—whatever that meant. Reno wasn't sure England would care too much for that. Seemed to Reno that ownership of all that country up north was being debated between the king—or was it a queen now?—and whoever was president of these United States.

But the surveyors kept talking about a war brewing between the states. It had something to do with freeing the slaves or, to hear one of the men who spoke with a Mississippi drawl, it had to do with "a bunch of damn Yankees pushing us good Southern folk around." That got Reno to figuring that there was no way the United States would put up a railroad across country that might not be part of the United States in a few years. So he paid even closer attention to the surveyors.

Around 1853, some surveyors had been hauling their boxes and making their maps along what most folks called the Buffalo Trail, led by some captain named Gunnison. Something the surveyors called the Thirty-fifth Parallel Route. Reno figured that one died when Ute Indians killed some of the soldier boys, but he also met another one of those young whippersnappers who called himself an engineer. Went by the name of Lander, Frederick W. Lander, who worked for some outfit called the Eastern Railroad of Massachusetts. Lander told Reno that there could never be a railroad in the South, but a railroad had to connect the Pacific with the Atlantic because if war came—not among the states, but against a European power with a strong navy and mighty army—the United States would not be able to defend California without "an adequate mode of transit," whatever that meant.

So Reno decided to throw up a trading post along Clear Creek in the Unorganized Territory, take a gamble that Lander was right, and that eventually he'd be selling items to greenhorns stopping for a rest on this transcontinental railroad.

The post was a combination of logs—which he had

hauled down from the Medicine Bow country—and dirt. He had built it into a knoll that rose near the creek, digging out a cave that he knew would be cool enough in the summer and hot enough in the winter. The logs stuck out and made the post look more like a cabin, though, and gave it more of an inviting feel. Reno had never cared much for those strictly sod huts that looked, to him, like graves. This way, part log cabin, the post didn't seem completely like a grave to Jed Reno.

A few years later, Lander came back again, and this time he had some painter guy with him. That's when Jed Reno began feeling pretty confident about his investment. After all, if you hired some artist to paint some pretty pictures of you working, then you had to think that this was being documented for history.

Besides, even if it didn't happen, if the railroad went north or south or never at all, well, Jed Reno still had a place he could call home, that would keep him warm in the winter and cool in the summer. He had a good source of water, and could fish or hunt or get drunk or just sit on his porch—if you could call it a porch—and watch the sun rise, the sun set, the moon rise, the moon set. By Jupiter, he was pretty much retired anyhow, like ol' Bridger.

Of course, the war came—just like everyone had been talking about—and the surveyors and engineers stopped coming. Poor young Frederick Lander. He joined up to fight to preserve the Union, and from the stories Reno heard, the boy took sick with congestion of the brain and died somewhere in Virginia in 1862. Wasn't even shot or stuck with one of those long knives or blown apart by a cannonball. Reno wondered if that gent with the paintbrushes—some gent named Albert Bierstadt, who had dark hair, a pointed beard, and penetrating eyes—ever amounted to much.

* * *

Most of the blood inside the trading post had been covered with more dirt, which Reno packed down with his moccasins. The merchandise that had been busted, or soaked or stained with blood, he tossed into a canvas bag and hauled to the smelly dump that the settlers, who had not moved on with the railroad, had started up and was already attracting vultures and rats and coyotes and flies. But it was far enough away from Reno's post that the smell seldom bothered him too much.

He salvaged most of the merchandise, not that it really mattered. Since the railroad moved on, Reno had not seen much business, and since the trains brought only supplies and more workers, it wasn't like settlers were stopping to spend money on trinkets and blankets and tin cups. Reno began to doubt if he could ever sell anything else—not that he really cared one way or the other.

Fixing the hitching rail was probably the easiest thing, since he had hammers and plenty of nails and even some spare ridgepoles, located behind the post, he could use. The roof and the porch, however, were another matter. He had to use another pole to replace the one he and The Voice had knocked down, and then secure that with another pole, nailing one end to the vertical pole and ramming the other between two logs, which he then patched with chink.

After that, he had to climb onto the roof and throw enough brush down to cover the hole one of the bandits had made with his double-barreled shotgun. He could hear some of the dirt sprinkling from his ceiling and probably dirtying up his bolts of fabric and those nice woolen blankets. But he could beat the dirt out of them later. It would give him something to do.

While he was still on the roof, he heard a couple of shots from the settlement, which some citizens were starting to call a town. Reno ignored that, kept busying himself with the roof, and then piled dirt on top of the hole. He was satisfied with his handiwork. Of course, he had built a few cabins in his day up in the Rockies when he needed a place to winter, and some things Mr. Sneed, the wheelwright, had taught him back in Louisville still registered in his brain.

He had just finished, and was making his way to the ladder he had fashioned, when he spotted the dust. Reno remained on the rooftop, and checked the loads in the revolving Colt's pistol he carried these days—another sign of progress, he told himself. An Army Colt could shoot six times before you had to reload it. Back in Reno's day, a man had to do his job with only one bullet. Else he was dead.

Four riders, coming from the settlement. Four on horseback. A couple others followed afoot.

Tenderfeet.

Reno sighed. He hoped those fool city folks weren't coming to complain about him using their dump. Or maybe someone had found the bodies of the three men he had killed and were out to investigate another killing in Violence.

CHAPTER 3

Sitting on the roof, he filled his pipe, struck a lucifer against his thumbnail, and brought the match to the bowl, cupping his hands to protect the flame from the wind. Although he sold various tins of all types of tobacco, Jed Reno still preferred his homemade mix. The Shoshones called it *äñ'-ka-kwi-nûp,* but among the fur traders, it was known as kinnikinnick. Shavings from willow bark and crushed sumac, mugwort, sage, and a little carvings from his plug tobacco. It relaxed him. Just in case, though, the townsfolk weren't coming to chat, he drew his Colt revolver and laid it on the roof, behind his back, and out of sight.

They took their time, even those riding horseback. That could mean that the settlers riding meant to keep those afoot company. Or it could mean that not a one of them felt any pressing need to see Jed Reno. By the time they came close enough that Reno could make out their faces, he had finished his smoke. So he tapped the pipe against one of the cottonwood logs that helped hold his roof up, and stuck the pipe in the pocket of his buckskin jacket.

"Halloooo, Jed!" one of the men on horseback called out. "All right if we come for a talk?"

"Come ahead," Reno said. He waited on the roof.

The one who led the committee was Jasper Monroe. Maybe five-eight, fair-skinned, gray-eyed, and potbellied. By trade, he was a barber, and he had been pressed into undertaking. Both jobs, though mostly the latter, kept him busy—especially when the railroaders got paid and, after baths and shaves, took to drink. Jasper Monroe hailed from Davenport, Iowa, or so he said. Kept talking about the Mississippi River, how green things got in Davenport, and how humid, and saying things like he couldn't believe how dry things were in this territory, or windy.

Although he always held his tongue, Jed Reno wanted to warn that greenhorn that he hadn't seen wind or dry yet—but just wait. Having spent a few of his formative years in New Madrid—on the Mississippi River—Reno would grant that this territory wasn't muggy or sticky or anything close to humid, even when Clear Creek flooded.

Monroe had been appointed or elected or volunteered— Reno didn't know or care which—the mayor of the settlement. Another of the men on horseback was Eugene Harker, a freedman who basically helped Jasper Monroe by keeping him supplied with hot water when he was barbering or by emptying the spittoons. When Monroe took to his undertaking duties, Harker did the grave digging and singing a hymn and acting as the official mourner. Almost always, except for Monroe, the black man was the only person at the funeral—unless you counted the deceased. Harker had been laying track for the Union Pacific before he decided to draw his time and stick around and make a home in this windswept country. He could sing, though, a deep bass, soulful. His voice carried all the way to Reno's post, unless the wind blew the other direction.

The other two men, riding sorrel mares, one saddled, the other bareback, were Cutter—Reno couldn't recall the man's first name—and Henry Yost. They had partnered in a hotel, which only did business when some big gent from the Union Pacific stopped by.

They had hauled in framed lumber and put up a false front to make the log cabin look a bit classy—until you stepped inside. Well, the owners swore that once the town got on its feet, they would make their hotel the grandest establishment between Omaha and San Francisco, which caused Jed Reno to wonder just how many hotels were there right now between Omaha and San Francisco. Probably not one.

Now that the tracks and most of the workers had moved on west, there wasn't that much business in town, which had stopped the hostlers' expansion plans. Cutter, in a broadcloth suit covered with a linen duster and stovepipe hat, rode the saddled sorrel. Henry Yost, in a plaid sack suit and no hat, came along bareback. He had amused Reno with his riding, bouncing this way and that, sliding left and right, but somehow managing not to fall off the fat mare. When they finally stopped in front of Reno's post, Henry Yost slid off the horse's back, began stretching his legs and back, rubbing his buttocks, and wiping his sweaty face and bald head with a silk handkerchief.

The two men afoot called themselves land speculators: a fat man from Boston named Aloysius Murden and his skinny, bespectacled partner, Duncan Gates. Gates also owned a mercantile and served as the postmaster, since the mail was all dumped at his store. Murden was a federal land agent, and the real estate agent for any lots bought in the town of Violet—often referred to by the town's residents as Violence.

"Fixing your roof, Reno?" Gates asked.

Idiot, Reno thought. "Admirin' the view," he said.

Murden turned around and looked back at the settlement. "It is pretty, isn't it?"

Reno answered by spitting from his perch. The place looked like Hell. When he had put up his trading post, you couldn't see anything but sagebrush, prairie grass, hills, and distant mountains. Maybe a Cheyenne or Shoshone Indian every once in a blue moon. Buffalo grazed alongside antelope. Now the damned terrain was littered with tents and trash and sod huts and shoddily constructed cabins. Iron rails and wooden crossbeams and leveled land. And one hill dotted with wooden crosses, many of which had already toppled over from winds and rains.

"There's been another killing, Mr. Reno." Jasper Monroe's statement caused Murden to turn around, frown, and stick his hands inside the deep pockets of his striped britches.

Reno studied the six men and leaned back, adjusting his right hand so that it rested closer to his Colt revolver. He carefully shot a glimpse toward the arroyo and trash heap, where he spotted a few buzzards swooping in as others flew off, having filled their bellies for the time being on the dead thieves Reno had left there.

"Actually, two." Monroe corrected himself.

Reno gave the mayor a closer look. Unless the fool couldn't count . . .

"One at Slade's," Monroe said. "Another at O'Rourke's."

With a nod, Reno brought his right hand away from his revolver, and rested it on his buckskin trousers. They weren't here about the men he had killed after all.

"Good business for you and Harker," Reno said.

The mayor frowned. "This is serious, Mr. Reno. Violet has a chance to be a beacon on the U.P. line. This is fine country. We'll be getting more and more settlers here soon. But if men like Slade and O'Rourke . . ."

With a yawn, Reno looked at his fingernails and hands. Needed a good scrubbing. He let the mayor speak his mind, but paid no attention to anything the city dude had to say.

That two men had died in Slade's bucket of blood and O'Rourke's gambling den came as no surprise. The hilltop cemetery had been populated mostly by men who died in one of those—what had Henry Yost called them? Dens of antiquity?"

Micah Slade had fought on the losing side during the War of the Rebellion, and came west from Alabama with a patch over one eye and a left arm that just hung uselessly at his side. Jed Reno, of course, had only one eye himself, and no one called Reno an invalid. No one called Micah Slade one, either, unless he wanted to die. He dressed in black, wore a brace of Navy Colts stuck butt forward inside a green sash, and served whiskey and beer in the front room of his sod saloon, and ran some sporting girls in a hog ranch right behind his place.

Paddy O'Rourke came from County Cork, by way of New York City, where—if you believed anything Cutter said—he killed a policeman during the draft riots in '63 and fled west. Apparently—again, this came from Cutter—O'Rourke had run some gang in the Irish slums of the city, and had been following the railroad at every Hell on Wheels camp since Omaha. He employed ten cardsharpers and confidence men who fleeced the Irish and black workers for the railroad at the faro layouts and roulette wheels and poker tables in his place, which wasn't anything but a tent made of canvas and poles, although he said he planned on making things permanent here. He was hurrying, too, because O'Rourke was no fool. Fall had settled on Clear Creek, and winter would not be far behind—not in this part of Dakota Territory.

"We want Violet to become the greatest city in the territory," Mayor Monroe said.

Reno stopped looking at his dirty skin and fingernails and trained his one eye on the barber. "You mean Violence."

Which was what everyone called that Hell on Wheels practically since the rails first arrived, the first tents went up, and the first man got himself shot dead.

"I mean Violet, sir." The mayor was already stumping for the next election, like there would be another election. "If we do nothing to stop the bloodshed, sir, Cheyenne will win and Violet will be second to that Hell on Wheels in this part of the country."

Cheyenne lay down the railroad tracks about twelve miles east. Back in July, General Grenville M. Dodge, heading a U.P. survey crew, had platted out the railroad camp as a city, at a place Reno had always called Cow Creek Crossing. They named it Cheyenne, after the Indians who lived in the region. Reno had not been to see the city that had sprung up first as a bawdy, violent railroad camp and had kept growing, once the tracks reached the city a few weeks ago.

Most Hell on Wheels camps moved with the railroad, but Cheyenne had always been considered a permanent place, a city that would last as long as the iron rails, maybe even longer. Violet—which everyone except the mayor had corrupted to Violence—wanted to steal Cheyenne's glory.

"Homesteaders won't settle here as long as those blights operated by those two ruffians control Violence," Mayor Monroe said, not even realizing he had slipped and called his town by its more accurate name.

"Homesteaders?" Jed Reno laughed. "You think you can farm this country? Mister, it's November, by my reckoning, getting close to December. You've had the mildest fall I've ever seen in this country. But you wait till winter comes hitting us with full force."

"Our wives, sir, and our children are coming in on one of the next westbound trains." That came from Henry Yost.

"It's true," Harker confirmed.

"You're bringing in womenfolk and kids?" After fetching his Colt and holstering the weapon, Reno climbed down the ladder. "To this country? With winter coming on?"

"Not only that," Duncan Gates said, "but by the first of January, we expect the arrivals of the first colonists for the Clear Creek Emigration Company."

"The what?"

"Homesteaders, sir," Aloysius Murden sang out excitedly. "Adventurous spirits who, after having toiled in the harsh climes of Europe, are leaving Boston for a new life in the West, to better themselves, better our country, and better this land."

Reno leaned against the wall and shook his head.

"You gents are all daft."

"I beg to differ, sir," Mayor Monroe said. "We are dreamers. And we dream of a better country. We dream of establishing a great town, and since the Rebellion has been put down, and the Negroes like Mr. Harker here freed, you are about to witness, Mr. Reno, a great migration of settlers."

"I witnessed that already, bub." Those prairie schooners, most of them bound for Oregon, had ruined this country. At least, that's how Jed Reno saw things.

"A trickle," Murden said. "Think how fast railroads can bring settlers. This whole country will be populated with whites." He remembered Harker next to him. "And Negroes."

"Once," Duncan said, "the Indians are all buried."

Which got a chuckle from Cutter.

Reno shook his head.

"And Violet," the mayor said, "will replace St. Louis and San Francisco as the gateways to the American West."

"I see." Yeah, Jed Reno saw all right. He saw that these white men from back east were all crazy.

"But we need help, sir," Jasper Monroe said. "We need to bring law to our fair city."

City? If those fools didn't start building something substantial, they would be blown away and buried underneath mountains of snow. Reno put his hands on his hips. They wanted him to do something. Something foolish. He waited.

"We need a town marshal, sir. We want you for that job."

Reno blinked. He spit. He blinked again. Then he laughed. It was a great belly laugh, something he had not enjoyed for months, maybe even years, perhaps not since he had gotten drunk with Jim Bridger and shared old lies and made up some new ones about trapping and fighting and drinking.

"Son," Reno said when he had recovered, "I am seventy-one—I mean . . . I am fifty-nine years old. Too long in the tooth to become some lawman wearing a tin star or something like that."

"We need help!" Harker sang out. "Those were not railroaders murdered the other night. One was an executive with the Union Pacific itself. The other was a priest. A priest, sir, bound to save the souls of the heathen Cheyenne redskins."

Reno frowned. A man of the cloth, some black robe, murdered at one of those "blights." It brought back memories of Pierre-Jean De Smet. Reno remembered when old Bridger had, along with Andrew Drips and Henry Fraeb, brought the priest to the Green, the Siskeedee-Agie, back in 1840. The last great rendezvous of fur trappers. De Smet had performed a mass. Reno wasn't Catholic himself—he didn't know exactly what he'd call himself, maybe a "heathen," like the Cheyennes—but he had admired De Smet's grit and gumption. The black robe had gone to the Gros Ventre Range, to preach the word to a thousand or maybe more Indians: Flatheads, Nez Perce, and Pend d'Oreilles.

"A priest?" Reno said.

"Yes," Cutter answered. "A man of the cloth. Who stood outside O'Rourke's awful establishment trying to keep those wastrels from the railroad from damning their eternal souls."

"Shot in the back," Harker said, bowing his head. "Twice."

"And then some fiend robbed the dead man of God of his crucifix and Bible," Monroe added.

"So you see," Murden said, "we need law. And we need it now."

"Help us." Monroe practically begged.

Reno studied all six men, looked them in the eye. Fools they might be, yet he could not doubt their sincerity.

He sighed. "I'm sorry, gents. I just ain't no marshal. Don't know nothing about lawing."

Every single one of those men's heads dropped. Their shoulders sagged.

Reno hated himself. "Well . . ."

They looked up, eyes filled with hope.

"I mean . . . maybe . . . well . . . I might know somebody who could help you out, though. Maybe. You'd have to get word to him. And . . . well . . . he's just a kid."

"A kid?" Monroe cried out incredulously.

Reno spit. "Well . . . no . . . I knowed him when he was just a shirttail young'un, greener than spring grass. But I don't reckon you'd call him a kid no more. Not by a damned sight."

CHAPTER 4

Tim Colter kicked free of the stirrups as soon as the report of a rifle caught his ears and the blood bay gelding shuddered and fell in midstride of a lope. As he sailed to the left of the trail, Colter caught a glimpse of the six-year-old gelding somersaulting horrifically down the ruts, sending up dust and grass and blood before the horse slammed into a tree. Then Colter hit the ground.

He came up, spitting out grass and blood from his busted bottom lip. A bullet trimmed several locks of hair. Blinking, he dived to his right as another bullet buzzed past him. That shot came from Colter's left. The first shot—since his horse had been shot out from under him—had barked out from the woods straight ahead. Likely from the same gunman who had killed Kilroy, the bay he had paid seventy-five dollars for just four months back.

Colter kept rolling until he landed in a depression, which would offer him a bit of protection from either of those two gunmen. But not from anyone behind him.

The first bullet ripped the collar of his Mackinaw. The second burned his side. Spinning around, but keeping his head low enough so the first two squat assassins couldn't blow his head off, Colter saw the little line shack maybe thirty yards off the trail. He also saw the man in Mexican denim britches and a checked shirt running at him. White smoke obscured the man's face, but only momentarily, as the Henry repeater belched and sent another lead slug in Colter's direction. That bullet went high and wide. It was, Colter knew, difficult for anyone to hit a man, even a sta-tionary one, while running, gasping, jacking the repeater's level, and firing from the hip. But even an idiot could get off a lucky shot—and the running man was covering a lot of ground, closing in on Colter quickly.

He had already cocked the pistol in his right hand. In fact, the revolver was in his hand even as he was leaping from the saddle, in midair, trying to see who the hell was shooting at him.

As if he didn't know.

The gun bucked in Colter's hand, and the charging man let out a little scream as he pitched to the left, and sent the Henry crashing into the grass maybe fifteen or twenty yards in front of him.

Behind him, maybe behind one of those boulders, some-one let out an oath, and followed that curse with two shots that kicked sand onto the brim of Colter's black hat.

How the hat stayed on his head after leaping from a dead horse, rolling across the grass and rocks, and being shot at from practically every direction would remain a mystery.

Coming to his feet, Colter ran, shifting the revolver to his left hand, bending forward, and making a swipe at the stock of the Henry rifle as he ran past it. His fingers man-aged to graze the walnut stock, but he couldn't quite grasp it. And he knew he had no time, no chance, to make a sec-ond try.

The man with the Henry was lying faceup. Tim Colter's slug had caught him right in the center of the chest—hardly any blood—and the outlaw had lived only long enough to make that little cry before leaving this cold morning for the warmer climes of Hades. Colter got a good look at the dead man's face—enough for him to know who was shooting at him, as if he had not already made a pretty good guess.

Old Man Carter. He wouldn't be robbing any more banks with Stewart Rose's gang ever again. Unless Hell had banks.

A bullet spanged off a rock in front of Colter. Two more dug up grass at his heels. His lungs burned from the cold air as he ran toward the line shack.

His side felt sticky. Apparently, that bullet had done more than just burn him, but Colter figured it was only a scratch, just a minor irritation. If the rest of Stewart Rose's boys were doing the shooting, Colter would have much bigger irritations shortly. He needed to make it to that line shack.

Another bullet knocked off his hat. Now that he got closer, Colter wondered if that shack would provide any cover. With those gaping holes between the picketed slabs of wood, the place was well ventilated, but it had a door. And it was the only thing that might keep Tim Colter alive.

The door swung open, and Young Man Carter, the Old Man's behemoth son, came out with a double-barrel shotgun. Young Man Carter, who wore a dirty beard that stretched halfway to his belly, grinned a toothless smile, as he thumbed back both hammers.

Colter shot the fool and watched him crash against the front of the shack. The big man managed only to knock off one wooden shingle from the roof as he slid to his left and landed atop the big scattergun.

Colter swore. Young Man Carter weighed a few pounds less than an Oregon steer. There was no way Colter would be able to roll over the body to get the shotgun, and a quick glance told Colter that the dead outlaw carried no sidearm. A bullet splintered part of the door, but Tim Colter had reached it by then, and he pulled it shut.

He started to look for a bolt—if a bolt would do any good—when a muzzle blast almost blinded him and the roar of a massive rifle deafened him. Tim dropped to his knees, and blinking back spots of orange and red and purple and white, which flashed and burned his eyeballs, he squeezed the trigger, pointing his pistol in the general direction of where the gun blast had almost blown his head off.

"Arrgggghhh!"

Wood splintered. A heavy crash. An "oomph."

Silence did not last long.

Several gunshots popped the walls of the shed. However, despite how weak the building looked, the wood was not rotting, and none of the bullets managed to pierce the walls, although two or three went through the holes in those walls and dug up the dirt floor.

Colter could see now. He saw the soles of the boots of the dead man who had shot at him at point-blank range, somehow missing with the .50-caliber Sharps rifle. Colter had managed a scratch shot that hit the man in the belly and sent him crashing through the west wall. That man, Blondie Kidd—Colter could tell from the dead man's corn-colored hair—still clutched the Big Fifty, and Colter's shot had blown him too far out of the shack for Colter to risk a grab at the rifle. Which was empty anyway, Sharps being single shots.

Colter ran his free hand to his side. He felt the tackiness of blood, and despite the cold, the wound burned. Colter was also sweating. He came up and slid to his right so that he no longer would make an inviting target for someone on the west side of the cabin. Blondie had made a pretty big hole in the wall for such a slender young punk.

Once he positioned himself against the door—the strongest part of the cabin, since the door had been made of hardwood and had no gaps for bullets to come through—he tried to figure his chances of getting out of this mess alive.

Zero.

That didn't take long, and math and statistics had never been Tim Colter's best subjects.

CHAPTER 5

"Colter!"

He recognized the voice.

"Tim Colter," Stewart Rose bellowed. "I've been doing some ciphering."

Colter wet his lips. "Without your abacus?"

Stewart Rose had killed sixteen men—if you believed the wanted dodgers—robbed twelve banks, four stagecoaches, at least one omnibus, and, in Virginia City, Nevada, he and his gang of cutthroats had even robbed a gambling parlor before riding off and stopping at a brothel to rob it, too. But the outlaw appreciated a sense of humor.

He laughed.

"You got style, Colter," Rose shouted. "I'll give you that much. You got style. Yes, sir. Plenty of style. But you got three shots left."

Colter glanced at the heavy revolver in his right hand. He thumbed back the hammer.

"What makes you think I haven't reloaded?" Colter called out.

"Because my left boot's pressing your powder flask into the dirt."

Colter reached into a pocket on his jacket, but all he felt inside was scratchy wool.

"And everybody knows you never have trusted paper cartridges."

Colter had to smile. "What else do you know about me?"

"Not a thing, Marshal. I just know about guns. A Colt and a Remington hold only six beans in the wheel, pard. And that's if you ain't caring too much for safety. Most folks keep an empty chamber under the hammer. But I figure, you on our trail, you'd shun safety. So I say you got three shots left."

"What if I have a Paterson Colt?" Colter said. He glanced through the openings, but no sudden movement—no unnatural things like flashes of sunlight from spurs or knives or revolvers . . . no red flannel or pale muslin. Just the normal sights of late November in the state of Oregon.

Stewart Rose laughed again. "Then you'd have only five shots anyway, which would reduce you to two."

"Two or three shots might be all I'd need," Colter said.

"But I got four men left with me. And then there's me. And I don't die easy."

He heard the click—wear a star long enough and you recognized that metallic sound of a Colt revolver being cocked—and caught a glimpse of flannel, though it was green, not red, and therefore harder to spot. Tim Colter brought the revolver up as the man in the green flannel shield-front shirt swung around and fired through the opening Blondie Kidd had left in the west wall.

The bullet slammed into the door and sent splinters digging into Colter's cheek. But his own gun bucked in his hand, and Green Flannel fell to his knees, spit out bloody phlegm, almost fell forward atop Blondie Kidd's body, but somehow managed to push himself up, and then bring up the Remington revolver in his left hand.

Left hand. Then that would be Drew Livermore. Colter aimed carefully, steadying the heavy revolver with his free hand, and squeezed the trigger again. The pistol belched smoke and Drew Livermore fell backward, sending his Remington sailing far behind him. The outlaw kicked twice, shuddered, and farted as he died.

The shack now smelled of sulfur, and smoke irritated Colter's eyes almost as much as the sweat. His ears rang for a while, but slowly that noise died down until all Colter could hear was the wind moaning through the cracks in the shack's walls.

"Drew didn't die too easy, neither," Stewart Rose said. "Which means you got just two shots."

Colter eared back the revolver's hammer. "And you're down to four men, counting you."

"And here we come, Marshal."

It was no bluff. After seven weeks on Stewart Rose's trail, that was one thing that Deputy U.S. Marshal Tim Colter had learned about the man he was pursuing. Stewart Rose never bluffed. He was a cutthroat, a killer, a robber, a thief, and a plunderer, but he was a man of his word. Hailed from Virginia, the dodgers and the writ in Colter's other pocket all said. Virginians held honor up there with God, mothers, and Robert E. Lee.

Most of Rose's gang had ridden with Mosby's boys in the war, raiding for the Confederacy. Tim Colter had never heard that fabled Rebel Yell.

Until now.

Oh, Colter had joined up to put down the rebellion and free the slaves. Back in 1862, he had tendered his resignation as a deputy marshal to his boss, Dolphes B. Hannah, and ridden to Fort Walla Walla, where he quickly found himself elected lieutenant of Company D, 1st Oregon Volunteer Cavalry. But he missed all the glory and fame and carnage that had taken place back east. About as far east as Colter had gotten was over to Idaho Territory in the summer of '65, well after Robert E. Lee and all the other

Rebel generals had surrendered. Colter had seen only action against Indians, and little of that. Mostly, he had led
troopers on patrols along the emigrant roads to protect
the settlers. And for much of Colter's duty, he had been
sick with various complaints, seeing only bedpans and a
drunken doctor at Fort Walla Walla, Fort Vancouver, and
chasing Indians—but seldom seeing any at Coos Bay and
along the Malheur River until finally being mustered out
early in '66.

Stewart Rose and his boys were veterans of some of the
most savage fighting the United States had ever seen. And
now they were screaming as they charged the line shack.

Shrieking, that unnerving, earsplitting Rebel Yell. Sound-
ing like a bunch of sick coyotes. But coming from three of
the shack's four sides. On foot. A bullet punched a hole in
a slat over Colter's head. He ducked, saw the figure coming from the west, so Colter ran out to meet him, ducking
as he made his way through the rough hole in that wall.
The pistol came up as another shot blew a hole through
the tail of his jacket. It roared, and the man staggered, still
clutching his revolver in his right hand, weaving like a
drunkard. Another bullet buzzed over Colter's head. Again
he thumbed the hammer, aimed, and fired. The weaving
man collapsed in a heap. Colter turned to see two other
men running at him from the road.

Both men held repeating rifles, the one with the checked
trousers shooting a Spencer, the one in the red duck pants
holding another Henry.

Colter brought the pistol up. His first shot missed. He
had rushed his shot, jerked the trigger, a foolish mistake
that often cost a lawman his life. But Colter had always
been lucky. The Spencer's next round merely nicked the
side of his head. He blinked back pain, shook his head to
clear his vision and his mind, and squeezed one shot that

dropped the man with the Spencer, right in the forehead. Somehow the man fell forward and to his left as he died, and tripped the guy carrying the Henry.

On the other side of the cabin, Stewart Rose cursed, but kept on charging, his twin Remingtons punching holes that splintered the shack.

Ignoring the leader of the gang for just a moment, Colter aimed the smoking-hot revolver. The man who had tripped came up, searched for his rifle, but saw it was well out of his reach. Thus, he reached down and jerked a Navy Colt from his waistband.

His yellow shirt exploded crimson, and the man fell back.

"What the hell!" Stewart Rose yelled. "You ain't got two guns!"

Colter leaped back through the shack's door. As he did, he worked the big pistol, flipping the lever that moved the pivoting striker. He dropped to his knee, tightening the grip on the curved handle of the revolver, bringing up his left hand to steady the big pistol.

Stewart Rose rounded the corner, brought up one of his revolvers, his face masked by anger and confusion.

The grapeshot barrel of Colter's handgun sent a twenty-gauge charge that, at this range, practically tore Stewart Rose in half.

Tim Colter held the smoking gun over Stewart Rose's body. The outlaw lay on the dead grass, shuddering, spitting out blood, practically choking to death on his own blood. His stomach was a bloody mess, but his eyes managed to focus on Colter.

"It's not a Colt. It's not a Remington." Colter held up his pistol for the dying man to see. "It's a LeMat. Nine-shot cylinder," Colter explained. "Forty-two caliber. Plus a smoothbore secondary barrel. Sixty-caliber." The smoothbore barrel had sent the twenty-gauge buckshot into Stewart Rose's middle.

Somehow, Stewart Rose managed to shake his head. Underneath all that blood, he appeared to smile.

"Good thing you didn't have one more man with you, Rose," Colter said. "Because—now—I am empty."

Stewart Rose might even have laughed just before his eyes glazed over and his chest stopped rising and falling.

The LeMat was relatively new, designed in New Orleans by a gunsmith and doctor named Jean Alexander Francois LeMat, with a push by an army major named P.G.T. Beauregard, who went on to resign his commission when the Southern states started pulling out of the Union. Beauregard joined the Confederate Army as a general.

Although a few of the massive weapons—weighing more than three pounds before they were loaded and with an overall length of 13¼ inches—had been produced in Philadelphia, most of the LeMats were manufactured in Belgium and France before they went back to Birmingham, England, to be proofmarked and shipped to the Confederate States of America—if the ships could run the Union blockades.

Blue-steeled with checkered walnut grips, it was a pretty weapon, and quite deadly. Although a few generals, like J.E.B. Stuart had carried LeMats in the war, it had never been popular among the regular soldiers. Cavalry troopers preferred to carry two or more revolvers rather than a heavy LeMat. And the Union blockade prevented too many of the pistols reaching Southern hands.

Apparently, John H. Mosby never carried a LeMat. If he had, maybe the late Stewart Rose might not have been quite as confident before his bloody departure.

* * *

It took a while for Deputy U.S. Marshal Tim Colter to get everything in order. He bandaged his wounds—neither serious—the best he could, but only after he had reloaded the LeMat, both the .42-caliber cylinder with its nine rounds, and the twenty-gauge underneath barrel with more buckshot. That took longer because he had to find his copper powder flask.

Always honest, so to speak, Stewart Rose had not been lying when he said he had been standing on the flask. Tim also collected his saddlebags, rain slicker, saddle, blanket, bedroll, and bridle from Kilroy. He wasn't about to leave a horse like that, a seventy-five-dollar horse, for wolves and bears and crows, so he covered it with dirt and rocks, having found a shovel inside the shack.

By the time he had found where the outlaws had stashed their horses, it was getting too dark to travel, so Colter took advantage of the line shack, and dragged all of the dead men inside it. He found most of the money that had been taken from the bank in Grants Pass, which Colter figured would make everyone in that little town happy.

He mounted the best horse, a black stallion that wasn't anything close to the now-dead and partially buried Kilroy, and rode up the trail a while, then turned and picked a path down to the Rogue River, where he bathed his wounds, re-dressed his bandages, and drank greedily. He also managed to catch a couple of fish, which he took back with him to the line shack and fried for supper.

The outlaws had also carried hardtack, jerky, and corn dodgers, so Tim Colter ate like a king that night. The fire was warm, and cut the night's chill, and the coffee Colter had packed in his own saddlebags made him relaxed.

He slept well, got up before dawn, heated up the coffee and the leftovers for breakfast, and then wrapped the dead men in their bedrolls, strapping them on the horses, two dead men for a horse. He rigged a lead rope and set out east to Grants Pass, leading the horse with the dead men, and those with only saddles and packs.

It snowed twice before he got out of the high country, and carrying that load, it took Colter five days before he rode into Grants Pass. Luckily, the weather remained cold—though the snow hadn't followed him out of the higher elevations—so the bodies of the dead outlaws did not stink too much when he left them at the constable's office in Grants Pass.

He filed his report with the constable, a bespectacled man named Talent, and the local judge, a fat man with a forked beard who called himself Malcolm Prine. He gave a traveling journalist and artist named Vale Baker an interview, even let the fellow draw his likeness and he kept a sketch of him leading his strange cargo into the town for himself. Vale Baker said he contributed to *Harper's Weekly*. Colter gave him an address to send a copy of the magazine if it ever got published.

Colter doubted if it would.

And after having the dentist examine his wounds, and shaking the banker's hand for the umpteenth time, Deputy U.S. Marshal Tim Colter left Grants Pass on the black stallion he decided might as well replace Kilroy.

He rode north, roughly 140 miles to Eugene. Then turned west and rode through the thick forests for another sixty miles.

He rode home.

CHAPTER 6

Home.

It didn't feel like home for Tim Colter. It had not for some time now.

Waves crashed against the rocks, spraying him with the salty mist as he stood by the bougainvilleas, only vines now at this time of year, so brittle, so fragile, that it appeared as though they might crumble in the cold. Dead. Which fit Tim Colter's mood.

His house stood a couple of hundred yards away from the Pacific, miles from his nearest neighbors, in part of Lane County. Actually, it had been part of Umpqua County when he had moved here back around 1852. The Klamath Exploring Expedition had established a town near the old Hudson's Bay Company trading post, which eventually would be replaced by an army post during the final days of the Rogue River War in 1856. The fort had been abandoned during the Civil War.

The settlement, well east of where Colter now stood watching the morning waves usher in high tide, was called Elkton, which vied with Scottsburg for the county seat until Elkton finally took that over, permanently, in 1855. County seat—but never a courthouse. Umpqua County didn't last long enough to have a courthouse. Like the gold rush that had brought Tim Colter here.

Tim Colter had not come alone. Patricia, his wife, had been the one who wanted to leave their farm in the Willamette Valley. She had always been the adventurous one. Colter had thought she would not want to risk anything, especially remembering everything she had gone through on their way from Pennsylvania to Oregon Territory back in 1845, when they were still in their teens. But Colter had listened—after all, she was carrying their child—and they had sold their farm to Colter's sister, Nancy, and her husband, Chase Burgess, and joined the flood of settlers, taking a line among the pack trains and freight wagons that crossed the Umpqua River.

They found just enough pay dirt to keep from starving, and then rode out to see the Pacific Ocean, and all those wrecked ships lining the coast. That's where Colter found his success. Salvaging cargo from wrecked ships.

He did all right. Built a house—the only house on the coast in Oregon, probably—pampered his wife, and his son. Then a daughter. Until the gold camps began fighting each other, and Elkton sent a citizens committee to ask Tim Colter to serve as marshal.

"What would I know about marshaling?" Colter had asked with a laugh.

"You know about guns. That much we know of you," the leading merchant, a mercantile owner named Horace Friedman, had said. "Everyone in the territory has heard about you, sir. How you rescued your wife, your sisters, and others from renegades. What you did at Colter's Hell."

Colter had frowned. "I had help."

He thought about that Cyclops he had befriended—Jed Reno. The mountain man had saved Colter's life, taught him how to survive, and, yes, taught him how to kill a man who was trying to kill you and not feel any regret.

"Yes. Of course. And you'll have help, too. With our Vigilance Committee."

"I'm no lawman," Colter had argued.

"But you're a legend, Colter. And we need you. You're the best man with a gun we know."

Patricia had told him to do it. She could take care of the children. And Elkton was offering him two hundred dollars a month in gold. Which certainly topped anything that he had pulled out of wrecked ships. Patricia said she would stay here, out of harm's way, and watch the children and the bougainvilleas.

She loved the spring and the summer here. The purple flowers. The rains. The wind. The smell of the salt air. To her, it was paradise, and Colter could not deny that. After growing up among the coal mines, furnaces, and foundries of Danville, Pennsylvania, and then laboring sunup to sundown on the Oregon farm.

So Tim Colter left her and the children and pinned on a gold-plated badge in Elkton.

If what he had done in the Wyoming country—surviving a massacre by white and Indian renegades, burying the dead with his own hands, leaving South Pass afoot to rescue the women captives, joining a mountain man, fighting the elements, black-hearted villains, crossing mountains he would have thought impossible, and then rescuing the women (with much help from Jed Reno and some Cheyenne Indians)—had made him a legend along the Oregon Trail, what he did in the Umpqua's gold country secured his fame.

"You're the best man with a gun we know," Friedman had said.

The merchant was right.

Colter cleaned up those bandits—and without much help from the town's so-called Vigilance Committee.

Back home along the Pacific, he met Walter Forward around Christmas, 1858. Forward had just been appointed United States Marshal for the District of Oregon, and wanted Tim Colter to be his first deputy. Patricia smiled and told him to take the job, that there had not been any ships wrecked along the coast since the lighthouses had been built. So Colter rode with Forward back to Eugene, then on to Salem, Portland, Medford, Corvallis, Oregon City, farm towns, forts, mining camps, fishing villages, mountains, rivers, the dry country . . . wherever he needed to go—but always returning to the coast west of Eugene.

Dolphes B. Hannah took the marshal's job in August '59, a few months after the territory had been granted statehood—a free state, of course—and Hannah had been no fool. He could see the record of arrests, and he could read the articles published in the *Oregon Spectator,* the *Oregonian,* the *Western Star,* the *Statesman,* and the *Free Press.* Hannah kept Tim Colter on the U.S. marshal's office payroll.

Then, the Civil War erupted. Most federal troops in the state and up in Washington Territory left the Pacific Northwest for the East. A few men of Oregon went east to fight. Edward Baker, who had been a U.S. senator from the state, would die at Ball's Bluff, leading his troops in Virginia. A Jacksonville lawyer named James Lingenfelter, who had been in Pennsylvania when the war started, stayed there to fight with the 71st Pennsylvania Infantry and was shot dead while on the picket line.

But with settlers still making their way from the East, to join the gold camps in Oregon and over into Idaho Territory, organized in 1863, and with Paiutes, Shoshones, and Bannocks causing trouble, Tim Colter stayed in Oregon. When Governor John Whiteaker granted George Wright permission to form a cavalry regiment, Colter joined the 1st Oregon Cavalry.

Colter lasted longer than Colonel Wright, who was replaced by some half-wit Californian named Cody before Colter, or anyone else, even joined. Cody was gone, too, before Thomas R. Cornelius was commissioned in November 1861 and ordered to raise ten troops of cavalry.

Although Colter couldn't claim to have seen much action, he rode with the blue—when he wasn't sick from bad water or worse food or having caught some complaint from one of his fellow troopers—from the summer of 1862 to the summer of 1865.

It was after the 1st had returned from a little affair along the Malheur River and Camp Lyon in mid-July of '65 that he got the letter. Numbly, Colter had gone to Colonel Reuben F. Maury, who had assumed command of the 1st that January. Maury granted Colter a leave, and he would not return to active duty, even when he and everyone else in the regiment was mustered out in November of '66.

Tim Colter rode back to the Pacific.

To an empty house.

Diphtheria.

That's what the doctor had called it. The epidemic had swept through much of Elkton. Patricia Scott Colter had likely picked it up when she came to Elkton for supplies. Because she lived so far from any neighbors, no one had known she was sick, or that the children had come down with the disease. The old sawbones had said that, likely, Patricia had thought it was just the croup at first. Bad cough, sore throat, a touch of fever. Elkton or Eugene or anywhere else would be too risky to travel to see a doctor. By the time the noses started bleeding, it would have been too late, anyway, for even the best doctor to treat them. Certainly, Patricia could not have gotten herself or the kids out of the house.

Remembering that Patricia had come to town during the early outbreak of the diphtheria epidemic, Horace Friedman had traveled those rugged sixty miles down the river to the coast, then across the sand dunes to the mouth of the Siuslaw and the home Tim and Patricia had built with their own hands.

The merchant had buried them by himself.

Colter left the bougainvilleas and walked to the wrought-iron fence that surrounded the graves. The fence had been a gift from the people of Elkton, Marshal William H. Bennett, who had replaced Dolphes B. Hannah in '62, and Governor A.C. Gibbs.

He looked at the marble stones, small, just names, and ages, and the year.

> *Patricia Colter*
> *36 Yrs.*
> *1865*
> *Jed Colter*
> *13 Yrs.*
> *1865*
> *Matilda Colter*
> *10 Yrs.*
> *1865*
> *Claude Colter*
> *4 Yrs.*
> *1865*

Colter swept the hat off his head, keeping it in his right hand, and wrapping his left around one of the wet, cold iron bars.

"I won't be coming back," he told the graves. "You once told me if anything happened to you ..." He had to stop, let the tear slide down his cheek, swallow down the lump in his throat. "... to ... keep living. I come back here ... and ... I just remember you ... now. Dead. All of you.

And I know . . . even if I hadn't been gallivanting across the country play-acting like I was a real soldier . . . that I couldn't have done anything. I know that. But . . . I think . . . that maybe . . . if I'd just . . . if I wasn't here, that I'd remember you alive. And that's how I'd like to remember you. I love you. I'll always love you. I'll never forget you."

He felt a little better, oddly enough. Colter released his grip on the fence. He watched the ocean, the waves crashing, and he knew, come spring, this cemetery, this homestead, this whole beachfront, would be covered with bougainvilleas.

"You got a pretty place here," he said. "Real pretty. Just like all of you. Take care. I'll see you all . . . when it's my time."

When he left, a few hours later, the wooden home, the lean-to, the shed, and even the outhouse were burning.

Tim Colter did not look back.

That was another thing Jed Reno had taught him.

CHAPTER 7

The federal district offices were in Portland, but the state capital remained in Salem—at least it had since the 1864 election—and new marshal Albert Zeiber was meeting with Governor George Lemuel Woods, and had asked to meet Tim Colter at the capitol.

That suited Tim Colter well enough. He would rather spend time in Salem than Portland.

He stood that morning on the corner of Commercial and Ferry, staring up at the three-story building Joseph Holman had built, most people said, as a hotel. Then some arsonist or arsonists—at least that's what most of the citizens still claimed—torched the Oregon State Capitol a few days after Christmas, 1855, and Holman changed his plans. He was, after all, a fairly civic-minded gent—one of the trustees of Willamette University—had settled in the country around Fort Vancouver and up in Champoeg in the 1840s. His hotel was turned into a temporary house for the Oregon State Capitol, with the Oregon State Senate meeting on the third floor, the House of Representatives on the second, and other state offices on the first.

The original capitol remained on its site, a wreckage of ash and stones, although everyone in the state kept saying that—one of these days—folks would put up another building, maybe one with a dome. Yet no funds had been found to build such a magnificent building.

William H. Bennett's term as U.S. Marshal for the District of Oregon had expired back in April, and Senator J.W. Nesmith nominated Albert Zeiber as Bennett's replacement. Congress approved that appointment on November 6. Now, a few days before Christmas, Marshal Zeiber had arrived in Salem and sent word to Colter that he wanted to meet him.

Colter had no idea what his boss looked like. He stepped inside the building, out of the light but frigid rain, and removed his slicker. It was like most government buildings—this planned hotel turned into state offices. Not much different than the federal buildings up in Portland. Men in top hats and fancy suits scurried about with satchels and papers and this better-than-you'd-ever-hope-to-be expression on their faces. Colter had seen that enough from the previous marshals he had worked under—and most of those he had actually liked.

A U.S. marshal was an appointed politician. He served at the whim of the attorney general and the state senate, maybe even the president, and so marshals came and went. Republicans now. Democrats before. Yet one thing remained the same, no matter which party was running the show.

Marshals stayed behind desks. Deputies did all the work, served the writs, and made the arrests. Deputies did all the dying.

"Marshal Colter?"

Colter turned from the painting of Lewis and Clark that hung in the lobby of the building. He found a solidly built, bearded gentleman, holding a raincoat draped over his left arm, his left hand holding a military campaign hat from the late war. He did not look like he thought he was better than anyone. He could even have been a sheepman—like

Mr. Holman himself—wearing his Sunday-go-to-meetings clothes.

"Yes, sir."

The man extended his right hand. He had a grip like a sheepman, too.

"I thought so." The man gestured at the LeMat that hung snugly on Colter's hip.

Tim Colter had learned to always keep a revolver handy. Jed Reno had taught him that, too.

"I'm Albert Zeiber."

"Welcome to Salem, Marshal."

The politician smiled, but it wasn't the fraudulent smile Colter had expected.

"It's good to be here, sir. Grand to be in Oregon. And a pleasure to meet you."

Colter shrugged. He had never cared much for accolades.

"Is there a good restaurant nearby where we could take a bite to eat? Maybe sip some coffee? And talk?" He shook his head. "Someplace where the roof does not leak. I almost drowned talking to Mr. Cornelius."

A Republican from Washington County, Thomas R. Cornelius, for all practical reasons Colter's first commanding officer with the 1st Oregon Cavalry, was now president of the Oregon State Senate.

Tim Colter decided that he liked his new boss.

"I know just the place, sir."

Betsy McDonnell had been running the Bullfrog Café down on Ferry Street since her husband had died—of diphtheria—early in 1867. Anyway, that's how Colter had started talking to her . . . well, why she had started talking to him anyway. Maybe they had helped each other heal.

Maybe Betsy was the reason Colter had finally burned down that home that overlooked the Pacific Ocean. Patricia, he made himself believe, would want him to move on. He was alive. And if you were alive, Patricia often told him, you have to live. That's why they had sold the farm and struck out to the Umpqua in search of gold. And then followed the Siuslaw River to the Pacific to find another adventure.

She brought Colter and Marshal Zeiber two cups of coffee and two giant corn muffins, seasoned with cinnamon, all on the house.

"To welcome you to our lovely state, Marshal."

Zeiber stared up at Betsy. "Madam," he said, "I thought Oregon—this country—was of such a deep green that never would I find anything to match its beauty. Until I saw your eyes."

She smiled, but he blushed, noticing the black band around the arm of her gray dress.

"I hope you do not find my comment inappropriate, madam. I meant no disrespect and please allow me to offer my condolences to your—"

"Apologies are not necessary, Marshal," she said, "especially after such a wonderful compliment. Might I get you anything else?"

Colter stared. She did have stunning green eyes. Even on such a rainy, dismal, cold day as this, they shone. Her hair was red, bright and as warm as a Christmas fire. She looked at him, winked, and left after Zeiber shook his head.

"A fine woman." The marshal sipped his coffee. "My world . . . and this coffee is the best I've ever tasted."

"Wait till you sample her muffins, sir."

"She cooked these herself."

"She does practically everything in this restaurant herself."

Zeiber sampled the muffin, then studied Colter with a bit of scrutiny.

"Her husband . . . ?" the marshal asked after Colter had sipped about half his cup of coffee.

"Dead," Colter answered blankly.

"How did he die?"

Colter swallowed. He stared out the window at the puddles still being pelted by drops. "Diphtheria." He wasn't sure he could even say the word. Yet this time, when he did say it, he no longer saw his dead wife and children. This time, he did not even see the flames roaring through the home he had built with Patricia. He just saw the rain.

"I am sorry."

Turning away from the window, Colter shook his head. "No need, Marshal. My wife and children have been gone for more than two years."

As he lifted his coffee cup, Marshal Zeiber smiled. "And . . ." He sipped the coffee, lowered it, and shook his head. "Never mind."

"What is it?"

Zeiber leaned forward. "Sir, I was going to ask you—as a widower myself—about the availability of Mrs. McDonnell—as of the end of January, of course, giving her enough time for mourning for the appearance of respectability."

Now Colter stared at his boss with complete puzzlement.

U.S. Marshal Albert Zeiber laughed as he pulled off another bite of muffin. "But I know better than to trespass, Marshal Colter, especially when the owner of that property carries a LeMat pistol."

Colter's head shook. "Marshal, I think you are mistaken."

"I don't. I see beauty in Mrs. McDonnell's eyes, Tim. I see something totally different in yours."

They finished their muffins in silence, sipped coffee that Betsy came by to refill, and finally Albert Zeiber pulled the satchel off the floor, set it on the table, and unfastened the clasps.

"It's time for business, Marshal Colter," he said, and pulled out an envelope. Colter read only the Seal of the Attorney General of the United States of America.

"My first bit of business as U.S. Marshal of the District of Oregon," Zeiber said, "is to show you this letter. A request, sir. A plea for help."

Actually, the papers Colter saw in his hand came from various people. Requests. Forwards. Endorsements. First he held a letter from Henry Stanbery, the attorney general, written to Marshal Zeiber. Just a brief note about what he was forwarding to Oregon, although Colter did feel a bit honored that he now held a piece of paper signed by the United States attorney general, a man who worked close to President Andrew Johnson.

Next he held a letter from Laban H. Litchfield.

The name meant absolutely nothing to Colter, but the letterhead read:

Dakota Territory
Office of the U.S. Marshal

Dakota Territory had been created by Congress on March 2, 1861. It covered much of what had been the Unorganized Territory. That had been another mere forward, a letter of endorsement, sent to James H. Alvord, territorial marshal in Idaho. Most of these new territories had been carved out from other territories. Idaho, well, that's one thing Colter knew. The territory, carved out three, no, four years back, covered a lot of the country people were starting to call Wyoming.

The last letter, the one that had been forwarded to Washington City . . . to Yankton in Dakota Territory to

Boise in Idaho Territory and, finally, to U.S. Marshal Albert Zeiber in Oregon, was in Tim Colter's hands in a café in Salem on a wet, wintry December morning that was approaching afternoon.

> *Sir:*
>
> *We, the undersigned citizens of Violet—but representing the majority of the inhabitants of our fair city along the Union Pacific Railways, ten miles east of Cheyenne—beseech thee for relief.*
>
> *Our city, soon to be heralded as a great beacon to the Western territories, is besieged by ruffians, cowardly murderers, and the most vicious and evil rapscallions ever to lurk. We need law. We need help. We need to rid our great city of evil-doers and make it fit for our people, our women, our wives, our children . . . and those settlers who wish to help settle this great Western empire.*
>
> *We believe one man can help us accomplish this task. Therefore, it is our great wish—our only hope—that one of your federal lawmen, the renown marshal Tim Coulter, be sent to Violet. We can pay him fifteen dollars a month.*
>
> *Two men are at the root of our problems. Both ruffians with no moral values, a saloon owner named Micah Slade and a nefarious gambling operator known as Paddy O'Rourke. We are at their mercy, and fear for the lives of our town and all of us law-abiding citizens.*
>
> *Please, Marshal Coulter, please dear sirs, please ride to our rescue. Save us from being wiped off the face of the map.*

Colter read the signatures:

> *Jasper H. Monroe, mayor, Violet, Idaho Territory*
> *X (which someone, apparently the mayor, had noted as Eugene Harker, freed slave, good barber)*
> *B.B. Cutter*
> *H.R.R. Yost*
> *Aloysius Murden*
> *Duncan Gates*

Then Colter carefully refolded the letters and handed them, and the various envelopes, back to Marshal Zeiber.

"What do you think?" Zeiber asked.

"They spelled Colter wrong," Colter answered.

Zeiber's smile showed no amusement. "Marshal Alvord said he would welcome you in his territory, even on a temporary assignment, but he believed that this is not a federal matter. He says . . ."

Colter nodded. He had read Alvord's letter, and had to agree with him. Maybe it was federal as it was in U.S. territories, but this seemed to be more within the jurisdiction of a local lawman. Alvord said he had written Mayor Monroe, telling him the very same, but assuring him that he would forward the correspondence to the new district marshal for Oregon and a request to deliver it to Tim Colter.

"And fifteen dollars a month is not much pay to risk one's life," Zeiber said. Yet, Zeiber's eyes were as easy to read as Betsy McDonnell's.

Tim Colter's boss was disappointed.

"So your answer is . . . ?" the new marshal asked hopefully.

He already knew it. So did Tim Colter, who was watching Betsy bring more coffee and a couple of slices of pie. He saw her eyes. He knew. . . .

It was one thing to go after some hard case like Stewart Rose. That was his job. He had to do that. They had robbed the U.S. mail, which led to federal warrants for the arrest of Rose and his gang. Tim Colter had taken an oath. But to travel all the way to Cheyenne—wherever in blazes that was—and risk his life for people he didn't know, in a town he had never seen, which might even require him to resign his deputy marshal's commission, for fifteen bucks a month.

No. Colter wouldn't—couldn't do that. And there was another reason. She was refilling two cups of coffee and sliding two plates, each holding a slice of warm, bubbling apple pie, in front of Tim Colter and Marshal Albert Zeiber.

"I can't leave . . . ," Colter said. "Not after . . ."

CHAPTER 8

Winter. January. Three feet of snow on the ground, five below zero, a gale blowing with nothing to stop it from Canada, and Jed Reno had never been so busy since he had left the Green River. The latest U.P. train, following another smoke-churning monster of an engine with a snowplow attached to its cow-catcher, had brought seventeen more settlers—all who were either staying at the Yost & Cutter Hotel or in some of the sod huts that had been erected as temporary homes in the town Aloysius Murden and Duncan Gates had platted.

Reno couldn't understand a word any of the women or men said. Flemish, Mayor Jasper Monroe called it. It didn't matter, though. The sodbusters knew what they wanted, and they paid in silver and gold.

They weren't all farmers, though. And some of them spoke English. One extended family—a tough, sunburned army veteran from Texas and his three sons and their wives—planned on filing adjoining claims and ranching down south a ways. Warren was their name. A dentist named Gregory had rented the first office in the first completely wooden-framed house erected in Violence, and another gent named Custer—no relation to the Civil War hero—had started up a bank.

Violence was growing. Both the town, and the killings.

"Here."

Jed Reno slid the double eagles into his beaded buckskin pouch—he still had not bought one of those newfangled cash registers, or even a moneybox—and smiled at the woman with her hair in a bun, spectacles hanging on the bridge of her nose, and wearing a navy blue woolen dress, with a heavy coat and scarf. Reaching below the counter, he pulled out the jar of stick candy, unscrewed the lid, and held it out to the woman's mess of kids. Six of them, ranging from what appeared to be five years old to fifteen or so. Fat kids. She must be a fine cook.

"Iffen it's all right with you, ma'am," Reno told her.

She stared, and then smiled. Probably didn't understand a single word he had said, but she could see the peppermints, and how wide her sons' and daughters' eyes got.

Each of them timidly took out one stick, nodded at Reno. The last one said something on behalf of all those young'uns, which Reno took as a thank-you. He watched them file out of his trading post, closing the door behind them.

"That's right generous of you."

Reno turned, and that nice feeling that had settled over him vanished in a heartbeat.

"Slade," Reno said as he screwed the lid back onto the jar of candy.

He wore a Yankee greatcoat—probably one he had taken off a soldier he had killed—with the left sleeve empty, though Reno could see the black sling that held that crippled arm. Slade strode over from the shovels, spades, posthole diggers, and hoes to the counter. He withdrew a flask from the back pocket of his black trousers. He held it up to Reno.

"Thank you, no," Reno said.

"Haven't seen you in my establishment lately, Jed." The

man spoke in a thick Southern drawl. He unscrewed the pewter flask, drank greedily, and leaned against the counter.

"For what you charge," Reno said, "can you blame me?"

The gambler grinned. "Two bits for a stick of nickel candy. You want to talk about inflation?"

"Candy's hard to get in these parts," Reno said.

"So is whiskey."

Reno laughed. "Yeah. But not if you heat up pure alcohol and season it with rattlesnake heads, chewing tobacco, peppers, and gunpowder."

Grinning, Micah Slade gestured with his good hand toward the closed door. "You try findin' rattlesnakes when it's this cold, ol' hoss. 'T'ain't easy."

"Try taking a glance behind your bar. Plenty of rattlers. Just got to know where to look."

The gambler exploded with laughter. "I like you, Reno."

"Don't like you."

"I know that. But do you like that greasy little Mick more?"

Meaning Paddy O'Rourke, who owned The Blarney Stone, that awful gambling den across the street from Slade's Saloon. The Union Pacific had brought enough supplies that O'Rourke's joint had expanded. Gone were the canvas walls, which the wind battered, and the poles, ropes, and rawhide, which tried to hold the joint together. It now boasted a false front and two stories of whitewashed framed wood, trimmed green, made of logs hauled down from the Medicine Bow range, and even a gabled roof with wooden shingles.

"I don't give him no business, neither," Reno said.

"You're a man in the middle, Reno." Slade found his flask again, but did not offer Reno a drink as he took another healthy swallow. "You don't like me. You don't like O'Rourke. You don't like nobody. You don't even like this town. Why in hell did you start a trading post here?"

"Wasn't no town when I started it." Reno frowned. Actually, he had not expected the swarm of settlers so soon after the tracks had just been laid. Progress of the U.P. line had slowed down substantially with winter, and Violence—or Violet, if you preferred—had become even bigger as a railroad supply stop for the crews off to the west. Railroaders. Farmers. Townsfolk. And men like Slade and O'Rourke. And nowhere to go without freezing to death. Not a healthy combination.

"So . . . there was a meeting of Violence's best minds last night."

Reno had figured Slade eventually would get to the point of his visit. He had to give the saloonkeeper some credit. Earlier this afternoon, Paddy O'Rourke had sent one of his faro dealers to prod Reno for information. At least, Slade came himself.

"You wasn't invited?" Reno chided.

This time, Micah Slade did not smile. He pushed back the tail of the blue kersey coat, revealing the butt of one of the Alabaman's Navy Colts.

"You're not always funny, Reno," Slade said.

"You touch that hogleg, Slade, and you'll never laugh again."

"I'd just like to know what that meeting was all about."

"Ask the mayor."

"I'm asking you."

The door opened. Another family came in, led by a stout man who looked like he had just stepped out of some painting of the Alps—if that those were the right mountains. A tiny woman, who kept her head down, and two little girls, probably not yet ten years old, followed him. The door closed, cutting off January's icy breath.

"*Goede avond,*" the man said, as he removed his fur cap with the leather earmuffs. "*Hoe gaat het met jou?*"

"Uh," Reno said. "Yeah."

The man went to the food stores. "You need any . . . help . . . uh . . . yeah. . . ."

They paid him little mind, but the husband and his wife started carrying on a conversation, while the two girls stood at their mother's side. Well, they would be like the rest of those foreigners, Reno figured. They would get what they needed—rather, what they thought they needed—bring it to the counter, pay Reno in gold coins, and be on their way.

"We were talking about the town meetin'."

Reno turned away from the sodbusters and stared into Slade's cold eyes.

"You were doing the talking, remember? I wasn't at that meeting, either."

"In the middle, eh?" Slade's head shook. He pulled up his black hat, which had been hanging on his back, secured with a latigo lace.

"It suits me," Reno said. "I'm just a little old merchant."

"People in the middle get run over, Reno. You might best remember that. You're no fool. That's why I come to talk to you. A town like Violence, well, there can be only one bull of the woods. You don't want that title. Being an old man and all, with just a few more years left on this here earth."

Reno felt his ears reddening, but he merely clenched his fists and did not beat the one-armed Alabaman into the dirt. It might leave a bad impression on those Flemish-speaking newcomers, and Reno didn't want them to take their business into town. After all, he had become a bit of a capitalist, much like ol' Jim Bridger.

"This town'll be up for grabs, come spring. Me or the Mick. That's what it boils down to. It'll be a railroad town. Not full of damned idiots who can't even speak no proper English. Not a bunch of fool farmers. And not even ranchers. Railroaders. Gamblers. Whores. Saloonkeepers.

That's where the money is. And me or O'Rourke will run Violence. You savvy that, I know."

Reno scratched an itch above his eye patch. "Don't sound like there'll be room for me."

"There's always room for folks who mind their own business, Reno. Who don't get run over by a train." He turned around, headed for the door, and stopped by some crates the latest freight had brought and Reno had yet to unpack. "I hear tell that killer in Oregon didn't take the job."

"What killer would that be?" Reno asked.

"Tim Colter."

Reno just stared at the saloonkeeper with his one good eye.

"A man like Colter showed good sense. He knew what would happen to any marshal in Violence. He'd get buried. You don't want to be marshal of Violence, do you, Jed?"

So they were on a first-name basis now.

"A man with your brains, *Slade*." He emphasized the name, so the Alabaman would know that they were not on that first-name basis. "A man like you, he'd already know that they asked me to take that job back in November. And I said no." The farmer was bringing sacks of flour, coffee, sugar, and beans to the counter. "You see. I'm just a storekeeper."

The farmer asked, *"Kan je mij helpen?"*

Reno looked at him blankly, then again faced the gambler.

"I've got nothing against storekeepers, Reno," Slade said. "Especially those that can take care of themselves. Like this story I hear about one gent at a trading post who managed to kill three men trying to rob him. Then dumped their bodies, so that nobody would be the wiser. That's a man who's smart and strong. I'll be seein' you, Jed."

The door opened, quickly closed, and Micah Slade was gone.

Reno turned and tried to figure out how much he should charge for those supplies that kept coming to the counter-top, but his mind wasn't on business. It was on Micah Slade. So now Jed Reno knew who had sent those cutthroats to rob him back in November.

He didn't charge the homesteaders enough, but figured he had made enough money already. When they were gone, Reno pulled in the latchstring through the door, set the bolt, and wandered back to the storeroom, where his pallet lay on the floor. Warm and toasty. He found his jug of his own blend of Taos Lightning; then leaning against the earthen wall, he sipped his liquor, and picked up the copy of *Harper's Weekly*.

CHAPTER 9

Ferre Slootmaekers was a pretty good kid. Tall and gangly, but he had no trouble lifting forty- or even a hundred-pound sacks, and even heavier boxes. Plus he spoke passable English, and understood all that crazy talk the immigrants kept speaking. Which is why Jed Reno hired him. It was the first time Reno had paid anybody, unless you wanted to count that Nez Perce boy that Reno had helping him with the traps back in '38 and '39, or the fat Shoshone squaw he had wintered with way back in 1833 through 1834.

February came, and winter—real winter—roared in with it. The trains stopped coming. Most men stopped working. People died, just up and froze to death, and were stacked in one of the soddies that no one had claimed as a home, to wait till spring, when the ground finally thawed out again so that the dead could be properly buried.

And then, along toward the end of the month, a false spring arrived. Oh, Jed Reno could not tell anyone what the exact day was. Sure, he had a stack of those calendars the U.P. had dropped off to sell, but Reno never had looked at one, except the handful he sold to some Flemish folks, and even one of the Warren boys, back in December. Reno didn't need a calendar to know what time of the year it was, and he had been in this wild country long enough to know that this spring would not last, that winter would dump another two or three storms on Violence before it really warmed up.

But twenty-five degrees felt downright tropical after thirty and forty below. A train made its way to town, dropped off all manner of supplies at the U.P. yards, then chugged on west down Clear Creek toward wherever the end of the line was by now. Folks came out of their huts or their cabins or their balmy hotel rooms to see the first rays of sun they'd noticed in a coon's age. The piano at The Blarney Stone began playing again, and so did the banjo man at Slade's Saloon.

It brought folks to Reno's trading post, too.

When the last sodbuster left, Reno looked at his ledger, or what passed for bookkeeping to his way of thinking. He frowned. Like everyone else—except those working for the railroad, or Micah Slade or Paddy O'Rourke—most money had vanished. The Flemish-speaking foreigners had spent their last gold coins, and now Reno had to put them on credit or barter with them. He studied the recent entries.

Some family called De Vroom, if even Reno had spelled that right, owed him a bushel of beets. Jed Reno despised beets. Wouldn't touch the damned things, but he thought maybe he could sell some to Harker or Murden or Gates, come summer. The Joossens promised him two pigs. Whenever they got their pigs. He shaved a better point on his pencil and scratched through one name: ~~Vandroogenbroeck~~.

The old lady had gone crazy and killed her two kids at the end of January, and Mr. Vandroogenbroeck, after discovering what had happened, wandered off into the blizzard. Clint Warren, the old widower who wanted to ranch with his boys, had found the man, frozen stiff a week later.

Reno would not be collecting the barley from the Van-droogenbroecks' first crops.

"Boy," Reno called out as he closed the book, and tossed the pencil onto some pelts he had swapped Mrs. Jutta Claes for soap. Soap. Who would take a bath in winter?

Ferre Slootmaekers immediately put down the load of potatoes on a table and practically ran to the counter.

"Sir?" the kid said. The word was English, but the accent sure wasn't.

"How many times, boy, do I have to tell you not to go around 'sirring' me."

Ferre Slootmaekers blinked, and stared, his mouth open. His English had its limits.

Shaking his head, Reno reached below the counter and pulled out the beaded buckskin pouch. One of them. He had buried a few before the snows got too heavy, for safekeeping. Jed Reno didn't trust that guy Custer, and Reno had never cared much for banks anyway. Back in Bowling Green, Louisville, and St. Louis, he had seen plenty of those places go bust—or heard that the banker had left town in the middle of the night, after cleaning out the vault.

He pulled out a double eagle, felt the gold coin in his fingers, and, with a heavy sigh, finally slid it across the counter in front of the sixteen-year-old from Mechelen, wherever in blazes that place was, or the *Dijlestad,* which the kid also sometimes said had been his home.

Again, Ferre Slootmaekers blinked and stared. Although his mouth remained open, no words came out, neither Flemish nor English, or Mechelenish or *Dijlestadish,* for that matter, or whatever he was supposed to be speaking.

"Boy," Reno said. "They ain't no such thing as slavery in this country no more—not even way to hell out here in Idaho Territory. That's for you. You been working for me for right about a month now. That's your pay."

The kid blinked again.

Reno pushed the coin closer, and then pointed at the boy, even touching his chest. "For you."

Now, if Ferre Slootmaekers had been Cheyenne or Shoshone or Blackfoot or Arapaho or even Blackfoot or Nez Perce, Jed Reno could have carried on a conversation with the boy. But these sodbusters from wherever the hell Flemish was didn't even know sign language.

"Pay," the kid finally managed to say, "for me."

"That's right. Pay. You get paid. Once a month."

The boy smiled brighter and slid the coin into his pocket. Oddly enough, that sight make Jed Reno feel practically like he was becoming a real human being. But he was sure that feeling would pass directly.

"Remember," Reno told the boy as he went to the coatrack. "You got to work tomorrow, and so I expect you to be here right after your ma makes your breakfast."

The boy put on his coat, muffler, scarf, and gloves, pulled open the door, and let another coated man inside. Ferre Slootmaekers stopped and stared past the newcomer's shoulder at Reno.

"That's all right, boy. He ain't here to buy nothing. Are you, Marshal?"

Cutter, part owner of the town's hotel and with a new job since the first of February, chuckled as he pulled off his woolen scarf. "That's right."

Reno had to wave at the boy, to let him know it was all right to leave. The door shut, and Cutter walked to the counter, his new badge gleaming.

"What do you make of this weather?" Cutter asked.

"I don't."

"Reckon it'll last?"

"No."

"No?"

"Too early."

Cutter pulled out a cigar, bit off the end, and spit into

the cuspidor. He then fished out a cigar from one of his frock coat's inside pockets and held it out toward Reno.

"Pipe man," Reno said, shaking his head.

The cigar disappeared.

"Town's coming alive," Cutter said. "Warm weather. Train came in and dropped off some more railroad workers. I might be about to earn the fifteen a month I get paid to wear this." He pressed an index finger on the five-point badge, then wiped off the smudge with the cuffs of his shirtsleeve.

The cigar was fired up, and Cutter took several pulls before the end finally glowed. He drew in a deep breath, held the smoke, and sent it skyward in a perfect smoke ring. Jed Reno always marveled at men who could do that, but he kept his amazement to himself.

"This'll be a big night. For the law." Cutter removed the cigar. His eyes narrowed. "I figure I might need some help. I'd like to offer you the job as my deputy. Even if it's only for tonight, or, well, maybe as long as the weather holds."

Reno's head was shaking before Cutter even finished the sentence.

"I can pay you ten dollars. I mean, the town council will pay you ten. You know how much I get."

Reno kept shaking that head.

"O'Rourke and Slade are trying to get control of this town, Jed. This'll be our chance to show them that the law has come to Violet, that they need to move on down the line, to the next Hell on Wheels."

"Like I told you gents last fall, I ain't no lawman."

"But you can't just stand in the middle, Jed."

This time, Jed Reno laughed. "Cutter, you ain't the first person to tell me that. But I been doing pretty fine just tending my trading post."

Micah Slade had told him that. So had the main faro dealer at The Blarney Stone. So had Mayor Jasper Monroe. So had Paddy O'Rourke two weeks earlier. Hell, so had Jed Reno himself. Only Jed Reno seldom listened to anyone, even himself.

"Well, I thought I'd ask," Cutter said.

Reno pointed. "On account you don't carry a gun yourself."

"You don't need a gun, Jed," Cutter said, "when you're the law. The law speaks for itself."

"A forty-four Colt speaks louder."

"If I carry a gun, the law gets no respect. I have to show men like Slade and O'Rourke that the law is bigger than the gun."

Reno studied Cutter harder now. The man ran a hotel, but he had sand. "Cutter," Reno said after a long thought, "I wish you well."

"See you tomorrow, Jed."

He sat on his pallet, sipping his whiskey—real bourbon whiskey shipped all the way from Kentucky, and not the hooch he made himself—and reading, for the countless time, the *Harper's Weekly*. He had to thank his parents and Mr. Sneed, the wheelwright in Louisville, for teaching him his letters and how to read and even to a bit of ciphering. That gave him an advantage, he had learned. Jim Bridger and even Kit Carson couldn't write their own names—not that being illiterate had hindered Bridger or Carson.

This time, though, Reno looked at the drawings that illustrated the magazine. He rubbed his fingers through his beard. He thought back two decades, and looked at the picture again. And he started to re-read that article when he heard the gunshots.

For a while, Jed Reno ignored what he had heard. Two more shots sounded. He sipped more bourbon out of his tin cup. "Welcome to Violence," he said to himself, and he made himself laugh at his joke. "That ain't funny," he said. He started to refill his cup from the bottle, but then cursed, and pulled himself to his feet.

"Man who starts talking to himself is loco," Reno said. "Ain't he? Yes, sir, he is. And Jed Reno ain't out of his mind. Not yet. Is he? Damn, stop this silly talk."

Once he had pulled on his coat and hat, he grabbed the .44 Colt, stuck it in his waistband, and thought of something else. When he stepped outside into the cold night, he was gripping his Hawken rifle.

CHAPTER 10

Yellow light cast an eerie light on the street that divided Violet, or Violence, in half. Aloysius Murden and Duncan Gates had named it Union Street, in honor of the U.P. Railroad. On a night like this one, most of the railroaders called it Hell Street.

As Jed Reno rode his piebald mare down the street, he saw the shadow he assumed was black-clad Micah Slade standing in front of Slade's Saloon, flanked by several spectators. The men, in sleeve garters and fancy vests of shiny brocade, were all well-illuminated by the lanterns hanging inside the saloon—except for Micah Slade, of course. Yet most of the attention lay directly across Union Street, at The Blarney Stone. A crowd had circled around the boardwalk made of excess railroad ties, spilling onto the street of snow, ice, and mud. A few of the men heard Reno's horse and turned around. One of them held a floppy-brimmed felt hat in his hands.

As he dismounted the mare, Reno nodded at Eugene Harker, the freedman who had an assortment of jobs in town. The black man returned the greeting, and Reno led his horse to a hitching rail by the Yost & Cutter Hotel, next door to Paddy O'Rourke's gambling den. The hitching rail was vacant. Town was bustling, but few people in

Violence owned horses. Even the sodbusters who spoke Flemish were waiting till spring before they brought in their old nags or stout horses and mules to try to turn this country into farmland. Violence, or Violet, was a railroad town. The train brought people here . . . or carried them away.

Reno, still wielding the Hawken, walked through ankle-deep snow until he reached Harker. A big man, Jed Reno had no trouble seeing over the shoulders of most of the men who stood in front of him. They had formed a semicircle around the front of Paddy O'Rourke's gambling den, and there, standing before the front doors of his new building, stood O'Rourke himself, thumbs in his waistband, talking to two of his faro dealers on either side of him.

Reno looked away from O'Rourke and at the man who commanded practically everyone's attention.

That man lay facedown in the mud and muck and snow, arms outstretched over his head, the hat crown-side-down in the snow.

"Hell." That was Reno's way of begging his pardon as he pushed his way through the throng of mostly railroaders, about three-deep, until he made it to the clearing. Eugene Harker came right behind him, mumbling something that Reno didn't quite catch. Well, one of Harker's odd jobs was undertaking, and he had business this night.

Reno knelt, keeping the Hawken balanced on his thighs, and took in a deep breath. The cold air burned his lungs. Steam rose from the two bloodstained holes in the dead man's coat. Bullet holes . . . in the man's back.

It was a frock coat, tan with navy stripes, with a collar of black velvet. Jed Reno recognized the coat. Keeping his left hand on the Hawken, he lowered his right to the dead man's neck, past the woolen scarf, and moved forefinger and thumb down to the throat, feeling for the throbbing of a vein, which Reno knew he would not feel.

"He's dead, ain't he?" Eugene Harker whispered behind Reno.

"Yeah."

The freedman came over and helped Reno roll the dead man over. The badge pinned to the lapel on Marshal B.B. Cutter's coat reflected the light shining from inside The Blarney Stone and on the two lampposts on the columns before the gambling den's doors. B.B. Cutter stared up at the night, but those eyes were dead now, seeing nothing.

"Good night for you, darky!" O'Rourke's heavy Irish brogue called out from the doorway to his crooked gaming house. "Another man to plant, come spring." The gamblers flanking the big Irishman chuckled.

"What happened?" That came from a newcomer. Mayor Jasper Monroe stepped into the mud, making his way through a parting sea of railroad stripes and Mackinaw coats.

"Your marshal got killed," O'Rourke said. "In the line of duty, of course."

One of the gamblers, a bald man with shaded eyeglasses despite the darkness of midnight, hooked his thumb inside. "But he got the kid who killed him."

O'Rourke laughed again. "An even better night for you, darky," he told Harker. "Two in one night. Violence is good for your business, boy."

Reno was staring at the freedman, and he saw something in Harker's eyes that he admired and respected. But now was not the time. "Let it slide, Harker," he whispered. "Been enough killing for one night."

"Yes, sir," Harker managed to say stiffly.

"There was a disturbance?" Mayor Monroe asked.

O'Rourke and his gamblers laughed. So did a few chirpies who stood in what some folks might have called clothing, albeit not much clothing, beside the doors to The

Blarney Stone. "Yeah, Mayor," O'Rourke said, "I guess it was a disturbance."

"The man that killed your marshal is inside," the gambler with hair, and two Colt revolvers in shoulder holsters, said. "We'd appreciate it if you'd fetch him out of here, boy. It puts a damper on the spirit of things inside our gem."

"Kid inside was drunk," O'Rourke began. "Cutter there . . ." He gestured with an unlighted cigar at the corpse in the street. "He came in to arrest the boy. Got shot twice for his troubles. But Cutter put two bullets in his killer. All's well that ends well, I guess, as the Bard said. A man murdered, but his murderer killed, too."

"With what?" Jed Reno rose, and this time aimed the Hawken from his hip in the general direction of Paddy O'Rourke.

"You mind pointing that cannon elsewhere, Reno?" O'Rourke said.

"With what?" Reno asked again. The barrel of the Hawken did not move.

"What do you mean?" the bald gambler asked.

This time, Eugene Harker answered. "Y'all say that Mr. Cutter here killed the man who killed him. Ain't that right?"

"That's right," the two-gunned gambler replied.

"How? Cutter here . . . he didn't even pack no gun."

"He had one tonight," O'Rourke answered. "Isn't that right?" The Irishman turned toward the gambler with the brace of Navy Colts.

"That's right." The gambler pulled out his Navy .36 from his left shoulder, and Reno slowly aimed the Hawken in that man's direction. "This revolver." He held the barrel under his nose. "Yep. This is the one. Fired two shots. Dropped it on the floor as he staggered outside to die in the street. I picked it up. Here." He pitched the gun, which landed and sank through the snow that had yet to melt into mud.

Reno spit onto the one step that came from the street to the boardwalk.

"Reno," O'Rourke said, "there are twenty witnesses inside who'll swear that's how things happened."

"That's right. We swear. I swan, we swear." One of the girls laughed. Jed Reno figured he could smell the opium from the girl from where he stood.

"Let's see the other," Mayor Monroe said, and Jed Reno left the dead B.B. Cutter with Eugene Harker, and followed the procession inside.

The light hurt his eyes. He had never been inside The Blarney Stone, especially not at night. It surprised him that not everyone had left the gambling parlor. Roulette wheels still spun. Dice rolled across felt tables. Glasses clinked, tobacco splashed in saloons, and as soon as Reno pushed his way inside, the piano began playing again. It wasn't crowded—not like the street—but it certainly was not dead.

Except for the body on the floor near an overturned poker table.

"Oh." Reno stopped. The Hawken suddenly felt like a cannon, and he almost dropped it onto the muddy floor. He felt as if a Blackfoot spear had punched through both lungs and his heart. People stopped up short behind him, cursed, and went around him. The chirpy who had spoken outside—the one who Reno would have bet fifteen Cheyenne ponies that she had been smoking opium in one of those upstairs rooms—stepped around him, but this time she stopped.

"Oh . . ." Her voice cracked. "Oh . . . my . . . goodness."

Another chirpy, one with red hair and a face heavy with rouge, came over, took the opium-dazed soiled dove, and practically led her to the staircase.

By then, Eugene Harker had made his way inside, and was moving toward the corpse by the poker layouts. Jed Reno made his legs work and followed. He smelled whiskey and beer, sawdust, tobacco smoke; and as he neared the dead body, he smelled urine and excrement. The kid lay faceup, and like B.B. Cutter, his eyes were open, too. Sightlessly staring at the punched-tin ceiling.

Reno dropped to the floor heavily, and pushed past Harker, touching the boy's forehead, and then gently closing Ferre Slootmaekers's blue eyes. The bullets that killed the sixteen-year-old farm boy, who had left the *Dijlestad,* also known as Mechelen, for a new life in America, had not been as well-aimed as the two that had killed Marshal Cutter. One in the stomach, another in the throat. The blood formed a lake around the kid's body.

"Does anybody know this . . . ?" Eugene Harker stopped, suddenly recognizing the kid. He stared, struck dumb, at Reno. In turn, Reno could barely nod.

"The boy?" Mayor Monroe asked. "The boy killed Braxton."

Braxton, thought Reno. Braxton B. Cutter. Now he had learned the dead man's name.

"Aye," O'Rourke answered. "He came in with a twenty-dollar gold piece. Started drinking the best rye we serve. Dottie was with him, but he . . . Well . . . the kid didn't have the nerve." Laughing evilly, O'Rourke looked around for Dottie, but Reno figured that was the one befuddled by opium who had been rushed upstairs.

The Irishman kept talking. "Then the kid came to try his hand at poker. Boy couldn't hold his liquor. Lost. Got angry. Started disturbing our place."

"That's when your brave marshal came inside," the bald gambler said. "The kid pulled a pistol. Got off two shots. And Cutter got his pistol and returned fire. Bam-bam-bam-bam. Just like that."

"We can hold a miner's court if you like, Mayor," O'Rourke said. "Not that we're miners, or anything. Just an expression out here on the frontier."

"Where there's no law," said another gambler, one working a poker table a few feet behind Reno.

"I reckon . . ." Monroe's head shook. "There's no need for that."

Reno leaned forward, closer to the dead boy's white face, and came up, cursing himself. He smelled liquor on the boy, and those dead eyes were red-lined. Maybe he had come in to drink, spend that twenty bucks Reno had just paid him. Maybe he had gotten drunk. Maybe this never would have happened had Jed Reno not felt so damned generous. Maybe. A thousand maybes.

He looked straight into Paddy O'Rourke's eyes.

"And where did Ferre get his pistol?"

"Who?" O'Rourke asked.

"The boy here. Ferre Slootmaekers. Kid never owned no pistol, wouldn't even know how to shoot a damned Colt."

"Musta got lucky," the two-gunned gambler said. "Because you could cover the two holes in Cutter's back with a golden eagle."

Reno's thumb started to pull back the hammer of the Hawken, but this time it was Eugene Harker's hand that touched Reno's forearm. Reno stared angrily at the freedman, until he heard the black man's whisper.

"Now ain't the time, Mr. Reno."

Reno calmed himself. "And the pistol?"

"He stole mine." The gambler at the other poker table rose from his seat, and walked to the crowd, slowly withdrawing a Remington revolver, the barrel sawed off until it was barely a stub, from a holster near the small of his back. He spun the pistol expertly and handed it, butt forward, to Jasper Monroe.

"I am sorry, truly, boss," the gambler told O'Rourke, who grinned.

"Aye, Dan. But such things happen. Such things happen in a town like Violence."

A smattering of laughs filled the parlor. Reno pushed himself up. He nodded at Ferre Slootmaekers. "I'll be taking him to his folks' farm. First thing in the morn."

"You do that," O'Rourke said. "And tell the boy's folks that their drinks will be on the house for all of next month. As a way of showing my condolences. We try to run a clean place here. Too bad their son had to soil The Blarney Stone's reputation."

"Well," Mayor Monroe said. "I guess that settles everything."

Reno stared at him. Decided that Monroe was either worthless, an idiot, or in O'Rourke's back pocket now. Maybe, probably, all three.

He walked outside, feeling a wetness in his eyes that he wasn't sure when he had last felt. Before he got outside, however, he managed to kick over two spittoons, hoping those stains would be as hard to clean from The Blarney Stone's floors as Ferre Slootmaekers's blood.

CHAPTER 11

When he reached the trading post, he brought in more wood for the stove, found his bottle of bourbon, turned up the lantern, and found the *Harper's Weekly*. Jed Reno's book-learning had ended when he ran away from the Sneeds, back when he was fourteen or fifteen. Some of the big words he couldn't quite manage, but he got most of the story figured out. Besides, the six pictures accompanying the article that fascinated him helped Reno figure out what the writer was trying to say.

It made Jed Reno think. He had not heard from Tim Colter in years. Two letters in twenty-two years. One of those had been sent to Bridger's trading post shortly after Reno had sent the boy off to join the rest of his people. Well, the kid's ma and pa had been massacred, and his two sisters were with him, along with that gal he'd been sweet on and her mother. But the rest of the members of that wagon train had moved on, and so Reno watched the boy ride away.

Boy? Hell, Tim Colter was a man by then. Even if he was only sixteen or seventeen or something like that.

So that first letter had been short and sweet. The kid said they had arrived safely at the Willamette Valley, and that he and Patricia were engaged to be married. Tim wrote that Reno should come visit them anytime he wanted, that Oregon was beautiful country. Mostly, Tim Colter thanked Jed Reno for all he had done, saving his life, helping Tim rescue his family and girlfriend.

Hell, that boy had saved Jed Reno's hide—and more than once.

Reno tried to remember. . . .

It had all started at Bridger's Fort, summer it had been, getting late in the season, too, back in '45. Reno had gotten into quite a fight against a little rat named Malachi Murchison, who was in cahoots with another scoundrel, a half-Métis renegade named Louis Jackatars. Murchison had gotten away, and Reno rode after him.

When Reno arrived at South Pass, he found another old trapper Terrence "Just" Jenkins. Jenkins was a good man, but times being what they were back then, he had been reduced to guiding those damned fool emigrants across the Plains and Rockies to that promised land everyone called Oregon. Another wagon train had come upon the site of a massacre, being captained and guided by some half-wit whose name Reno had long forgotten. Just Jenkins had ridden back to check on a couple of wagons that had remained at South Pass for repairs. Those were the two wagons that had been ransacked.

There were two graves, but neither Jenkins nor any of the men from the following wagon train had dug those. Man and wife—turned out to be Colter's folks—were buried in one of the graves, and some gent named Scott— the pa of the girl Tim Colter had been sweet on—was in the other.

Looked like Indians had done the deed, and not just one tribe. Jed Reno had met up with some Cheyenne Indians, and then, remembering what Murchison had told Reno, things started to make sense.

If you looked at the sign, you would have thought that a confederation of many tribes—Cheyennes and Arapahos . . . Sioux and Blackfeet . . . Nez Perce and Shoshone . . . maybe even others—had killed those poor fools. But it had been Louis Jackatars and some of his renegades, red and white. Jackatars, a madman, had this plan to turn the Oregon Trail into the biggest graveyard ever known to mankind. Have a war going on, a war that would wipe out the Indians and ruin this land. This little massacre was that blackheart's way of getting the war started.

There had been another sign, and another body. Jackatars had left behind one of his men to kill a boy who must have survived the massacre. Only instead, that boy had killed the renegade, then set out—afoot—following the trail of Jackatars and his boys. That damned fool kid was going after his sisters and his girlfriend and his sweetie's ma.

Reno remembered what Just Jenkins had said of the kid. "Good boy, though greener than a tree frog."

A tree frog named Tim Colter.

And Reno's own words sang out from his memories: "Boy's got a ton of guts. I'll give him that."

The emigrants, being the fools that they were, wanted revenge. Get that war started. Wipe out all the redskins in the territories. Reno had sent them on to Bridger's Fort, asking Jenkins to give him two weeks. Two weeks to stop a war. Two weeks to catch up with Louis Jackatars and kill that son of a bitch.

So Reno rode north and west. He didn't think he would find the Colter kid. Alive, that is.

Yet, he had—with a thunderstorm about to flood the country, and the kid and another of Jackatars's men, a rapscallion named Abaroa. Reno had shot down that darkskinned killer. Reno had hoped to send the boy down to Bridger's Fort, but the kid had other notions. He was coming with Reno, or going after Jackatars himself.

Reno let him tag along. For a while, he regretted it. After all, he had to teach the boy how to shoot both rifle and pistol, how to saddle a horse, how to pack a mule, how to cook, clean, live, survive.

They had made their way along the Big Sandy . . . and across the Red Desert . . . climbed into the mountains . . . found the Siskeedee-Agie, better known as the Green River. And had met up with three more of Jackatars's killers, with one of those being Malachi Murchison. Oh, Jed Reno somehow survived that scrape, too; but with two arrows in him after those villains were dead, Reno was done for. He knew he would bleed to death, or the rot would set in, and he would die slow, painfully, from gangrene. Reno had been coherent enough to tell Tim Colter what to do, and the kid had managed to cauterize those ugly wounds, get the bleeding stopped, and even do some other pretty fine doctoring for a green tree frog.

Reno woke up alive, but he wouldn't stay that way for long.

So the Colter boy had managed to fashion a travois, and they had taken off along the Green River, until they turned to climb through some of the most brutal mountains in this country that some folks were starting to call Wyoming. Finally they made it to the South Fork of the Shoshone River.

And then they had gone straight to Hell.

Colter's Hell. Named for a mountain man who had hunted and trapped this country back when Jed Reno himself had been some snot-nosed kid in Bowling Green. People still talked about John Colter. Of course, Tim Colter was no relation to the famed trapper who had traveled for a spell with Lewis and Clark, but the green tree frog did fine enough.

Colter's Hell was a smelly pit of geysers and sulfur lakes and hot springs. Medicine country, some called it. Others found it bad medicine. That's where Louis Jackatars planned to trade his women captives to some Blackfeet Indians, and then load up on gunpowder and blow the country to another level of Hell.

Jed Reno, Tim Colter, and some Cheyenne Indians had surprised Jackatars and his men. Colter had managed to make his way along a chasm carved by some of the foulest-smelling water know to man. He had gotten the girls out of there, safe and sound, while Reno had managed to kill Jackatars and blow up the gunpowder.

The boy, the girls, and the Indians were supposed to have tried for Fort Union, way up on the Missouri near the Yellowstone. They'd be safe there. Well, that had been Reno's plan, because he figured he would be killed in the explosion. But God favored fools.

Reno caught up with them. He had planned to take the white greenhorns back to Bridger's Fort so they could make their way on to Oregon. But Reno, the Cheyennes, and young Tim Colter had not killed all of Jackatars's villains. Dog Ear Rounsavall, perhaps the meanest of the lot, had followed them. He had challenged Reno to a duel, but it was Tim Colter who accepted the fight.

Now, that was a fight to remember. Reno had marveled at how much Tim Colter had grown. The boy killed Dog Ear Rounsavall, pretty easily, too. So they had returned to Bridger's trading post, said their good-byes, and Tim Colter had left Reno's life.

Left his life forever.

Reno gripped the bottle, and took another pull of bourbon. Of course, it didn't have to be forever. The kid had invited Reno to come visiting, but Reno had never been much for visiting. He figured his home was in the Rockies. Carson, Bridger, and many other trappers—even Terrence

"Just" Jenkins—had been back to St. Louis, or at least Independence, but never Jed Reno. He always said he had
been born . . . reborn, maybe . . . in this country.

"That country," Reno corrected himself. Violence, Idaho
Territory, lay maybe three hundred miles east of Fort
Bridger. Probably two hundred to maybe even five hundred
miles from where he had trapped all those years in the
Rockies.

He corked the bottle, and looked back in the storeroom,
which also served as his bedroom, his living quarters. A
couple of older ledgers lay somewhere beneath the old
hides, robes, and some of his trapping equipment. If his
memory was right, and there was no guarantee after
drinking three-quarters of a bottle of bourbon, he had
stuck the second letter Tim Colter had written him in one
of those old books.

That letter had arrived during the War to Save the
Union. It, too, had been delivered to Bridger's Fort, which
had been forwarded on to Reno's own post. Took probably six months for the letter to reach Jed Reno.

It wasn't much of a letter, either. Tim Colter had been
marshaling in Oregon—a federal job—before he had
joined the army. He said he doubted if he would stay in the
army, and as soon as the war ended—by then, from everything Reno was hearing, that would not take too long—he
would return to being a lawman. He did say one of the
scouts reminded him of Reno, which was why he had
taken pencil to hand to check up on his old mentor.

"Mentor": Reno had asked a dragoon what that word
meant. It had made him smile.

Something else in that letter had made Reno blow his
nose, although he blamed it on the dust and cold. Colter
and his wife had three children. The oldest was a boy,
twelve years old when Tim had written the letter. The kid's

name was Jed. Named after "my dear old friend, loyal comrade, teacher, mentor, hero."

Reno looked at the *Harper's Weekly.*

The story said that Colter, who had single-handedly wiped out an outlaw gang led by some cutthroat named Rose, was a widower. A disease—that word Reno could not make out—had taken Colter's wife and three kids back in '65. Every time Jed Reno read over that passage, his chest tightened. The boy Tim had named after Jed Reno . . . he was dead.

Reno inhaled deeply, and made himself stand. He went back into the trading post, to the counter, found his ledger, and ripped out a blank page in the back. He figured he was just drunk enough to write a letter. Probably be the first letter he had ever written, and his last.

When he had suggested Tim Colter as the lawman of Violence, all he had known about his old traveling pard was that Colter had been a federal marshal in Oregon. But the way that magazine story put things, Colter was a good lawman. Well, Reno made himself smile, the boy had one good teacher twenty-odd years ago.

Reno cursed himself. Two letters Tim Colter had written, but Jed Reno had never written the boy back. Colter probably figured Reno was six feet under by now. Reno looked at what he had written: *Dear Tim.* He looked back at the canvas opening to the dugout part of the post. He thought about wadding up the ledger paper and tossing it into the stove. Jed Reno was not one to beg. And he was not the kind of man to bring a friend into a situation that could get that boy killed.

"They asked me to be that lawman," Reno said to himself.

He looked at the pencil in his hand, at the misshapen knuckles. Hell, it hurt him just to stand here, and he was leaning against the counter. He knew he had been right to turn down that job offer. "I'm an old man. Seventy years. More than seventy."

Again, he looked at the paper, the pencil.

"Hell's fire," he said. And he began to scratch out a few more words.

CHAPTER 12

This wasn't Tim Colter's favorite place in Salem, Oregon.

Guards armed with Spencer repeating rifles marched along fourteen-foot-high concrete walls, with cupolas on the corners housing more guards, and more guns. The main brick building, two stories, looked foreboding itself, and a tall iron fence surrounded it. The Oregon State Penitentiary had been completed back in 1866, replacing the original pen in Portland. It was a state prison, of course, but Oregon had no federal penitentiary, so federal prisoners were also confined here.

Colter stood in the warden's office, watching two guards lock a Gardner Shackle on Jake Long's right leg. One iron band locked just above Long's ankle, with braces coming down from the sides and underneath the heel of the shoe. This one, Warden J.C. Gardner bragged, weighed only eighteen pounds.

"Get used to it, boy." Standing behind his desk, Gardner smiled. "Some of my inventions weigh close to thirty pounds. But that's for the real bad boys."

Long glanced at Colter, who kept his eyes locked on the warden. One of the guards placed a heavy key, used to lock the boot into place, into his jacket pocket. Then both guards escorted the prisoner out. Jake Long walked like a man who had suffered a stroke. Hardly any balance. And Colter knew that iron band and braces would be wearing through the denim trousers and woolen socks, rubbing Long's skin raw.

"Is that necessary, Warden?" Colter asked once the last guard had closed the door.

"You know how many prisoners escaped, Marshal, before I came up with my shackle?" The warden did not wait for Colter's response. "They don't run anymore."

Colter shook his head, picked the receipt for the delivery of Jake Long to the Oregon pen off the warden's desk, and headed for the door.

"Just a moment, Colter," the warden called out.

Keeping his hand on the doorknob, Colter turned back.

"I'm glad it was you who brought in our latest guest." J.C. Gardner stood over his desk, sorting through a pile of mail. "This came yesterday." He pulled up a crumpled, wet and then dried, well-worn tan envelope. "I was going to give it to the deputy who brought in Mr. Long to hand to you. But since it's for you." With a grin, he held out the envelope.

Colter could just make out his name in the faded ink.

Tim Colter
Dep. Marshal, USA
Staat OF Or-E-gun, USA

And beneath that, the sender had penciled in:

Maal Bos: Need heLp getTin thiS to Colter, pleez, Sir

Colter gave the warden a questioning look. "It came here?"

Laughing heartily, J.C. Gardner sank into his plush chair. "Marshal, it's a miracle that thing even got to Salem, don't you think?"

Colter had to nod at that assessment.

"If I were you, sir, I'd buy every postmaster a Daniel Webster cigar between Salem and . . . and . . . and wherever in blazes that thing came from."

He looked at the fragile envelope in his hand. There was no return address, and the several cancellation stamps on the envelope were too faded for him to even make out where the letter did come from.

"Thanks," Colter said, and walked out the door.

He nodded at the guard as he passed through the iron gate out front, still studying the envelope, and quickly, though carefully, slipped it inside his coat pocket when the wind picked up and the misting rain began to fall. Colter swung into the saddle, then rode away from the prison.

It was past dinnertime, almost two o'clock, so he road to Ferry Street and found an open rail in front of the Bullfrog Café. After tethering his horse, he ducked underneath the awning and looked through the glass in the door. Not crowded. The rush was over by this time of day, so Colter went inside, removing jacket and hat. After withdrawing the envelope, he sat at the table closest to the overhead lighting.

"Hey there."

Colter looked up and smiled. Betsy McDonnell had already filled a cup with coffee and slid it in front of him.

"Hungry?"

"Stew," he requested, and she left.

He was still holding the envelope when Betsy returned with a bowl that smelled great. She had brought an extra cup of coffee, too.

"Mind if I join you?"

He grinned. "Well, it would be imprudent for a man to tell his fiancée no. Right?"

With a laugh, she sat across from him.

Oh, they had played everything with the strict formalities. Waited a full year after Betsy's husband had died before they began what one might call a courtship. In March, they had agreed to marry—Colter wouldn't actually call it a proposal—and had set a wedding date in June. Two months.

"What's that?" Betsy asked.

"I don't know, exactly," Colter answered.

"You going to open it?"

"It might disintegrate in my hands."

Her head shook. "It's not that far gone."

He found a knife by the place-setting and slid it through the corner. Two pieces of paper were folded inside. One looked like it had been ripped from a newspaper or magazine. Slowly he pulled the papers out, and laid them in the center of the table. Immediately he recognized the clipping.

"*Harper's Weekly* made you famous," Betsy said.

"I never should have agreed to let that artist do those drawings, or write that story."

"You can't stop the press."

"Wasn't thinking clearly." Hell, who would have been thinking with clarity after all he had been through? That gunfight should have left Tim Colter dead. One man against a gang of thugs led by Stewart Rose? He still didn't know how he had lived through that, and sometimes he thought maybe he had gone after Rose and his blackhearts because he had wanted to die. He had known Betsy McDonnell then, but he had not found love till after that set-to.

"Well?" Betsy asked.

Colter slid the page from *Harper's Weekly* aside, and stared at the letter, still folded, brittle, stained from water.

A corner fell off as he unfolded the paper—from a ledger, it appeared—and he brought it up to read.

At first, he beamed, and said, "Well, I'll be damned."

Quickly, however, that smile died on his face.

Tim
Yes Plenti Medesen IS stil Aliv & hop U is 2
Harper's Weekly tels me that I taut U good
Run a post ON the UP lin
we need help killins thieves bad tims
if U cud come Help, wood B a bles-in
yer pard
Jed Reno
Violet, Idaho Ty.

"His spelling is atrocious," Betsy said after Colter had passed the letter across the table. "I would know that. I taught school before I married Elliott."

Colter liked that. Betsy could mention her dead husband now without grieving. And Tim Colter thought, for the most part, he had put his wife and children in a good place. A good memory. He and Betsy could get on with living, and not mourning. "What is this Plenti . . . ?"

"Plenty Medicine," Colter answered. "His Indian name. And I think his writing's pretty good. Clear, at least. Concise. Considering he probably hasn't written a letter since he was . . . since . . . well . . . forever."

She studied the letter again, but finally placed it gently on the checkered tablecloth. "Violet?" she asked. "Idaho Territory?"

"Imagine Jed copied that off some building, or a signpost on the Union Pacific rails."

Again, Colter looked at the letter, but this time he read it without those memories from two decades ago coming to him. He analyzed the letter, and he sighed.

"Jed must've told the city leaders about me." Leaning back in his chair, he recalled the letter that had come to U.S. Marshal Zeiber. They had read that letter in this very restaurant, just a few tables over, several months ago. He remembered what Zeiber had called the letter.

"A request, sir. A plea for help."

Colter had easily dismissed such a plea, such a request. He wasn't leaving Oregon for Idaho Territory. He wasn't leaving Betsy McDonnell.

"Tim," Betsy said. "This Reno . . . he would not have known about the gunfight with the Stewart Rose bunch back then. I remember when that letter came. It was our first meeting with Marshal Zeiber. There is—"

"I'd written Jed before," Colter told her. "Gosh." His head shook. "That had to be an eternity ago. During the war. Before Patricia and the kids were called to Glory." He had done it, too. He had managed to say that without feeling his heart break, or the tears well. "Told him I had had a job as a federal deputy, that I'd likely go back to marshaling when the war finally ended."

He was smiling. Hearing from Jed Reno did that. By Jupiter, Reno was still alive. That Cyclops in buckskins would have to be seventy years old by now. No, probably a year or two beyond seventy. And running a trading post, following in Jim Bridger's moccasin tracks. Colter tried to picture what that vagabond would look like after all these years.

Across the table, Betsy McDonnell was not grinning at all.

Tim pressed his lips together.

"If I remember correctly," Betsy said stiffly, "you told Zeiber that Idaho Territory had its own lawmen. Your commission is with the district of Oregon. Isn't it?"

He leaned toward her, put out an open hand, hoping she would meet it.

She didn't. Her eyes blazed, and her face reddened.

"A man writes you for the first time in twenty years and you . . ."

"Betsy," he said, trying to stay calm.

"It is hard enough for me to watch you ride out after some evil man and go traipsing across this state. Not knowing if you'd come back again to me. Now you want to go to some—what do they call them, Hell on Wheels?—all the way in Idaho Territory. To some savage wilderness?" She pointed at the letter. "Where killings, thieves, and bad times are rampant?"

Tears began running down her cheeks.

"Betsy," he said again.

"Tim . . . we're to be married in two months."

"I imagine I'll be back in two months."

"Alive? Or in a pine box?"

That punched him in the gut. He pulled his hand back, taking the letter with him, but leaving the *Harper's Weekly* page.

"You're going." It was a statement.

"I have to."

She wiped away her tears.

"Why?"

"I owe Jed. I wouldn't be alive if not for him."

Betsy had some will. Tim Colter was amazed when she shut off those tears as if closing a spigot, and she shook her head. "Well . . . I suppose the wedding might have to wait." Her voice was calm. He could tell she was forcing this, of course, but then her expression changed again, and she blurted out in excitement, "I could come with you!"

CHAPTER 13

He remembered the roads as he followed the ruts, sometimes so deep he found it hard to believe. The closer they got to Oregon, the worse the roads had become. Sagebrush and dust, dust and sagebrush. Most of the people Tim Colter had traveled with hated the stink of sagebrush, but Colter had always found the aroma pleasing. Sagebrush and dust, dust and sagebrush. No, the country had not changed, just the ruts seemed so much deeper than they had been back in 1845. When you finally reached water, the mosquitoes seemed as big and as hungry as crows.

That had not changed twenty years later, either.

Oregon was behind him now. The last supplies he had bought had been back in Baker City. He rode easy, a pack mule trailing the black stallion he had finally gotten around to naming Plenty Medicine. And that had been long before Jed Reno's letter had reached him at the Oregon State Penitentiary.

Marshal Zeiber had regretfully accepted Colter's resignation as a deputy marshal, but promised him the job would be his when he returned. Zeiber had stressed *"when."*

"You could get an appointment in Idaho Territory," Zeiber had said. "I'll be glad to write an endorsement."

Colter had considered it before declining. "Then I might get pulled away from Violence."

"Which wouldn't be a bad thing," Zeiber had said with a frown. "At fifteen bucks a month."

"Keep that letter handy, Marshal," Colter had told him. "If I need it, I'll send word to you." Yet, Betsy McDonnell had changed Colter's mind about that. A federal commission might come in handy, she had argued, or at least give some ruffian second thoughts before pulling a trigger. Killing a town law was one thing. Having every federal lawman on your trail for killing one of their own was another. She had changed Colter's mind about the commission, but he had not backed down on refusing her offer to come to Violet, Idaho Territory.

"They don't call this place Violence for nothing," he had said.

A barren land Colter had crossed. He remembered those rough parts of volcanic rock, the smell of salt along the desert ranges, and some of the most rugged mountains he had ever seen—jutting up like teeth from some storybook monster.

Even today, all those years since the last of the Conestoga trains had brought settlers to Oregon, Colter remembered how tough it was crossing the Snake Country, where broken rocks could lame oxen and horses, or how long it had taken him to clean hooves with his knife of packed-in volcanic ash.

Oh, rain fell here. But the land soaked it up like a sponge, and that precious water disappeared into sinks in the desert. Even when they followed along the Snake River, water was hard to find. The river cut through the black basalt and ran wild far below the trail, maybe a hundred, maybe two, perhaps even more, impossible to reach.

Colter remembered Jed Reno telling him what French-Canadian trappers had called the Snake: *la maudite riviere enragee*, "the accursed mad river."

That part of the Oregon Trail might have been the worst, especially for those settlers who had endured so much on those endless miles from Independence to Fort Hall. You would hit, if you were lucky, that desert wasteland in July or August, and it could break your heart. Of course, when Tim Colter had first seen it, his heart had been broken by the massacre of his parents. And he had grown up a lot since that day at South Pass.

Now, the country, still brutal, seemed tame.

As Colter traveled east, beyond Fort Hall, came a stunning paradise of wonderful mountains, cool breezes, timber, water, grass for livestock, fish and ducks and geese to eat. This was Bear River. Sheep Rock and Soda Springs. Katydids, which the settlers had called "Mormon crickets." Annoying to many of the emigrants on the trail, but Jed Reno had taught Tim Colter that they made fine eating, and a key ingredient to the pemmican that kept them alive. Colter caught a few as he made his way across the country and put them into a kind of soup he cooked up. The protein was needed, even if they tasted like dung.

Steamboat Spring and then the Sheep Creek Hills. How nightmarish that had been back in '45, climbing up, then sliding down with the wagon wheels locked with sawed logs.

It was a lot easier on horseback.

He made it across the Utah country, passing many abandoned stations that had once fed and housed riders for the Pony Express, around Salt Lake, and neared Bridger's Fort. Bridger wasn't there anymore. The Pony Express had used it as a station back in 1860 and '61, but the army had taken over the post during the Mormon War in the 1850s. When that ugly incident had ended, the government had not let Bridger take back his property. Colter wasn't sure what kind of deal Russell, Major, and Waddell had negotiated with the army to get that Pony Express station. The army had left for the war, but the blueboys were back when Colter rode to the post. Infantry boys, Colter noticed. A lot of good foot soldiers could do in horse country.

"I'm looking for the U.P. rails," Colter told the post commander, a major who looked as if he needed to march a lot with his soldier boys.

"Well, sir, it's not here."

Colter waited.

"Not yet anyway. A year from now, perhaps. If the Indians stay peaceable."

Colter took the coffee a sergeant brought him.

"It doesn't follow the old Oregon Trail, does it?"

"Not exactly. At least, not east of here. The rails are being laid mostly south of the old trail."

"And a Hell on Wheels, or a town called Violet?"

The major shrugged. He had that bulging red nose of a hard drinker, but the sergeant, standing behind his commanding officer, kept nodding at Colter, letting him know what was right.

"When the U.P. . . . or maybe the Central Pacific . . . reaches Fort Bridger, then maybe I can tell you. If this Violet is a Hell on Wheels town on the U.P. line, by grab, I'd have to guess that the citizens there are more in touch with civilization than we are."

At the stables, he found two soldiers admiring Plenty Medicine. Colter could smell the whiskey on their breath.

"I'll be taking my leave now, boys," Colter said. "With my horse and my mule."

"Fancy rig you got there," the corporal said, a big brawler with a misshapen nose and several missing teeth. "Ain't seen a pistol like that since the war."

Colter waited.

"And it had been on a dead Reb."

"You a Reb?" the private said, a tall man who leaned against the fence, and cracked his knuckles.

"All I want is my horse," Colter said. "And my mule."

"You don't sound like no Reb," the corporal said.

"I served with the First Oregon Cavalry, boys. Wore the blue like you two are wearing now. And I was born in Pennsylvania. That satisfy you?"

"No," they said at the same time.

He had to concede that both men had gumption. No sense, but plenty of grit. They came at him quickly, bringing up their fists. Two men ready for a row, but with fists. Coming against a man armed with a LeMat revolver on his hip. Colter caught a glimpse of something shiny, and then learned that this fight wasn't so one-sided to his advantage after all.

The blow from the tall man split Colter's cheek, almost broke the bone, and blood rushed down his face as he fell against the mule, which snorted and kicked. The next blow, also from the private, hit the back of Colter's head, and more blood flowed, and more pain shot through his head.

"Let me have at him, Grover!" the corporal yelled.

"I want his gun," Grover sang out.

"I want his boots."

"I'll take the mule."

"And I get the stallion."

Colter felt an iron fist ram into his stomach. He doubled over, and through blurred vision, he saw the corporal, drawing back his elbow to fire another punch. Colter tasted blood, and felt the coffee he had been drinking in the commanding officer's quarters coming up his throat. But at least the corporal wasn't using brass knuckles like the tall private.

The corporal slammed another fist, that somehow, vaguely, Colter managed to deflect, but then the soldier latched another hand on Colter's collar. Colter tried to shake his vision clear. The big brute's right clawed onto the gunbelt, and for a moment, Colter thought that the corporal was trying to pull the LeMat. But no. Instead, the big man was lifting Colter off his feet. The man's strength astonished Colter as he felt his boots leave the ground. The mule sidestepped, snorted, and kicked, but the corporal shoved Colter and the mule until the animal was pinned against the corral fence. Then Colter was lifted up and thrown over the mule, and felt himself crashing into the corral.

He came up quickly. This time, he reached for his LeMat, only to find it gone. The mule kicked up dust and bellowed. Both soldiers cursed. Ducking underneath the railings, Colter could sense the men trying to get around the mule, but that mule kept kicking and braying, madder than Tim Colter was getting himself.

"I got the gun, Grover," the corporal yelled.

"Then let's finish that ol' boy. Before Sergeant Meriden spoils our fun."

Colter moved to the kicking mule. He found the leather sack, somehow managed to pull it from the thongs holding it in place. It weighed a damned ton, and strained his muscles as he cleared away from the angry mule.

Voices rang out. Shouts. Someone even blew a whistle. Colter couldn't make out the words, and didn't try to. He focused on Grover with the brass knuckles and the corporal with Colter's LeMat.

The corporal came out of the dust first, holding the LeMat in his right hand. Grinning. Even as Tim Colter swung the heavy, clanging sack. Bones crunched when the sack connected against the corporal's arm, and the man screamed, and fell into a heap. The momentum carried Colter past with such a force that Grover's swing with the brass knuckles carried him away. The tall man rammed into the fence, and turned, but he was too late. Because Tim Colter had found more strength, and the heavy sack crashed against Grover's chest. The man wheezed, and slid into a heap, spitting up blood.

"You need stitches," Sergeant Meriden said.

Colter dabbed the cuts on his face and head with a whiskey-soaked bandanna the major had given him. He cringed at the burning.

"Doc Weston ain't too bad," Meriden said, "if he's sober."

Pressing the bandanna against the back of his head, Colter used his other hand to splash water on his face from the horse trough.

"Your doctor will be busy with your corporal and private, Sergeant," Colter said. The LeMat had been wiped free of most of the dirt and returned to Colter's holster. The mule had stopped kicking. Plenty Medicine looked ready to leave Fort Bridger, which certainly had been a lot friendlier when Jim Bridger had been running it.

"Probably right," Meriden said. "Turner's arm's so busted up, he won't be salutin' nobody for a spell. And with as many ribs as Grover busted up, he might not even be alive in a few days iffen one of those ribs sticks into his lungs."

"Better him than me." Colter had not forgotten what Jed Reno had taught him.

Most of the foot soldiers kept a lot of distance from

Colter, as he hoisted the sack and secured it onto the pack-saddle.

"What, may I ask, do you have in that bag, sir?" the major asked.

Turning around, Colter smiled. "Just some Oregon Boots, Major. Just some Oregon Boots."

CHAPTER 14

He followed Groshon Creek out of Fort Bridger, and then kept along Blacks Fork as he made his way east. When eventually the creek merged with Smith's Fork, he left the water and moved through the hard country, swimming the Green, which was heavy with snowmelt at this time of year, and then staying close to Bitter Creek as it meandered through the southern part of the Red Desert. Purple sage guided his way as he rode, the days disappearing, the cuts on his face and head scabbing over, no longer throbbing. Past the Continental Divide, Point of Rocks, Table Rock. South Pass lay to the north of him, and now the west. This country was new to him, but he figured the directions Sergeant Meriden had given him would get him to the Union Pacific at some point. If he wasn't killed.

In a few days, he saw the smoke signals rising from distant hills.

A man alone, traveling with a pack mule, would make an inviting target for any Cheyenne Indian, even if that tribe wasn't on the warpath. Yet the Indians must have found him a curiosity, or maybe deemed him crazy. What honor was there in taking the scalp of a man driven insane? That would bring only shame to the Cheyennes, and a good black stallion and a mean-spirited mule was not worth that. Even if mule made a good supper for a village.

It took him a week from Fort Bridger before he crossed the North Platte River. Five days later, he rode into Fort Sanders, an army post of wood that looked as though the wind might blow it away. And there certainly was wind. The soldiers there showed little interest in Plenty Medicine, the mule, or him, but a chatty sergeant informed him that he would find the railroad a short ride east.

"They be expectin' the rails here sometime in a week or so," the soldier said. "Maybe even sooner."

That much seemed obvious. Canvas tents flapped in the gusts, and wagonloads of wood were parked along what folks were turning into streets. Already some sod huts had been dug out, and log cabins built. Colter looked and marveled. He was watching the birth of a town.

"Gonna call it Laramie," the sergeant said. "Laramie City."

"Another Hell on Wheels?" Colter asked.

The sergeant shrugged. "For a spell, I reckon. But towns grown out of them sort of shenanigans. The law comes to a place, in good order. Or the town just dies and folks move along. Where you bound?"

"Violet," Colter answered.

The sergeant almost choked on the bulge of tobacco in his cheek. He wiped his lips with the back of his hand, turned, and spit.

"That's one town I'd like to see die."

Colter looked, but he knew to keep his mouth shut. The sergeant liked to gab, and would need no prodding.

"It's a hard day's ride from here. Real hard. Day and a half, maybe two probably take you with that mule. Too many of my boys, they get to hankerin' for some female company, or to drink and gamble and lose all their pay. So they ride or walk or practically run the forty miles to Vio-

lence. That's what we call it. What everybody calls it. Not
Violet. Because Violence is what it is. You'll meet the U.P.
rails long before that. Then you just follow the iron till
you come to it. Till you come to Hell."

"You can't do anything about it?" Colter asked, although he knew the answer. "Clean it up?"

"No. It ain't the army's matter. And there's another post
closer, Fort Russell. Near Cheyenne. I got to think they got
a much bigger problem with Violence than I do, being it's
just ten or twelve or fifteen miles from there."

Colter held out his hand, and liked the sergeant's firm
grip.

"Sergeant," he said, "you've been most helpful, and
quite kind. This is a much better reception than I got at
Fort Bridger."

The noncommissioned officer spit.

"What you plan on doing in Violence, mister, if you
don't mind my asking?"

"I'm going to be the town marshal."

The sergeant stared, waited for the joke to be admitted,
and when it did not come, he turned his head to spit again.
When he looked back at Colter, he sized him up, glanced
at the holstered LeMat, and said:

"Wait till you see what kind of reception you get in Violence . . . Marshal."

He knew he was nearing the Union Pacific. A faint line
of smoke streamed into the pale sky past a few rolling,
treeless hills. Not smoke signals from Indians. No, this
smoke was black and thick, and fairly steady. A locomotive, Colter figured, likely with a load of supplies.

Yet, when he crested the hill and came to the flats, he
saw the first railroaders. Colter reined in, wet his lips, and
swallowed down the bile that was rising in his throat. He
kicked the black into a walk and pulled the mule behind

him. There were no rails, no train, no telegraph poles, but six white men, two saddle horses, and a wagon. A surveying crew, Colter thought as he pushed back his coattails for easier access to the LeMat.

There was another horse, too, but it seemed out of place. A pinto, more white than brown, with an Indian saddle and hackamore, tied to the right rear wheel of the wagon.

One of the men, a bearded man in plaid britches stuck inside work boots, nudged another man and spoke to the others, who seemed preoccupied with their task. They had unhitched the wagon, led the team of mules a few yards away, and pushed up the wagon tongue. A rope hung down from the top of the wooden log. The end of the rope had been fashioned into a loop. That loop was being fitted over an Indian's head.

"Howdy." Colter stopped the horse, and hooked a leg over the saddle horn as he pushed back the brim of his hat.

The bearded man pointed a rifle, an old Enfield, in Colter's general direction. Another drew an Army Colt from his waistband. As far as Colter could tell, the rest of the work crew carried no weapons other than surveying equipment and knives.

"Where in hell did you come from?" the bearded man asked.

"Oregon," Colter answered with a smile. He looked, however, at the Indian.

"The hell you say," said a pockmarked worker as he mopped his sweaty face with a rag.

"Salem, Oregon. Been riding a long way." Colter gestured toward the black smoke. "Got a job in Violence."

"Gambler?" the bearded man asked.

"Well . . ." Colter looked away from the Indian. "I reckon you could say it's a gamble. Yes, sir. It's most definitely a gamble." He pointed at the Indian. "Trouble?"

"Redskin," the man in blue denim and a collarless shirt said. He was the one with the Army .44. "And redskins are always trouble."

"LeRoy caught him snoopin'," said the shortest one. His right hand rested on a wooden tripod, which held an interesting device, that ten-inch-or-so telescope affixed to a circle. This instrument had a six-inch horizontal circle, and a five-inch vertical circle and needle. A surveyor's transit, at least, that's what Colter thought the gadget was called.

"We figured to make him a good Injun," the sweaty man said with a laugh.

"Causing you trouble, eh?" No one answered. So Colter figured that meant that the Indian had not been doing anything. "Let me see what I can get out of him." He dismounted easily, but even before his feet settled in the tall grass, the Enfield was pointed at his midsection.

"This any of yer affairs, stranger?" the man said.

"Yeah. And yours, too. You ask this Indian anything?"

"He don't speak no English," the bearded man replied.

"And he might have twenty or forty friends waiting over one of those rises." Ignoring the Enfield, Colter moved toward the Indian. But even as the two surveyors closest to the Indian and the wagon tongue backed away a few feet, Colter could feel the rifled musket and the Army Colt being aimed at his back. He heard the metallic click of the .44's hammer.

"*Vé-ho-é-nestsestotse?*" Colter asked.

The youngest one, a freckle-faced redhead, asked in an Irish brogue, "You speak that talk?"

"That's the limit of my Cheyenne," Colter answered.

The Indian shook his head. He looked to be somewhere between forty and fifty, his braids showing threads of silver, his face scarred, forehead knotted, eyes hard. He was

Cheyenne. That much seemed obvious, and he looked straight through Colter, studying him, even tilting his head.

Colter signed his name. Well, not really his name, although he said, in English, "I am Tim Colter." The sign he gave was that of a star. It was the closest Colter could think of explaining that he was a lawman.

"Tim . . ." The Indian's voice was guttural, but easy to understand. "Col-ter."

"That's right."

Then the Cheyenne said. "Plen-ty . . . Med-cine."

Colter blinked in astonishment. This warrior knew Jed Reno, and he seemed to remember Tim Colter. Colter had not known many Indians in all of his life, and he couldn't say he had known any when he had been traveling along the Oregon Trail or searching for his sister. But . . .

"I thought that buck didn't speak no English," the bearded man said.

"He doesn't," Colter said, waving his left hand to make the bearded man keep quiet. Colter concentrated on the Indian as he moved his leathery hands and fingers, as the Cheyenne rubbed four fingers in a circle, counterclockwise, along his right cheek, and, immediately afterward, held two hands in front of him, the palms up, and spread those hands apart. "Red Prairie." Colter could not believe it.

"He said that," the Irish boy asked, "with nothing but hands and fingers."

"Red Prairie," Colter said again.

"What's that mean?" the man with the Colt said. "That this prairie's gonna run red with our blood. Why, that dirty red Injun. String him up, boys."

Colter spun, the LeMat in his right hand. The gunshot roared, and down went the man with the Colt, clutching his right thigh. Before the bearded man could blink, the LeMat spoke again, and this bullet winged off the Enfield, sending it spinning skyward while driving the bearded man onto his buttocks. Next, the heavy pistol, already cocked, pointed at the redhead and a tobacco-chewer, the two closest to the wagon tongue.

"Fun's over, boys," Colter said.

The one with the bullet in his thigh moaned. The bearded man shook his stinging hands.

The sweaty man's jaw dropped open, but he did not speak.

Colter waved the smoking cannon in his right hand at the Irish boy.

"Cut Red Prairie loose," he said.

"But . . ."

The LeMat's barrel lifted, and the boy pulled a pocketknife from his pants pocket.

"Get your horse, Red Prairie," Colter said, and watched the Indian, massaging his wrists to get the circulation going again, move toward the wagon and his pinto pony.

"This wasn't none of your affair, mister." The bearded man, still on his butt, had found his voice.

"The army, from what I hear, is supposed to protect you from Indians," Colter said. "But you figured to string up an Indian who was just watching you, curious, to see what you were doing. If you'd hanged Red Prairie, you're right, this whole country would be running red with blood. Starting an Indian war is a bad idea, boys."

"You sorry son of a . . . ," the bearded man started.

Colter stopped him by aiming the LeMat. "Don't make me sorry I didn't kill you. Because I could have. And I still can."

"We'll see you in Violence, mister!" the man with the bullet in his thigh wailed.

"If you do, it'll be the last thing you ever see."

First, Colter gathered the Enfield and the Colt, which he heaved into the grasses as far as he could. Red Prairie was busy, too, getting his knife back from the sweaty man, and the bow and quiver of arrows back from the fattest of the bunch. Next, Colter moved to his horse, made sure Red Prairie was mounted and waiting, and swung into the saddle.

"We'll find you," the sweaty man said, but he was bluffing.

"Look me up in Violence, boys. I'll be at the town marshal's office."

Then he kicked the black into a lope, pulling the mule behind him, and followed Red Prairie over the closest ridge.

CHAPTER 15

"Twenty winters?" Red Prairie signed.
"More," Colter answered.

They smoked Red Prairie's pipe.

Tim Colter had met the Cheyenne brave through, of course, Jed Reno. Reno had given Colter that quick lesson in sign language, and later, Red Prairie had taught Colter a little more. Other lessons had come during the Civil War, when Colter had been with the Oregon volunteers chasing Indians instead of Confederates.

If Colter remembered correctly, Red Prairie had met up with Jed Reno when the trapper had first started chasing Malachi Murchison. It was the Cheyenne who had told Reno about the massacre of Colter's parents and Mr. Scott. Then Red Prairie and some of his braves had joined Colter and Reno near Colter's Hell. They had helped save Patricia Scott, Colter's sisters, and Mrs. Scott from Jackatars and those fiends with him. Reno and Colter could not have saved those women, if not for the Cheyennes, and the Cheyennes would not have helped, had it not been for Red Prairie.

He didn't know what the Cheyenne thought, but Tim Colter figured that he owed Red Prairie plenty, and, despite what he had just done, probably would never be able to repay that debt.

Colter signed a question about Plenty Medicine, but the warrior merely shook his head and signed back that many, many winters had passed since he had last seen the one-eyed trapper. The Cheyenne used fingers and hands and some throaty grunts to ask Colter if he had seen Plenty Medicine, but this time Colter shook his head. He wondered if he could tell him that he had heard from Jed Reno and that he probably would see him in the next couple of days. But that seemed beyond Colter's knowledge of signing, not to mention the dexterity of his fingers and hands.

Red Prairie then spoke and signed of the years that had passed since that day at Colter's Hell, which had made Red Prairie quite the wealthy Indian back in his village. They had captured a lot of horses from the thieves and killers, not to mention a few scalps. But since then . . .

It had started several years back, long after Colter had made his way to Oregon, but he had heard the story. Everyone in the United States and her territories knew what had happened.

Around 1854, an Indian brave—he was not Cheyenne, Red Prairie stressed, but a Sioux, a Miniconjou—had come across a stray cow that had wandered off from the wagon train, and the hungry Indian had killed the cow. The cow's owner complained to the army at Fort Laramie. Some greenhorn lieutenant rode out to an Indian camp to find out what had happened.

The Indians were at peace. The Sioux had never troubled the white men, and rarely if ever tormented any of the emigrants heading west in their wagon trains. They were living and abiding by the Treaty of 1851, camping near Fort Laramie as they were supposed to do.

The camp was another branch of the Sioux, Brulé, and the chief was named Conquering Bear. The officer wanted the man who had killed the cow to be turned over to the army, so he could be arrested and tried. Conquering Bear tried to explain that he was Brulé, and had no authority over the Miniconjou. Talks went on, but Conquering Bear could not bend, so the army soldier went back to Fort Laramie.

The officer of the post sent another officer back to Conquering Bear's camp. His name was John Lawrence Grattan, a foot soldier with the 6th U.S. Infantry, Colter recalled, who had recently been graduated from the U.S. Military Academy at West Point. Grattan seemed to be spoiling for a fight, and rode out with just about thirty men, a half-breed interpreter named Auguste, who was pretty fortified with liquor, and two cannons.

Auguste didn't like the Sioux, and the Sioux did not care much for him. The half-breed called out, "Where are your warriors? I see only women." And laughed. He said, "These bluecoats that ride with me have come to kill you all. We shall clean up this country by and by." Not that anyone could understand what Auguste was saying. He spoke little Sioux, and the booze slurred his words. But Conquering Bear and the other Sioux did not need to understand but a few words. They could see what Auguste meant in his eyes, and in the face of the shavetail lieutenant leading his men.

Grattan demanded the cow-killer.

Conquering Bear, ever the diplomat, said he could not turn over the brave, but would give the lieutenant a horse, as a token, as a replacement for the dead cow.

About this time, a trader named Bordeau came along to help ease the tension. Bordeau spoke fluent Sioux, and the Indians liked and respected him. Bordeau spoke some, but he could see the Indians and the soldiers and Auguste. Anything he said now, Bordeau later explained, would have done nothing. It was already too late. He rode back to his trading post, drew in the latchstring, closed and bolted the shutters, and loaded his gun. A fight, he said, was as certain as winter snow.

Grattan yelled at Conquering Bear, saying that the U.S. Army knew how to deal with lawbreakers, and walked away. One of his men raised his rifle and fired at an Indian. Conquering Bear screamed for peace, but he was cut down. Even belligerent Lieutenant Grattan yelled at his men, trying to stop an ugly incident—or, more likely, trying to save his own life. But any hope at peace had disappeared.

Grattan fell dead, his body pincushioned with arrows. Auguste was caught and chopped to pieces. Eleven soldiers fell beside the dead lieutenant. The others tried to run back to Fort Laramie, but a party of Sioux cut them off. All were killed except for one, and he would die a short time later back at Fort Laramie.

Newspapers called it the "Grattan Massacre."

Red Prairie said it should have been called the "Place Where Conquering Bear—and Peace—All Died."

"You're probably right," Colter told him in English, but the Cheyenne did not understand.

The U.S. Army retaliated, of course. That was the army's way. A colonel named Harney took to the field. Colter remembered reading in a newspaper that Harney had said, "I am for battle. No peace."

Harney's troops caught up with some Sioux at Bluewater Creek in Nebraska in 1855, and pretty much ended what the newspapers kept calling an uprising. The First Sioux War. But not the last.

The Santee Sioux, starving and having not been paid or fed as prescribed by a treaty, rebelled in Minnesota and Dakota Territory in the early years of the Civil War. Colter couldn't remember how many settlers had been killed, but he did know that several Indians had been hanged in Mankato, once the army had stopped that rebellion.

Nor had the Cheyenne been spared.

During the cold months in the later half of 1864, a Methodist minister named John Chivington, commissioned colonel of some Colorado militia, had attacked a peaceful camp of Black Kettle and cut down more than a hundred Indians, perhaps as many as two hundred. Most of those were women and children. And what the white soldiers had done to the dead, and the living, was uglier than anything Tim Colter would have imagined.

So the Cheyenne Indians joined the Sioux and other Plains Tribes. Julesburg, a white settlement on the South Platte River, was almost wiped out by a combined Indian force of Sioux, Cheyenne, and Arapaho. Rock Creek Spring . . . Platte Bridge Station . . . Tongue River . . . Sawyers Fight . . . the Fetterman Massacre up at Fort Phil Kearny, where another glory-hunting soldier had led his command to death. Even as far west as Washington Territory at the Bear River Massacre, war had spread. Peace came in spurts, but rarely lasted. Usually, Colter had to concede, it was his people—not the Indians—who had started the wars. But, alas, likewise, it was his people—and not the Indians— who had the firepower and numbers and the temperament to finish those wars, too.

Sometimes Colter found himself wondering. Louis Jackatars, that demented, violent half-breed, had dreamed of turning this territory into a sea of blood, a place where peace would never settle, a country that would be awash in violence for years and years to come.

"This is Jackatars's dream . . . fulfilled," he said.

Colter blinked. He wet his lips and nodded at Red Prairie.

*   *   *

The past twenty-plus years had been hard on the Cheyenne warrior. His eyes seemed ancient; his skin was cracked with deep crevasses and scars. Most of the Indian's teeth were gone, and those not were rotten. He did not smile. One earlobe was missing, and his bottom lip was deformed by what appeared to be a bullet wound. His right pinky was missing, as was the tip of his left pointer finger, and deeper scars had been carved into his forearms. Probably during a mourning period. Indians often cut themselves when they had lost a loved one. Wife? Sons? Colter could only guess, and he would never ask.

Red Prairie pointed at the black smoke, still soiling the blue sky over one of the hills.

"When the whites first came in their prairie schooners," the Cheyenne signed, "we let them pass. Even though we knew that eventually they would not pass, but stay. Some, like Plenty Medicine, we welcomed. For they lived as we did. They knew and respected our ways. Our lives. Yet, more and more passed through, and the buffalo, the elk, the antelope, eventually even the rabbits, they left the country. They moved on. Often my people had to move away, too.

"So now comes this new thing of you white people. This iron horse. We have been told that it will only pass through our country, too, but we have seen the tracks left by the prairie schooners years before. The tracks run deep, but it was our hope that, with time, maybe many, many winters, these ruts will be filled with sand and mud and the seeds that make grass. And the tracks will disappear. But these new tracks, these iron rails, these do not look like will ever go away. They will always be here. They are too heavy for even a good spring rain to wash away. And we see more of your villages along these iron tracks. More of your people come. Our buffalo—which we depend on to feed our women and babies and even ourselves—wander away, never to return. This makes it hard on our people. But this is our land. We will fight to keep our land. We will fight to stay alive. This . . . do you understand?"

Colter nodded.

"It is good." Red Prairie rose, walked to his horse, and mounted. "For I would hate," he signed, "to have to kill you."

CHAPTER 16

For what had started as just a Hell on Wheels, Violence, aka Violet, had exploded since the passing of winter. A steam-powered saw whined as its blades cut down logs. Some fool might think this was forest country, Jed Reno thought, even though a man would be hard-pressed to find any trees except along the creeks and rivers. No, greenhorn fools kept hauling lumber from over in the Medicine Bow country. Hammers pounded on nails, handsaws scratched through the planks the lumber company provided—at outrageous prices—and people busied themselves making a town.

Oh, most of the homes and businesses remained crude dugouts and soddies, or canvas tents that popped in the winds of late spring. What was that old saying he recalled back in Kentucky? March comes in like a lion and goes out like a lamb. Whoever said that had never been in Idaho Territory, or whatever they were calling this country these days. Along Clear Creek, March blew in like a dragon and never stopped blowing. The dragon's breath was the only thing that changed, hot or cold.

Yet, frame buildings—with false fronts—kept sprouting up like ungodly wildflowers along Union Street. The Blarney Stone and Slade's Saloon looked halfway respectable, and other buildings had joined them. The Railroaders Lounge. Jake's Place, Licensed Gambler. The Cheyenne Saloon. Mattie's Place. Keno House. Most of the new buildings were just raw pine, but some had been whitewashed, and one or two were painted the gaudy colors that would turn a sober man's stomach. Even the Yost Hotel—renamed now that Marshal B.B. Cutter, once co-owner, was dead, buried, and forgotten—had grown up. Numbered side streets ran north-to-south from Union Street. Mostly south. Nothing had sprung up on the other side of the Union Pacific tracks except for what passed as a depot, some storage sheds, trash heaps, and a side track for the trains that ran through.

Reno wasn't sure what the founding fathers of this blight along Clear Creek had in mind; and since he had run away from civilization in Kentucky before the railroads had reached there—before, in fact, anyone really thought train transportation would amount to much—he couldn't exactly guess how train towns should look.

But the rails lay just north of town. Then, just south of the tracks, came Union Street, but the buildings on the north side of Union did not face the railroad. Nothing faced the railroad tracks except the sheds and what everyone called a depot, but it looked just like a boxcar without wheels and had railroad ties for a porch and boardwalk. Well, Reno guessed the buildings on the south side of Union Street might have looked across at the railroad tracks, but now had nothing but south-facing buildings on the north side of the track to stare at.

All that cogitating made Jed Reno's head hurt.

And then there were those other streets, well, not that anyone who had ever seen Louisville would have called them streets. Roads, maybe. Ruts, perhaps. Winding trails over flattened grass. First Street through Sixth Street, moving westward. If the town kept growing, Jed Reno feared, it would eventually incorporate his trading post.

"What do you think, Jed?"

Turning on the heel of his moccasin, Reno saw Henry Yost leaning on the wooden column of his hotel, smoking a cigar, grinning like some greenhorn who had been out in the sun too long.

A locomotive hissed, belched, and squeaked. Piano music rang out from one of the saloons or gambling joints. Prostitutes called down from the top two floors of Mattie's Place at the railroaders, even the sodbusters who, for some crazy reason, thought they could turn this country into Iowa or Alabama, depending on what uniform they had donned in the late war.

"I don't think," Reno answered. But, since Yost had withdrawn another cigar from his coat pocket and was holding it out, Reno did walk over to the hotel.

"We're growing, Jed," the hotel man said. "I don't think Cheyenne over to the east will survive. Nor that town they think they'll build west of here. What are they calling it? Lamar? Lamar City. Larimer? Laramie? Laramie City. Something like that. Violet will be the gem of the Union Pacific in Idaho Territory. Mark my words."

A gunshot rang out.

Reno had bit off the end of the cigar and spit into the street. Now he turned, dumbly holding the match Yost had given him, and looked toward Slade's Saloon. Reno wasn't exactly certain where the shot had come from, especially now that several other dens of iniquity lined Union Street, but it was a good guess. Especially seeing how many people were suddenly moving away from the saloon, even backing up tentatively as far as The Blarney Stone.

The batwing doors pushed open, and a man stumbled

out, clutching a revolver in his left hand. Even with only one eye that had seen more than seventy years of hard living, Reno could see that no smoke drifted from the 7½-inch barrel of the Colt. The batwing doors banged back and forth as the man fell against the hitching rail, dropping the unfired Colt into the mud. He held there for a moment, before he somehow managed to push himself up, and staggered backward against the wall of the saloon, to his right of the swinging doors.

A thin, rawboned man in duck trousers, black stovepipe boots, red shirt, and a Union Army shell jacket with brass buttons. His hat, some shapeless mass of dun, had fallen off in front of the saloon's entrance, and still lay there, crown down. Like many men in this country, the man sported a beard, unkempt and dirty, and hair that would give even the best tonsorial artist in the world plenty of fits.

For some reason, the thin man bent over, trying to fetch his hat. Hat? Why not the Colt? Reno shook his head, struck the match against his thumbnail, and fired up the cigar. Another figure appeared in the doorway of the saloon, and stopped the pounding batwing doors, but this man was nothing but a silhouette, watching at the spectacle of the man as he tried again for his hat.

The coat fell open, and that's when Reno realized he had been mistaken. The shirt wasn't red. That was blood, spreading across the homespun shirt of dirty white. The thin man had taken a bullet in his belly. Gut shot. Reno removed the cigar and spit in the dirt. Awful way for a man to have to die.

But the shot man kept trying to pick up the hat, until, finally, the man who was watching from behind the batwing doors made his way through and kicked the gut-shot thin man in his rear end, sending him sailing off the boardwalk and into the mud. He rolled over, his face now coated with the muck in the streets, and clutched his belly as he coughed, moaned, and spit out bloody phlegm.

Reno looked at the man standing in front of the doors. He held a long-barreled Colt, too, in his right hand, but his weapon still smoked. His Prince Albert, the tails tucked behind the empty holster on his right hip, was black, as was his ribbon tie and flat-brimmed, low-crowned hat. Black boots kicked away the dying man's hat. The man's pants, however, were gray woolen with blue stripes along the outer seams. The pants of an old Johnny Reb soldier. The man in the street, unless his shell jacket betrayed him as a liar, had served with the Union.

"Anybody else wish to make a disparaging comment about the late Confederate States of America?" the man in the doorway called out. "Or my honor and integrity?" The accent was thick as hominy, but nowhere near as sweet as molasses. An icy voice, cold, without mercy.

Now the man stepped away from the doors to the saloon, and his black boots kicked the hat again, this time sending it sailing into the street, a few feet to the left of the dying thin man.

"God," the thin man croaked. He cried out in agony, shuddered, and turned his head again. "Have . . . oh . . . please . . . mercy . . . mercy. . . ." His head moved skyward, and he shrieked again, which startled a horse tethered to the hitching rail a few doors down from Slade's Saloon.

Reno looked away, toward The Blarney Stone, where owner Paddy O'Rourke, one of his gambler-gunmen, and two of his prostitutes stood on the boardwalk, watching.

"This cur of a coward," the man in front of Slade's gin mill said, "insulted me and the country for which I fought. I brook no insults from any man." He pointed the barrel of his Colt in the general direction of the saloon. "Ask anyone inside and they will tell you what I gave this man." Now his black hat tilted in the direction of the dying thin man. "I gave him the opportunity to withdraw his insult and apologize. Instead, he reached for the Colt." A long finger pointed at the weapon lying just below the board-walk.

"Self-defense." Micah Slade had stepped out past the doorway, holding one of the batwing doors with his left hand. "I swear to it." The saloon owner was staring at Paddy O'Rourke, but then he turned his gaze until he found Yost and Reno. "Swear to it," he said again. "Mix Range had no choice in the matter."

Mix Range. Reno wet his lips. That *Harper's Weekly* magazine a few months back, the one that had contained that fancy story and fancier drawings of Tim Colter, had also published an article on Mix Range, some terrible gun-man from Alabama who had killed a few peace officers in Texas. The state had offered a pretty good reward for Mix Range's head. But this was Idaho Territory, not Texas, and Mix Range was showing Violence what might happen to anyone here who might think about trying to collect that three hundred dollars.

"Anybody here got something to say to me?" Mix Range asked.

"God . . . ," the man in the street said. "Mer-cy."

Mix Range stepped off the boardwalk and into the mud. He spread his legs apart and slowly raised the Colt. The thumb eared back the hammer. The man smiled. So, Reno observed, did Micah Slade. The revolver boomed, and a .44 ball tore into the thin man's forehead. Right be-tween the man's eyes, which now remained open, one looking skyward, the other at his lips. The horse at the rail kicked out and whinnied. No other noise came from town until Eugene Harker stepped onto the street.

"You shot that man dead," the freedman said.

"That I did," Mix Range answered. "You want to say something about it?"

Harker shook his head. "Just that we got a law in this here town."

"Yeah? I put him out of his misery. I done him a favor. You heard him beg, didn't you, boy?"

Harker's head nodded. He started to speak, but froze at the sight of the Colt in Mix Range's hand, which was now trained on Eugene Harker's forehead.

"Hell." Jed Reno tossed the cigar into the mud—the flavor had turned vile—and moved down the muddy street. Mix Range saw him coming, but he did not move the Colt's barrel.

"Range," Reno said.

"Yeah. You got a problem, too, One-Eye?"

"Nope," Reno lied. "Just explaining the law of Violence to you. Ask your boss behind you." He tilted his head toward Micah Slade. "He knows the law. Been in place here since our last marshal got himself buried."

Reno stopped. He had placed himself between Mix Range and Eugene Harker. Behind him, he could hear the freedman whispering, "Mr. Reno, you ain't got to do that, sir. Don't get yourself blown to hell on account of me."

"Ask him," Reno said.

Mix Range did not lower the Colt, but he did shoot Micah Slade a curious glance.

The saloon owner cleared his throat.

"Reno and Harker are right, Mix," Slade said. "That's the law of Violence. *The one law.* Kill a man. You have to pay for his funeral."

CHAPTER 17

There was another thing about civilization, the railroad, this town called Violence, that sickened and saddened and downright angered Jed Reno. Now, folks might say that Jed Reno wasn't the cleanest person, and maybe he had dumped or left a few dead bodies around, but he never let trash ruin the country. Oh, he had trash—plenty of it—but he burned it in a pit behind his trading post, or in the fireplace or stove. As he walked away from the booming town, he picked up one beer bottle and several newspapers that sagebrush had snagged. The papers he shoved into his pockets. The bottle he kept in his left hand.

He stopped when he saw the horse, a good black, tethered in front of the trading post, and a pack mule hobbled in the grass near an extra water trough. He cursed himself, walking into that dung heap of a town, when he had a customer. Maybe even one that would pay, not like those Flemish sodbusters who wanted—well, actually, they had no other choice—to live on credit.

He pitched the bottle into the bucket by the front door, pulled the papers from his pockets, and tossed those also into his trash bin, and opened the door. A tall, lean, broad-shouldered man sat on the top of the counter, long legs bouncing about, while the man chewed on a peppermint candy. He still wore his hat, and Reno even saw a penny on the top of his cashbox. This gent wasn't one to live on credit. By Jupiter, he even paid for his candy. Usually, Jed Reno gave those away free—or ate them himself.

The man stopped chewing, his legs stopped kicking, and he swallowed the candy in his mouth, wiped his fingers on his trousers, and smiled.

"You haven't aged, Plenty Medicine."

Reno closed the door.

"Well, I hope to blazes that I have. That I ain't been dead all these years."

The tall man slid off the counter.

"You got my note," Reno said.

"Took a while."

Reno shrugged. "Well, never was much at writing letters or nothing. Wasn't sure how to go about it."

"You did fine. I got it."

"And you still come?"

The tall man removed his hat and laid it on the counter. When he faced Reno again, his smile had broadened. "I figured it was what friends do."

Then Jed Reno whipped off his hat, sent it sailing to the ceiling, where it crashed and dropped behind him. He let out a war whoop and charged, lowering his shoulder, just catching a glimpse of Tim Colter as he leaned forward and held out both hands. Not to stop Reno. Shoot, that would be as foolish as trying to stop a charging bull buffalo, or one of those locomotives that kept ruining this land. Reno lifted Colter and straightened, then spun around until he felt dizzy, while Colter laughed and playfully pounded on Reno's buckskin shirt. Eventually he had to stop, and lowered the tall man onto a cracker barrel. Then Reno collapsed into the rocking chair, which he left out for weary sodbusters and lazy, worthless no-accounts. He often swore he would never sit in one of those things, but, well, this one was so damned comfortable.

When the inside of the trading post—and Tim Colter— stopped spinning around, Reno stared and wet his lips.

"Now that you're here," Reno said, "I ain't rightly sure I'm glad to see you."

"I've heard," Colter said. "Town like this already has a reputation."

"You heard?" Reno blinked. "All the way in Oregon."

"Nah. But Fort Bridger. And most of the places between there and here. Violet doesn't sound like a nice place to hang your hat."

"It ain't. That's why we call it Violence. That fits better. A damned sight better than Violet. Crowding up, too. Both the town and the cemetery."

"No law."

Reno shook his head. "They tried it. Didn't cut. Man who pinned on the star thought that was all he needed. He got cut down. Cold-blooded. But . . . well . . . one gent says it was one thing, and that's all it takes. Makes me long for the days back in those wonderful mountains. Like when Kit Carson settled matters with some old cur who wasn't worth a cuss." Reno's fingers snapped. "Or like you done to Dog Ear Rounsavall."

"That was a long time ago."

"You've growed up a lot, though."

Meaning, you've killed a lot.

"Give me the lowdown," Colter said.

Reno frowned. He spit onto the floor, wiped his mouth, and stopped rocking in the stupid little chair. The coffee and stew in his stomach soured, and he felt like a stupid fool, and no friend to this fine young man at all.

After a heavy sigh, Reno said, "Boy, this here's the lowdown. You get on that fine-looking horse of yours, take that mule with you, and you ride back to that Oregon country you call home. You forget the ramblings and letter—if you could even call it a letter—that you got from me. Violence ain't worth it, boy. It ain't worth dying for."

For the longest while, Tim Colter just looked across the room, his eyes locked on the one eye of his old friend.

"Would you come with me?" he asked at last.

Reno grinned. "Can't, boy. This here's my home. Maybe not Violence. Maybe not Clear Creek. But this here territory. Those hills. Them mountains. The rivers and any beaver that might have survived somehow. I gotta stick here, boy."

"Well." Tim Colter sighed. "I guess I'll stick awhile, too."

Reno's tone sharpened. "Boy, I just watched a man come staggering out of a saloon with a bullet in his belly. Watched the assassin who shot him kick him in the butt and knock him into the street. Then I watched that devil put a bullet in the dude's head as he lay dying in the mud. And you know what the fellow who done the killing had to do?"

Colter absorbed all that. He did not answer. He waited for Reno's reply.

"Paid a dollar. A dollar for him to get buried."

"Cheap funeral," Colter said.

"This town's cheap."

"That why you picked it for your home?" Colter tried to bring a little humor inside the darkened post.

Reno's big head shook. "Wasn't no town when I started digging and rolling in logs. Wasn't nothing but antelope and some Indians who'd happen by every now and then. Nice place. Good water. Hills to keep the wind off, not like it is over in that town. I kept thinking about old Jim Bridger. You remember him, don't you?"

"One doesn't forget Jim Bridger," Colter said. "Just like no one ever forgets Jed Reno."

The old fur trapper waved off the compliment.

"Well, I started to thinking about Bridger, about how fine he was living after he give up the good life. Sipping whiskey. Telling lies. Making money off fool emigrants, like you was once. Beaver was all played out, of course, and not much living off wolf pelts and bearskins. Then I met up with some government men plotting that big railroad everyone thought this country needed. Keep the oceans together." His head shook. "Man, if you want to keep the two oceans together, just dig a damned ditch from the Atlantic to that there San Francisco town I've heard about."

"That's a fine idea, Jed. You should run for Congress."

"Don't sass me, boy. I'm seventy . . . I'm sixty years old or thereabouts, but I can still whup you to crying for mercy. So I let greed get the better of me. Greed and laziness. Made a mistake. Didn't figure that railroad would bring all this trouble. But that's my headache, and none of your own. So you ought to do like I told you—I saved your hide I don't recollect how many times all those years ago. You remember that? Don't you, boy?"

Colter grinned. "Yeah. And I remember me saving the hide of some one-eyed old reprobate."

For the first time, Jed Reno seemed to notice the hogleg holstered on Colter's right hip. He leaned forward in the rocking chair, and lifted his jaw in that direction. "What kind of cannon you got on your leg, boy?"

Rising, Tim Colter pushed back the tail of his coat, and withdrew the big revolver.

"It's called a LeMat," Colter said. "Nine-shot revolver with a smoothbore load, too."

"You ain't learned what I taught you, boy?" Reno slid back into his chair. "One shot."

"I remember you always told me to reload immediately. Don't wait. An empty gun doesn't help you do anything except get killed."

Reno grinned. "I was some teacher, wasn't I?"

"The best." Tim Colter was dead serious.

Silence. But it lasted for just a few minutes.

"There's no law in Violence?" Colter asked. "No lawman, I mean. Constable. Sheriff. Policeman. Marshal. Whatever you want to call it."

"Never got around to replacing this gent named Cutter after he got plugged." Reno shook his head. "There was a boy that everyone said killed the marshal, but I knowed that kid. He didn't do it. They just killed the lawman to run this town the way they want to. Like all those Hell on Wheels, which I'm sure you've heard of."

Colter nodded.

"Kid worked for me. Good boy. From some foreign country where everyone's called Flemish. At least, that's what I'm told. Farmers."

"Farmers?"

Reno grinned. "I didn't sell them the bill of sale that brought them here. Dumb as you once was, but good folks. They won't last, of course. Well, one of them might, but he ain't no farmer. He and his boys have a ranch south of town. Want to raise cattle."

"That's better than beans," Colter said. "At least, in this country. I don't have any prejudice against beans."

More silence.

"Who should I see about taking over for your dead marshal?"

Reno's frown hardened. "Mayor's name is Monroe. Jasper Monroe. Well, he's the mayor unless he has been replaced."

"You mean you've already had an election?"

"No." Reno shook his big head. "There ain't no elections. Nothing like that. What I meant was that maybe Micah Slade or Paddy O'Rourke replaced him. Made themselves mayor."

"They run the town?"

Reno cursed himself. There would be no getting rid of Tim Colter. Hell, he should have known that even before he wrote that stupid letter for help. Why, back when he had first found Tim Colter, back then a wet-behind-the-ears city boy from some burg in Pennsylvania, Reno had tried to talk some sense into the kid. Get him back to Bridger's trading post, away from Dog Ear Rounsavall, Malachi Murchison, and Louis Jackatars. And plenty of other cutthroats.

"Well, they ain't exactly married to each other," Reno said. "One wore the blue. That'd be the Irishman. Runs a gambling parlor and brothel. The other, Micah Slade, he runs a bucket of blood right across the street. He wore the gray."

"Still fighting the Civil War, eh?" Colter asked.

Reno nodded. "Like even today. The fellow who got killed. He was a bluebelly. Or so said the man who killed him. Mix Range." Reno whistled. "Why, I'd bet twenty prime plews that that's what Micah Slade has in mind. He wants to put a badge on Mix Range. Make him the lawman. Get control of Violence before Paddy O'Rourke can take it over."

Colter was standing now, checking the percussion caps on his big revolver.

"I guess we should stop Mix Range first."

CHAPTER 18

The façade of The Cheyenne Saloon had been painted purple. Maybe it was supposed to be violet, after the official name of the town, but it looked definitely purple. In fact, one of the ugliest shades of purple Tim Colter had ever seen. The lettering spelling the name of the saloon was black, making it hard to read, but Colter figured that most people who came into a place like this did not read anyway. They could tell what could be found inside by the crude painting of two foaming mugs of beer, and the lewd outline of a naked, plump woman.

Colter turned back and looked across the street at the barbershop and undertaking parlor. Jed Reno leaned against the wall and nodded.

So Tim Colter pushed through the batwing doors.

He saw the man with the gray trousers of an ex-Rebel soldier leaning against the bar. Not that it was much of a bar, just a series of whiskey kegs that covered the length of fourteen feet or so, and not even a plank on the top of the kegs. A place like this joint in a town like Violence needed no such formalities as an actual bar. The back bar, if anyone called the wobbly shelves behind the whiskey kegs a back bar, displayed only clay jugs.

The man in the gray pants and black hat was carrying

on a conversation with a man with a dirty green shirt and red sleeve garters. No, it wasn't a real conversation. The man named Mix Range was doing all the talking.

"You see, friend, we don't mind you working in this town. But you got to pay the permit fee."

The man who owned, presumably, The Cheyenne Saloon wiped the river of sweat off his face with dirty green sleeves.

"It's for protection, you see. A small price to pay. Ten percent of your profits, paid monthly. I'll collect. Ten percent. And that way your place isn't burned down. Or your whiskey kegs don't get filled with holes." He kicked the keg nearest his right boot for emphasis. "You savvy, don't you, sir? I mean, you're a smart businessman. And you wouldn't want to . . . well . . . let's say . . . die. Because in a town like this, that can happen, too. It often happens. And it will happen."

The sweating man, who smelled riper than a corpse, suddenly joined the conversation.

"Yes."

"Yes, what?" Mix Range asked.

"Yes . . . sir." The sweaty man was guessing.

" 'Yes, sir,' what?"

The sweaty man wet his lips, wiped his brow again, and guessed once more. "Yes . . . sir . . . I . . . understand."

The gunman smiled. "So . . . ten percent. Agreeable."

"Yes . . . sir . . . Mr. . . . Range . . . I . . . understand . . . and . . . ten . . . percent . . . is . . . just . . . fine."

"Good." The gunman slapped the top of the keg. "You might as well pay the first month now. Say fifty dollars."

The sweaty man blinked.

"I'll wait." Mix Range pointed at a jug. "And I'll have some of that there top-shelf dust-cutter while I wait. On the house."

"Of course."

The sweaty man backed away toward the cashbox, until Mix Range snapped his fingers.

"Oh." The man hurried back, grabbed the jug, put it in front of the killer, started to move, before he recalled that he might need to put a glass in front of Mix Range. He did that. And started to move again. That's when he noticed Tim Colter.

The sweaty man froze. His eyes widened. His mouth hung open, drawing flies, which were abundant in a place like this.

Slowly the gunman named Mix Range looked for a mirror, but there were no mirrors in The Cheyenne Saloon. He picked up the jug, poured a few fingers, and brought the glass to his lips. Before he turned around, he finished the rotgut.

Tim Colter sized the man up. Confident, hooking both thumbs in the gunbelt. The rig, Colter noticed, held two Colts, which did not match. The locations of the grips of both revolvers told Colter that Mix Range was right-handed.

"You're a quiet cuss," Mix Range said. "I'll give you that much. Quiet. Like a little ol' mousey that's scared of daylight."

"You're not," Colter said.

"'Specially when my sons start talkin'." The gunman pointed at the two guns.

"The way I see it," Colter said. "You were trying to extort money from the proprietor of this drinking establishment. That's against the law."

"'Extort'?" Range let loose with a loud belly laugh. "Hey, stupid," he called out to the sweating man, "this gent must be educated. I didn't know they let mouses into . . . what's that them places is called . . . uni-colleges?"

"Guess they don't have any of those in a backwoods place like Alabama."

The man quit laughing. His left hand came loose from

the gunbelt, the arm stretching forward, the finger pointing straight across the dark saloon at Tim Colter's face.

"You best watch what you say, boy."

"It's hard to watch . . . words."

Now Mix Range's right hand came away from the holster, and hovered over the .44-caliber Army Colt on the
man-killer's right hip.

"Iffen you know 'bout Alabama, then you must know
who I am."

"Mix Range."

The man seemed to relax, and let out a little breath. The
thin smile returned.

"So you've heard about me, eh?"

"Some."

"You . . . from Texas? Bounty hunter? Or you just like
them badge-toters I killed down south."

Colter remained quiet.

"I don't see no tin star pinned on your mousey chest,
boy, so I don't reckon you is a real lawman. But I've already buried one fellow this day—had to even pay a whole
dollar to get him planted—but, usually, I don't get no sleep
unless I kill me two gents. You look like a suitable candi-
date. Oh, wait. I said I killed two gents. I meant . . . I killed
two mouses."

"That how you want it?"

Now the sweaty man found his voice. "Please don't
start no gunplay in my place. You'll shoot up the whiskey
kegs. And it's expensive to haul that stuff by rail or wagon
all the way out to this infernal territory."

Tim Colter had to give both the owner of the saloon
and the cold-blooded killer credit. The sweaty man was a
businessman. And hailing from Alabama, the killer named
Range had manners.

"Suit you?" Mix Range asked.

Colter gestured toward the batwing doors.

"After you," he said.

Mix Range laughed as he walked through the doors and onto the warped, muddy boardwalk. But the laughter died just as Tim Colter, coming behind the killer, stopped the batwing doors from slamming.

"What the—" Mix Range's right hand darted for the holstered Colt, but instantly stopped.

Uneducated, an idiot, and a callous killer, but not that much of a fool. He was staring down the cavernous barrel of a Hawken rifle. That rifle was held, unwavering, in the hands of a one-eyed giant in buckskins.

"That's right, boy. 'Cause one more inch lower with that gunhand of yours, and your brains—if you got any— will be seasoning that drawing there of those frothy beers on the wall."

Colter slipped past the unmoving gunman. He took the Colt from the right holster, and shoved it into his waistband. He found the other revolver, a Navy .36, and slipped it inside the pocket on his jacket.

"This what you call a fair fight?" Mix Range asked.

"No. It's what I call an arrest." Colter drew his own LeMat and pressed the barrel against Mix Range's spine.

"Arrest. There ain't no law in this burg."

"Let's call it a citizen's arrest," Colter said.

"What the hell is that?"

"You'll find out."

They had a crowd. Men and women piled out of the saloons, brothels, gambling halls, and even some actual respectable businesses. Colter looked down the north side of Union Street, his eyes stopping when they reached Slade's Saloon. He saw the man standing out front, leaning against a wooden column, hands stuck in his deep front pockets. That man, from Jed Reno's description, would be the owner of that bucket of blood, Micah Slade. Micah Slade would have been the one who sent Mix Range to bully the owner of The Cheyenne Saloon. It wouldn't be the man in the green plaid sack suit and bowler hat out in front of The Blarney Stone. From what Colter had heard, Paddy O'Rourke would never hire a fool who had worn the gray during the Rebellion. The Irishman had not fought in the war, of course, for North or South. In fact, the tales said he ran away from the draft. But he was from New York, and like most New Yorkers, he despised Southerners and the South.

"What you gonna charge me with then?" Mix Range asked. "Other than extort?"

"Murder."

"You mean the Yank I killed this day. That was self-defense."

"You can prove that at the inquest."

"The . . . in . . . 'in-what'?"

"In*quest*. Let me explain the law, Mix. A crime or an alleged crime is committed. A coroner must determine what happened, and an inquest is held. Well . . . let's forget all about that. It'll take too long. Do you have a lawyer?"

"I've got a gun."

"You had a gun. Two guns. The Navy needs cleaning. Is that how you treat your weapons in Alabama and Texas?"

"Listen . . . I know all about miner's courts."

Reno stepped back, finally lowering the giant flintlock rifle. Colter shoved the gunman onto the street.

"This isn't a mining town, though."

"It's just a . . . Well . . . it don't mean nothin'."

Another prod sent the killer walking down Union Street toward The Blarney Stone and Slade's Saloon.

"And a miner's court is usually worthless . . . in the eyes of a judge. A real judge. With a real jury. And real lawyers. Besides, I'm sure the authorities in Texas will appreciate having a chance for you to defend yourself in the Lone Star State. You might even get off."

When they reached Slade's Saloon, Mix Range stopped, as Tim Colter expected he would. Colter kept the LeMat aimed at the killer's back, but he no longer prodded the killer. Range turned and stared at Micah Slade.

"You gotta get me out of this fix, Slade," Range said, and he no longer sounded confident, but like the poor piece of Southern trash that he was. "Them boys down in Texas. They'll string me up, sure as shootin', iffen I get hauled back down there."

Slade grinned. "You might hang here, boy. But I'm guessin' you know that already."

Micah Slade was easy for Tim Colter to size up. There was the patch over his left eye and a left arm in a black silk scarf that served as a sling. He, too, carried a pair of Navy Colts, but those were stuck butt forward in a green sash, and Tim Colter had no reason to believe Slade's guns needed cleaning. He dressed in black. His accent was just as Southern, but maybe more educated, than Mix Range's.

"But you's an Alabama boy your ownself," Mix Range pleaded.

Slade ignored the gunman, who appeared to be close to bursting into tears. Just like most gunmen. Most bullies. Take away their guns, and they were gutless wonders.

"So what exactly is going on here, sir?" Slade bowed slightly, but with no respect, at Colter. "Was there some disturbance in The Cheyenne Saloon?"

"There was a disturbance in Slade's Saloon earlier," Colter said.

Micah Slade grinned. "So to speak. But we buried that matter this morning." He nodded slightly at Mix Range. "He took care of it. You see, stranger, that's the law in Violence. I'm surprised that one-eyed rapscallion didn't let you know that before you came out here."

"That's the law?" Tim Colter sounded incredulous.

"That's the law." Micah Slade bowed.

"Well, Slade." Colter prodded the weak-kneed gunman again with the LeMat. "In case you haven't noticed, there's a new kind of law here in Violence."

CHAPTER 19

"Where is the jail?" Colter asked as they made their way down Union Street, past Second and Fourth Street toward Sixth, the last street on the western side of Violence. Odd, Colter thought, but the odd-numbered streets ran on the eastern side of town, with the town divided by The Blarney Stone and Slade's Saloon.

"Well, boy," Reno said, "I didn't exactly expect you to come back with a prisoner. Figured you'd kill him. Or I would."

"No jail."

"Nope."

Colter let out a mirthless chuckle. "And where was the late marshal's office?"

"Where he worked."

"Which was?"

"Hotel. But it wasn't nowhere nears as fancy as it is now."

They walked a bit more before Reno added, "But I reckon you could use my storage room as a jail." He let out a little chuckle.

"I'd rather not do that. Get your storage room all shot up when Slade tries to bust this two-bit assassin out of there."

Reno nodded. "I'd rather not get myself shot up when Slade tries that."

"Don't worry, pard. We'll see what the citizens committee says."

Reno stopped. "What citizens committee?"

"You'll see directly."

Tim Colter wondered how long it would take. He had barely fished the manacles from the pack mule, secured Mix Range's right hand to one cuff and the other to the solid bottom rail of Jed Reno's corral, had accepted a cup of coffee Reno brought out from the post, unsaddled his black stallion and taken just a few of the packs off the mule, and finally settled onto an overturned crate, leaning against the wall of the post, talking about this and that with Jed Reno, when he saw them coming.

"Oh," Jed Reno said, "you mean them folks. That citizens committee."

They were led by a man who introduced himself as Mayor Jasper Monroe. He stressed the *"mayor"* in his announcement. The roundness of his stomach told Colter that he drank too much beer, and his hands lacked any calluses. Barber and undertaker, he said, but Reno had already told him that Eugene Harker, the freedman, did most of the barbering and burying these days. There was no embalming. Not out here. And few coffins, either. Bodies would be wrapped in blankets, if the deceased had a blanket, and buried in the ever-growing cemetery on the hill behind the town.

Eugene Harker was there, too. His hands were tough, and his eyes wary. Muscles bulged from digging those graves and, before that, swinging a sixteen-pound sledgehammer for the Union Pacific.

Henry Yost ran the hotel, and collected a lot more

money now that his partner, B.B. Cutter, had been shot, killed, planted, and mostly forgotten. He wore a sack suit of navy and gray stripes, a bowler hat, with a nose and cheek that had been burned and blistered by the sun. He was also out of breath. Every single one of them had walked from town.

Aloysius Murden had to weigh close to three hundred pounds. He spoke with such a thick Yankee accent—Massachusetts, the fat man said—that Tim Colter gave up trying to understand half of what he said. He didn't need to listen to Murden, anyway, since his rail-thin partner, with the eyeglasses sliding precariously close to the end of his nose, repeated everything Murden said. The partner's name was Duncan Gates.

Gates and Murden ran the land office. They had platted the town. They had brought in all those foolish but hungry and well-spirited farmers. They had also invested in other businesses, and heaped praises on the Union Pacific as if it were the spirit of Abraham Lincoln.

The last member of the citizens committee surprised both Colter and Reno.

Paddy O'Rourke, the gambling kingpin and procurer of prostitutes, stood off to the side, grinning at Colter and Reno, and maybe even laughing inside at his fellow councilmen.

"I'll be blunt," Monroe finally said. "We don't want to turn Violet into a shooting gallery. So we'd like you to ride out of town. Back to Washington."

"Oregon," Jed Reno corrected. "And you come to me last year, begging for a lawman. I give you his name."

"He turned us down," Monroe said. "Remember?"

"He turned you down. When I writ him, he come. He's what you need."

Yost spoke up. "We had a lawman. Remember. Remember what happened?"

"That's why I sent for this kid," Reno said.

O'Rourke cackled. "Fifteen bucks a month, mister."
He eyed those beady eyes at Tim Colter. "A badge. Ain't
worth dying for, is it?"

"Don't plan on dying," Colter said.

"It doesn't matter," Monroe sang out. "The offer has
been rescinded. You have no authority. Not in my town."

So it was his town. Not Gates's and Murden's town, and
those men had put up a much heavier investment than
Jasper Monroe. Colter shot the mayor a curious look, wondering what had changed the barber-undertaker's tune.
Paddy O'Rourke? Or maybe Micah Slade?

"So if you don't have a badge," O'Rourke said, "then
you don't have the authority to hold that little vermin right
there. I'll take him off your hands. I'll run him out so he
never comes back to this sweet, peaceful little burg again."

Colter looked at his prisoner. Mix Range was sweating, and
fear crawled through his skin. Range knew what O'Rourke
would do to a man who had drawn pay from Micah Slade.
Actually, Tim Colter enjoyed seeing a blackheart like Range
sweat, but he dropped his fingers into his vest pocket and
pulled out a tin badge.

"But I do have a badge," he said.

He pinned it on the lapel.

Murden stepped closer. His lips parted as he read the
black lettering on the tarnished five-point star.

" 'Deputy U.S. Marshal'?" This time, Tim Colter had no
trouble understanding Murden's words.

Colter wasn't sure why he had changed his mind before
he had left Salem. Well, that wasn't exactly true. He had
not changed his mind, but Betsy McDonnell had changed
it for him. Getting that deputy marshal's job had been her
idea, and she had once taught school before she had married. Which meant she knew how to persuade folks to do
things they didn't want to do. If women could vote, Tim
Colter figured that woman would be governor of Oregon,

maybe even a U.S. senator. She had laid out some reasons, and they sounded good. A U.S. marshal had more clout, more authority, and if Violet, Idaho Territory, was just as tough as it seemed to be, well, then perhaps the Union Pacific executives would want it cleaned up, too. So Colter had gone back to U.S. Marshal Albert Zeiber and taken him up on that offer. Zeiber had sent a letter of recommendation to the territorial marshal in Boise, and an Express rider had raced back with a signed commission for Tim Colter as a deputy marshal for Idaho Territory.

"With the backing of Congressman Grenville Dodge, Thomas Durant, and the Union Pacific Railroad," Colter said. "The railroad, and a lot of other people, aren't too happy about what has been going on here, boys. Too many killings make things a bit harder trying to complete this grand project of a transcontinental railroad."

"I still prefer a big ditch," Jed Reno said without much interest as he tamped tobacco into his pipe.

"This gonna be your office?" O'Rourke asked in his thick Irish brogue.

"No." Colter shook his head. "Don't want my friend's place getting torn apart, and I don't think it'll be big enough for my jail. No, I figured you'd be coming to see me, and I wanted our first meeting to be away from town. More private, you see."

"Private?" the mayor asked.

"Just without distractions, such as men taking potshots at me. Or my prisoner."

"Why'd they do that?" the mayor asked.

"To keep him from talking." Colter rose. "Now, I don't think Mix Range is that type of gent. He hires on, he gives his loyalty to his boss. He knows he'll likely be going to the grave, probably by taking a long drop off the gallows, but he has known that a long time." Colter looked down.

Mix Range seemed about ready to soil his britches. "But he won't name his boss. He'll die game, die quiet. Even if he is promised a lesser sentence, he won't talk. That's not what a man like Mix Range is made of. So he'll die, alone, get buried in a pauper's field, and his boss and other killers will keep on making money and living and drinking and whoring and having a fun old time on this earth."

Now Colter walked away. "But his boss, he can't take that chance. So he'll come gunning for Range. Well, not him. The boss man won't personally come to kill Mix, to keep him quiet. If he were that kind of man, he wouldn't have hired Mix Range in the first place. So he'll send another killer to shut up Mix. And, probably, another killer to shut up the man who killed Mix. Gets to be a never-ending cycle, you see."

Colter was back at his spot.

"But I have a jail in mind."

The pack mule trailed the black horse as Tim Colter rode easily back toward the town known as Violence. The town leaders followed, a foot, but there wasn't much dust being kicked up, and the wind was blowing at their backs anyway. Trailing the strange procession was Jed Reno, on his favorite horse, keeping his Hawken trained at the shackled Mix Range, who staggered along in front of the old fur trapper.

When they reached Sixth Street, Colter reined to a stop, and waited for the mayor and his aldermen to catch up. When they had, he pointed to the corral and lean-to at the corner of Sixth and Union.

"What?" Mayor Monroe asked, took off his hat, and scratched his head.

Both corral and lean-to were empty, and the way the grass shot up from the corral and side of the little structure said no horses had been stabled inside for quite a while. Which was exactly what Jed Reno had told him when they had first walked to town.

Vern Carpenter had owned the corral, bought the lot from the land speculators, put up the corral and lean-to. Vern Carpenter figured that Violence would become that bona fide town on the U.P. line and he would make a fortune as a liveryman. But Vern Carpenter, the way Jed Reno put it, had a weakness for rye whiskey and raw women. He also had a temper. So it had surprised few people in town when Vern Carpenter's body was found lying in a frozen water trough in front of Jake's Place. Jake Trimble had sworn that Carpenter had not even set foot at his poker table that evening, and everyone believed Jake Trimble.

Not because Jake Trimble was honest, but because Vern Carpenter had been stabbed fifteen times in the back, arms, head, and chest, and everyone in this part of Idaho Territory knew that Jake Trimble never used a knife. He had killed, of course, four of the men buried on Violence's Boot Hill, but every one of them had died from bullets fired by the Sharps derringer Trimble favored. No one had ever seen Trimble with a Bowie knife.

"It's available, isn't it?" Colter asked.

Yost blurted out: "You can't mean to tell us that you want that lean-to . . . as your jail?"

Gates and O'Rourke laughed, too, at the sheer folly of such an idea. Mayor Jasper Monroe kept scratching his head. Mix Range stood with his mouth agape. Jed Reno grinned.

Colter chuckled. "Heavens to Betsy, no. Of course not. That lean-to wouldn't hold a rat or mouse. The corral. That's going to be the jail in Violence."

CHAPTER 20

He waited till the councilmen—if that's what they were—walked back to town, leaving him alone with Mix Range and Jed Reno.

"You gonna keep me in this?" Range finally asked.

"That's the plan," Colter answered, and made his way to the pack mule. With a grunt, he heaved the heavy canvas bag off the packsaddle, and, using both hands, carried it to the edge of the corral, where the prisoner and mountain man waited.

Reno opened the gate, testing the wood. "Sturdy enough, I reckon," he said. "For tame hosses. Maybe not wild mustangs or Indian ponies." His one eye locked momentarily on Mix Range. "Not sure about prisoners, though."

Mix Range stepped inside the corral, laughing so hard he almost doubled over. "You think you can pen me up like your mule, Marshal? Well, that's real funny. I thought you was a damned fool to try to bring law to this burg. Now you're provin' that you're dumber than my kid sister down near Horseshoe Bend way."

The bag clanged with iron banging against iron when Colter dropped the sack onto the dirt. Kneeling, he unfastened the opening to the canvas and reached inside. He pulled out a heavy oval made of iron, with iron braces coming out the bottom. A key remained inserted in a lock in the oval.

"What the hell's that?" Range fired out.

"A Gardner Shackle," Colter answered. "Or what we call back in Salem, an Oregon Boot."

Mix Range's protest was short because Reno clubbed him with the butt of the Hawken. When the killer finally sat up, holding the walnut-sized knot on his head, he looked at the device that had been secured above his ankle. Colter held up the key, then slipped it into his jacket pocket.

Range tried to lift his leg, but grunted in pain.

"That's the heaviest one I have," Colter said. "Thirty pounds. I think that'll keep you here for a while."

"He won't run far, that's sure as shooting," Reno said.

"It's already rubbing ag'in' my skin," the prisoner complained.

Colter pushed his hat up. "When I first saw those things, at the state pen in Salem, I didn't really like them. It was the warden's invention." He pointed at the "boot." "Even got a patent for them, but I'm not sure any other prisons are using these yet."

"He give those to you?" Reno asked.

Chuckling, Tim Colter shook his head. "J.C. Gardner doesn't give away anything. He sold them to me."

"How do I get it off?" Range wailed.

"If you're a good boy, I'll see about replacing this one with a twenty-pounder. Be real good, and maybe you'll be wearing the five-pound one before the Texas authorities come to fetch you back to the fine Lone Star State. Till then, you just find a nice spot in the corral and make your home."

"This thing won't hold me!" Mix Range shouted, and found a bit of defiance in his voice, but Colter and Reno knew that was nothing but bluff.

"Yeah," Reno said. "I recollect Big Thadd Hostetler." He gestured off to the northwest. "Trapped beaver with us back in '31, no, '33 it was. Well, Big Thadd was up in the Bitterroots one fall, stepped right into a bear trap. Couldn't set his right leg free." Reno tapped the inside of the Oregon Boot on Range's ankle. "Right about that same spot, I reckon." He whistled, and began searching for his pipe and tobacco.

"He die?" Range asked, his lips quivering.

"No. Big Thadd. Nah, last I heard he was hopping around Fort Hall, clerking at some store or some such."

"Hoppin'?" Range's face began to lose all color.

"Sure. Seen it happen to coyotes and wolves all the time. Get caught in a trap like that. Know they's done for. Nothing for them to do but gnaw off their leg. Reckon they'd have to break the bones, though. Teeth ain't that tough. Can't gnaw through bone. But if you break it. Man, that's gotta hurt. Hurt like blazes. And the way my leg feels, and from what I heard, ain't there two bones in that part of a man's body."

Colter tried not to grin. He answered. "Tibia and fibula."

"So he'd have to break the both of them first. Which one's the big bone?"

"Tibia," Colter replied.

Mix Range was now sweating.

"So he'd break the little one first. Just bend that leg back till the little . . . What was it?"

"Fibula," Colter answered.

"Right. Break the fibula first. But then he'd have to break the big one, and he'd know just how god-awful breaking that little puny bone hurt. Man . . ." Reno shuddered. "I don't see how Big Thadd done it. But he done it. Just like a coyote and a wolf."

"He cut off his own foot?" Mix Range wailed, wiped his face, and almost broke down crying. "He taken a knife and sawed off his own foot . . . after breaking those two bones?"

"Oh, no, boy," Reno said with a laugh. "You wasn't listening to me. He didn't have no knife. Dropped it when the teethes and clamps of that big iron trap snapped against him. Couldn't reach the damned blade. No . . ." Reno grinned, and ran a finger over his teeth. "He gnawed through his leg. Like a coyote or wolf, even a beaver or maybe even a silvertip griz. With his choppers. Like mine."

Colter grinned. Reno smiled. Only Mix Range saw little humor in the one-eyed trapper's story.

"Well," Reno said. "That ain't just no big windy, boy. I was funning a bit about using his teeth and all, but you head up to Fort Hall, and if Big Thadd's still living, you'll find him hobbling around on a crutch. He did taken off his own leg. Which is what you'd have to do to get shed of that thing."

"He has a bigger problem than the shackle," Colter said. "I still think Micah Slade will send someone here to kill him. Keep him from talking."

"I ain't gonna talk," Range said, finding his nerve again.

"I believe you," Colter said. "I just don't think Micah Slade can take that chance."

Range looked around. "What do I do if it rains?"

"You get wet." Colter walked out of the corral, holding the gate, which he closed, and slipped a bar lock through an opening to keep it shut once Reno had strolled out of the pen.

Colter pointed to the lean-to.

"We'll fix that up," he explained. "Put some blankets

over it, a tarp on the roof. That'll keep the rain out. And keep it closed. You'll be in there from time to time."

"I will?" Reno asked.

"If you want to be my deputy."

Reno grinned. "Ain't never been no deputy before."

"That way you can keep an eye on the jail. When you want to. The prisoners. They won't know when you're in there and when you're not. So if you need to go tend your post."

"Ain't much business there no how, not these days. Folks stay in Violence to do their shopping. And the sodbusters don't come in to speak that Flemish talk none. They's too busy trying to break sod."

"All right. Let's find a café, get something to eat, see what's stirring up in town. We might even bring back a few more prisoners. To keep Mix Range company. If he's alive when we get back."

"Think he'll be here when we get back?" Reno asked.

"If he's not, he won't be far away. Not with thirty pounds on his leg."

The restaurant wasn't as nice as the Bullfrog Café in Salem, Oregon. The food wasn't as good. The waitress wasn't as lovely as Betsy McDonnell. They ate fried potatoes with antelope steaks, corn bread, which was close to being stale, and drank weak coffee. Mostly, Jed Reno listened as Tim Colter talked.

As a deputy U.S. marshal, Colter could not swear in another deputy, not even a jailer. And as a federal lawman, Colter's jurisdiction was federal. But since Violence, aka Violet, had not been incorporated, and lay in a U.S. territory, Colter was going to push a few legal things and try to keep some semblance of law and order in the railroad stop. He had expected Mayor Jasper Monroe to complain, maybe even point out the difference between federal and local jurisdictions, but so far . . . so good. Besides, Colter figured that he could go into the mayor's office right now and get that town lawman's job.

Reno shoved a fork overloaded with greasy potatoes into his mouth. He spoke with his mouth open.

"You can be a federal deputy and a town marshal?" He swallowed. "At the same time?"

"Lot of lawmen wear more than one badge," Colter said. "More money. I've know deputy U.S. marshals who also had appointments as town lawmen, town deputies, county sheriffs, sheriff's deputies. Everything but maybe a Pinkerton agent, and I'm sure some have those jobs, too."

Reno picked up his tin cup, slurped some coffee.

"How'd you get to be so tough?" the mountain man asked.

Colter found the napkin on his lap, started to dab his mouth, but then looked a little closer at the ragged, dirty piece of cotton. Instead, he dropped the napkin on his plate and wiped his mouth with his shirtsleeve. No, this place definitely was not the Bullfrog Café. He thought about the question before answering.

"I was going to say that you taught me," he said after a moment.

"Was going to, but you know that ain't the truth." Reno finished his coffee.

"No." He thought some more, and finally shrugged. "You read about the little set-to I had with the Rose Gang."

"Yeah."

"And you know my wife died. And . . . our . . . kids."
Reno nodded.

"For a while, I guess, I just had no feelings whatsoever. No fear. No worry. Maybe I didn't care if I lived or died.

That's probably how I was able to get through that little scrape. Jed, I just didn't give a damn."

Again, the mountain man's head nodded. "I reckon I understand that a bit. Knowed some trappers who had similar thoughts, for different reasons. Knowed plenty of Indians who lived that way. They figured they had no say in when it was their time. So they just fought like blazes. That got you out of that scrape, maybe a few others, still breathing."

"Something like that," Colter said.

"I bet that there hogleg on your hip helped a bit."

Colter grinned. "A little."

"But," Reno said, "you feel a bit different now. Something else has come over you. That I see on your face, son. Even with my one good eye."

"Another woman." Colter smiled. "Betsy McDonnell. You'd like her. She runs a café in Salem. Lost her husband a bit over a year ago."

"So now . . . you're telling me that you do care if you live or die."

Colter nodded.

"So that there performance you been giving. You're just play-acting. Like that there John Wilkes Booth fellow."

Now Colter smiled. "I think you might choose an actor other than Booth. But you learn, Jed. You learn to bluff. Like we bluffed Mix Range."

Colter's head shook. "You think you put the fear of God . . . the fear of Marshal Tim Colter . . . into that man-killer? You think we'll find him still in that corral when we finish our dinner and walk back to Sixth Street?"

Colter answered with a shrug.

Reno reached into a pocket, pulled out a pouch, and dropped a couple of coins on the table. He nodded at the waitress, letting the bony woman know that this was for the meal. "Well, I got some sad news for you, Tim, my boy. We ain't gonna find that gent in that little pen."

Colter was standing, picking his hat off a vacant chair, and thanking the waitress for the meal—even if it tasted like sand and grass, and the coffee like water.

"I know that, Jed. I saw him limping into Slade's Saloon about four minutes ago. Let's go fetch him, shall we?"

CHAPTER 21

Tim Colter went through the batwing doors of Slade's Saloon with the LeMat in his right hand, cocked, and a saw in his left hand. He walked straight to the table, where Micah Slade sat alone, drinking coffee and smoking a cigar, and dropped the saw on the table. He had stopped at a mercantile and bought the saw. Cost more than it was worth, but that was the way things were priced in a raw town like Violence.

"Tell Mix Range this will help."

Slade just stared.

"The Oregon Boot won't come off any other way."

"Not without the key, right, Marshal." Slade rocked back on his chair legs. "The one you got in your pocket?"

"*Had*." Slade grinned. "*Had* in my pocket. Hid it."

Slade's chair came back to the floor. He laid the cigar in the ashtray, and touched the sharp teeth of the handsaw.

"Or," Colter said, "Mix could pretend to be a coyote or wolf. Start gnawing."

Micah Slade's eyes showed that he found no humor in Colter's joke.

"I'll give you five seconds, Slade." Now Colter pointed the big LeMat at the saloon owner's chest. "Send Mix back down here. Or you join him in Violence's new jail. Ten-pound shackle for you, I'd think. For harboring a fugitive from justice." A moment passed. Then the lawman added: "Unless you've already killed him to shut him up."

There was an icy calm to Slade's voice. "You think you can walk out of my place after sticking a gun at my heart. You only got six shots in that thing."

"Ten. But who's counting? The pin's set for the smooth-bore barrel, by the way. That's this big one underneath. They say you're a heartless bastard, Slade. Once I touch the trigger, at this range, they'll be proved right when they pick you up off that floor."

"Harry!" Slade called out.

The bartender answered.

"Fetch Range for the marshal, would you?"

"Sure, boss."

Now Slade smiled. "He just walked in here, Marshal Colter. We were just keeping him for you. Figured he wouldn't get far . . . not with that . . . what's it called, an 'Oregon Boot'?"

"That's what it's called. Appreciate your dedication to law and order, Slade. Helping us out and all."

A door opened, and two other men, with Harry the barkeep following, helped the limping Mix Range out from what Colter guessed was a storeroom. Range walked in obvious pain, so much, after the long walk from the corral on Sixth Street, that Colter wasn't sure he'd be able to make it all the way back to the jail.

Harry and the two other men stopped, and Mix Range, his face red with anger, frustration, embarrassment, and pain, limped a few more paces before stopping at the table. Colter motioned with his LeMat, and the surly Alabaman moved toward the batwing doors. Colter backed away from the table, turned on his boot heels, and backed out toward the doorway.

"Hey, Marshal," Micah Slade called out. "Don't forget your saw!"

"Consider it a gift, Slade," Colter said. "I figured you might have need of it before too long." He spotted the mop in a bucket against the wall, took the handle with his free hand, and tested the mop. "Or I'll just trade you the saw for the mop."

"Figure to clean up the town with that?" Slade asked, now smiling.

"No." Colter showed him the revolver and smoothbore barrels of the LeMat. "I'll do my cleaning with this."

Outside, he hurried Mix Range past the windows to the saloon, glanced across the street at The Blarney Stone, and waited. Jed Reno stepped around the corner. Colter handed the mop to Mix Range.

"What's this for?" the killer asked.

"Use it as a crutch. Or cane."

"That's worthless," Range said.

"I can always go back to Slade and get the handsaw."

The killer put the mop side under his armpit, and leaned against the long wooden handle.

"Well?" the old trapper asked.

"Middle of the street," Colter said.

"Ain't that dangerous?"

"No sense in risking any legitimate businesses," Colter said. "Or getting innocent people killed."

Jed Reno spit. "Boy, you'll figure out at some point that there ain't no legitimate businesses in a town like Violence. And ain't no innocent folks would call this place home."

They walked to the middle of Union Street, a wide street, made for the big freight wagons that would haul rails and crossties and telegraph poles as the railroad moved westward across the plains. But now that the railroad had moved, practically all the way to Laramie City, there was little traffic on the streets of Violence.

"Go," Colter whispered.

Leaning on the mop-turned-crutch, Mix Range began hobbling down the street, more like dragging his shackled leg, while Colter and Reno followed. Reno shifted the long Hawken and pulled the big Colt out of the holster, thumbing back the hammer. He shifted the Colt to his left hand, returned the heavy Hawken to his right. The rifle weighed a ton—so did the heavy Colt—but Jed Reno showed no strain. It looked as if he walked down Union Street with feather dusters in his hands.

"I thought you used to say that one shot's all a man needs."

"I used to say a lot of things," Reno said. "Times change."

They fell silent. Moved past the intersection of Union and Second. Reno and Colter could see the corral and lean-to now, at Union and Sixth, but those two blocks seemed miles away. With a thirty-pound weight on his left ankle, and having already limped from the corral-turned-jail to Slade's joint, Mix Range would not make good time. Colter thought about stopping, fetching the key from his jacket—he had lied to Slade about hiding the key—and unlocking the shackle. But that would take time, too, to get that cumbersome, heavy chunk of metal off the prisoner's ankle, and then Colter's attention would be on the Oregon Boot, and not the street, the wooden façades of the buildings, the windows, the corners, every place where a gun could be pointed at them right now.

Halfway between Second and Fourth. That's when they saw the smoke, thick and black.

"Sons of bitches!" Jed Reno roared. "They're burning my place."

Then the gunshots erupted.

Two men. One by the mercantile with the post office, up on the roof. Firing rapidly with a revolver. The other on the north side of the street, using a water barrel at the corner of the last building, still under construction, at the corner of Fourth and Union. He, too, fired a revolver.

The one on the roof, shooting down, would have the worst angle, so Colter trained the LeMat on the man behind the water barrel. Reno, even though he was closer to the shooter on the north side of the street, lifted the Hawken toward the roof. The man lifted his head, to take aim, and the big rifle roared. A pink mist wafted in the air, and the man was flying backward, tumbling off the roof, landing in the alley between the mercantile–post office and another building marked:

FOR RENT
SEE JASPER MONROE
BARBER-MAYOR

Colter felt a bullet whistle past his right ear, but he knew that that shot did not come from the guy behind the barrel or, especially, not from the guy whose head Jed Reno had just blown off.

"Behind us, Jed!" Colter shouted. He kept the LeMat pointed at the water barrel, and when the man came around the side, the big revolver bucked in Colter's hand.

The bullet caught the assassin in his shoulder, spun him out from behind the water barrel and into the dirt. He came up quickly, fanning the hammer and keeping his finger on the trigger. Bullets barked, but spit up mostly dirt— well short of Colter, Reno, or Mix Range, who lay on the ground, covering his head with hands and arms, while wailing like a newborn calf.

Colter squeezed the trigger again. It caught the wounded man as he ran past the water barrel. Another shot from the LeMat lifted the killer off his feet, and slammed him through the frames of the business that was being built.

Hearing a shot from Reno's Colt, Colter spun around.

Two more men were shooting, one from the roof on the north side of the street, the other with a Henry rifle at the near corner of The Blarney Stone.

The one with the Henry was the most dangerous.

"I've got the rifle," Colter cried out.

"Then get him, boy, before he gets us."

Reno shifted his Colt, squeezed the trigger. A lot of men, greenhorns, would have fired often. That was the good thing about a revolving pistol. You could shoot six times—though usually just five, if you kept the chamber under the hammer empty—without having to reload. But Jed Reno came from the flintlock and single-shot days. You never wasted a shot. One was all you need. Because one was likely all you had.

The bullet hit the man on the roof in the stomach. He straightened, tightened, but did not fall. Nor did he drop his Colt. He struggled to cock back the hammer, but before he could finish, Jed Reno had squeezed the trigger on the Colt again. That one caught the wounded man's throat, and a river of crimson sprayed as the man collapsed and disappeared. He did not fall off the roof, because that building had a flat roof. But Jed Reno knew that gunman was done for.

A bullet punched through the crown of Reno's hat. He whirled toward the man with the Henry repeating rifle, and called out Tim Colter's name.

But Tim Colter was no longer beside the old mountain man.

Reno blinked his one eye, swallowed down the fear and surprise, and yelled, "Boy, what are you doing?"

Tim Colter did not answer. He was too busy charging, running through the dirt and globs of drying mud, heading straight for the man beside the gambling den with a rifle that could riddle a man with .44-caliber bullets.

The LeMat barked. Smoke billowed like a cloud, and

Tim Colter ran through the white smoke. He pulled the trigger again.

Reno moved around, trying to find a clear shot at the gunman with the rifle, but he couldn't shoot for fear of hitting the running Tim Colter in the back. Then he remembered that there could be other killers. Four men already. How many would Micah Slade have sent? Or were these sent by Paddy O'Rourke? Or by someone else? Did Mix Range have any friends?

Seeing nothing, Reno turned back. Colter stopped running, turned around, aimed at a spot beyond Slade's Saloon. This time, it was the LeMat's ten-gauge that spoke just as a man stepped from that corner of the building. Buckshot drilled his chest, and the man fell backward and lay in a heap.

Reno blinked, and saw the man with the Henry rifle. He didn't know how Colter had managed, but he was still standing, apparently not moving, while the gunman with the repeating rifle sat, legs outstretched, leaning against the side of The Blarney Stone, head tilted to his right, maybe three bullet holes in the center of his white shirt.

A noise came behind Reno, and he spun, cocking the Colt, aiming, but not shooting.

Mix Range was raising up, mouth open, eyes blank, looking at the dead men on the street and beside buildings. He could not see the dead man on the roof, of course.

Walking back toward them was Deputy U.S. Marshal Tim Colter. His jacket flapped in the wind, and sunlight showed through the bullet holes in that piece of canvas.

CHAPTER 22

"You ain't hurt?" Reno asked when Colter stopped a few feet in front of him.

"Nope."

"How'd you manage that?"

Colter shrugged an answer, and began reloading the LeMat. Jed Reno crossed the street, picked up the dropped weapons of the dead man lying in the unfinished building, and brought them back before he began to reload the Hawken first, and then the Colt.

Finished, they looked back at Slade's Saloon, but by then, the streets were starting to fill with other people. Too many witnesses, Colter decided, for any more shooting. And with the streets littered with dead men, Tim Colter figured the chances of more violence in Violence were slim.

Now they looked down toward the trading post Jed Reno had built. Orange flames leaped from the building, showering the air with sparks that disappeared inside the thick plumes of smoke.

"It takes a mean son of a bitch to burn down a man's business and home," Reno said.

"Violence is full of mean people." Colter moved over to Mix Range, whose face remained without color and whose body kept shaking. Somehow, he had not been hit by the dozens of bullets fired, either. Maybe Slade's men—if they were hired by Micah Slade—hadn't been trying to kill the killer from Alabama, just Tim Colter and Jed Reno.

Kneeling, Colter fingered the big iron key from his pocket, and slipped it inside the hole. He turned, heard the click, and slowly separated the two U-shaped irons that formed the shackle.

"Have a seat, Mix," Colter said, and the frightened killer did as he was told, allowing the lawman to carefully remove the Oregon Boot.

"Might as well see if we can salvage something, Jed," Colter said as he stood. He held the heavy boot in his left hand, the LeMat still in his right.

"What about them?" Reno pointed the barrel of the Colt at one of the dead men.

Colter shrugged. "They're not going anywhere."

Nothing from the post could be salvaged, but Reno, Colter, and even Mix Range kept busy, soaking saddle blankets from well buckets and beating out the flames that the sparks started in the grass. The mule and Colter's and Reno's horses had moved away from the heat of the flames and the choking smoke, but the men who had started the fire had not bothered to steal the horses. Maybe they thought they would be able to get the horses easy enough, once Jed Reno and Tim Colter lay dead on Union Street.

Within a few minutes, some railroad workers jumped off a handcar and ran to help contain the fire. They were not about to see the flames rip across the tracks of the Union Pacific, maybe damage the crossties or even sweep down and burn a trestle a few miles westward. The Union Pacific would not care much for that kind of delay.

Railroaders, Colter thought. Not the mayor. Not the land speculators. Not even Eugene Harker. No one from the town, not that he had expected anyone from Slade's Saloon or The Blarney Stone. But the townsmen? The wind was blowing in the direction that could have pushed the flames straight into Violence.

Another handcar brought more railroad men, good, solid Irishmen. Colter had heard that the men building this railroad were nothing but burly drunks who cared nothing about what they were doing—helping a nation, still struggling to recover after a grueling four years of war, grow. They just wanted their paycheck, their beer, and their whiskey. And maybe, just maybe, they were just trying to save their railroad, and the work they had already done. But they were here. Helping.

Even Mix Range worked hard.

Maybe two hours passed before the cabin and dugout lay in smoking, charred ruins, and the grass, for perhaps fifty or sixty yards around the cabin, was bristled and black, smoking, the ground hot underneath the scorched earth.

Wearily Colter led the procession of men, their clothes drenched with sweat, faces and hands or gloves blackened with soot, away from the ruins, over fresh grass that had not burned. Colter sat on the iron rail of the track. The others sat on the rails or squatted on the grass. For perhaps five minutes, no one spoke. Two of the men—a burly redhead with shoulders almost as wide as the width between the iron rails, and a tall man with a bald head but long beard—walked to the livestock. When they returned, letting the horses and mule graze, they, too, sat down.

"I'd . . ." Reno had to stop, spit phlegm between his buckskin legs. "Give y'all some of my Taos Lightning, boys. But it all burned up."

"No need," said one of the railroaders. "Glad to help. Sorry we couldn't save nothin'."

Reno waved off the apology.

"Maybe we saved the town," the bald man, with the big beard, said.

They looked eastward, saw the town's buildings, sod huts, canvas structures. They heard the whining of the saws, the pounding of hammers, and the cacophony of voices. Music came from the saloons and gambling parlors. Even a few chirpies could be heard, calling out to men—possibly other railroad workers—as they walked past the brothels and cribs. The wind was blowing away from Reno, Colter, and the other firefighters. Which meant those soiled doves had to be screaming their catcalls really loud.

Mix Range coughed.

Two other men were bringing water buckets from the well. Sometimes, even railroaders, mountain men, and deputy United States marshals found water to be better than whiskey.

"Saved the town," another Irishman repeated.

"Yeah."

As they lined up to cup hands into the buckets and slake their thirsts, as no one even thought about just how dirty those hands were, just how refreshing that water tasted, they stepped back and looked across the rolling plains at the town known as Violence.

"You reckon . . ." It was Jed Reno who spoke. "That a town like that was even worth saving?"

"Good day for business," Tim Colter said as he stepped inside the undertaking side of the office of the mayor of Violence, Jasper Monroe.

It was a strange office. Two barber chairs and a bench for those men waiting for haircuts or shaves were on one side, with a Navajo blanket separating that part of the barbershop from a bathtub. The other side, which did not even have a blanket for separation or privacy, had one long table and two pine caskets leaning against the wall.

The caskets would be reserved for special customers, a luxury few dead men in this part of the world could afford.

The men Reno and Colter had shot dead on the streets certainly would not be resting for eternity in such comfort. Eugene Harker had laid the corpses on blankets, and those blankets were not Navajo, but cheap woolen rags that had been providing rats with food and stuff for their nests.

Monroe knelt over one body, the one Jed Reno had shot in the head with the massive Hawken rifle. That was the only corpse whose head and face had been covered with a vest. The other dead men were stretched out, arms folded across their chests, legs crossed at the ankles, boots removed—along with, Colter guessed, wallets, watches, watch fobs, greenbacks, coins, guns, and anything else of value.

Monroe's eyes were cold.

"I'm always busy in a town like this," he said. "But maybe not quite as busy until you came to town."

Colter looked at the dead men. "You recognize any of them?"

"No," Monroe said.

"How about you, Mr. Harker?"

The black man looked up in surprise. "Me, sir?"

"Yeah." He pointed to the one who had held the Henry rifle. "Him, for instance?"

Eugene Harker shot a nervous glance at Monroe, who pretended to busy himself with another corpse.

"Not by name, I reckon," the freedman finally answered, and reached up to mop his brow with a handkerchief he fetched from his back pocket. Finished with the sweat, he sighed. "Just seen him around."

Colter kept his eyes on Jasper Monroe. The mayor-barber-undertaker was not a good poker player.

"Any of the others?" Colter asked, still looking at the mayor.

"Can't say for certain. Folks tend to look the same in a town like this. Might have been on the railroad. Well, none of 'em was farmers. I know that much."

"They weren't gunmen, either," Colter said. "They sure couldn't shoot worth a nickel." He pointed at the one with the blood-soaked cloth over his head. "And him?"

"Nah." This time it was the mayor who answered. "He was a stranger." Rising, he stared across the hot room, already smelling of the dead, at the freedman. "Isn't that right, Eugene?"

"Yes, sir," the Negro said.

Colter grinned without humor. "How can you tell, boys? With his head blown off?"

Silence. Finally the mayor cleared his throat. "His face was fine."

So Colter knelt and removed the vest. Behind him came a heavy sigh from Eugene Harker. It had been an ugly wound, but Jasper Monroe had been telling the truth. The ball from the Hawken had hit the man above his right eye, traveled upward, blown out the top of his skull. It was an ugly wound, but most of his face, frozen in the hard death, remained easy to identify.

Colter had never seen him.

He re-covered the face and stared at the mayor.

"I'll be taking the marshal's badge now, Mayor."

Monroe squinted in a lack of understanding.

"You have a badge," he said, and pointed at the five-point star.

"Right. But I might as well be marshal of Violence, too."

"Violet."

"Violence." The mayor did not try to correct Colter again.

"Well . . ."

"Who gave the job to B.B. Cutter?"

Monroe did not answer.

Colter put the palm of his right hand on the butt of the LeMat.

"I reckon I did."

"So I figured you could appoint me marshal. I still have the letter you mailed, requesting me for the job." That was a lie. The letter had been forwarded on, with Colter's rejection, to the territorial marshal in Boise. But Colter had learned that white lies, or even bigger ones, sometimes came with the job as a lawman.

"I can send a telegraph to Council Bluffs." Colter changed his tune. "Towns don't survive without the Union Pacific's backing, you know. And the Union Pacific wants law and order in the town of Violet." This time he used the town's actual name.

"All right." Mayor Monroe moved from the undertaking part of the business to the barbershop, disappeared behind the rug that served as a curtain, or maybe a wall, and Colter heard the opening of a metal box, followed by the rustling of papers, the clink of metal, and then the mayor's feet on the wooden floor. He pushed through the split in the rug and held out a badge. Like Colter's deputy marshal's badge, this one was five-pointed, too. He stuck it in his pocket.

"You ain't gonna pin it on?" Eugene Harker asked.

Colter pointed to the federal badge on his lapel. "One target's enough, don't you think?"

The freedman cracked a grin.

"And I'll need a new office." Colter was turning back to the mayor.

"You have an office. That corral and lean-to. Remember?"

"That's my jail. I was going to sleep in Jed Reno's trading post, but . . . I guess you must have missed the smoke and flames. . . . You see, the place burned down. Somehow. And a town lawman ought to stay in town. Don't you reckon?"

Monroe's eyes narrowed until slits. So . . . Monroe wasn't one to be trusted, either. He wanted the town for himself, too. Just like Paddy O'Rourke . . . and Micah Slade. Those men, Colter could understand. So considering that O'Rourke was on what might have amounted to a town council, Colter had to guess that Jasper Monroe was in O'Rourke's back pocket. Or maybe it was the other way around.

"You got some place in mind?"

"Yeah. The one next door. The one where you picked up this gent." Colter pointed at the man who had been blown into the unfinished building, the structure with two-by-four frames, a floor, and a roof.

"They haven't even finished building it yet," the freedman pointed out.

"I know. But I got to thinking, after Jed Reno's place was torched, that seeing how that structure stands right next to this one, it's probably less like to get burned down."

He grinned as he backed out of the business.

"Don't you agree?" Before Colter left, though, he asked where he could find the post office. He wanted to write a letter to Betsy McDonnell, and tell her he was doing fine, without mentioning all the particulars of what he had endured so far in Violence, Idaho Territory.

CHAPTER 23

The man who ran the town of Violence rode in that night, tethered his horse outside of The Blarney Stone, but did not walk into the gambling parlor. Instead, he walked casually down the boardwalk, pulling up his collar and the brim of his hat down, and moving down the street. He stopped only to light his cigar, striking the match on a wooden column. Eventually, when a couple of railroaders staggered on past the building he stared at and stumbled inside Slade's Saloon, the man crossed the street, went down the alley, and entered the barbershop and funeral parlor through the back entrance.

The door was unlocked.

The man was expected.

He came into the bathing part of the business, where Mayor Jasper Monroe knelt on the floor. Sleeves rolled up, he busied himself scrubbing the washtub.

Looking up, Monroe wet his lips, then rose, leaving the scrubbing rag, still soapy, in the tub. Monroe found a towel to wipe his hands, and said to the man, "You got my message."

"I warned you about how to go about asking about me," the man said. He drew on the cigar.

"Yes. I know."

"Yes . . . what?"

Monroe lowered his head. His voice fell to a whisper. "Yes, sir."

"What happened?" the man asked.

Jasper Monroe slowly explained. About the new deputy marshal who came to town, arrested Mix Range. He told about the Gardner Shackle—the Oregon Boot—the lawman was using. How the marshal had—

"Does this lawdog have a name?" the man who ran the town of Violence asked.

"Uh . . ." Monroe was so flustered, he had trouble remembering. "Yeah. It's . . . um . . . Colter."

"A first name?" the man said, his voice icy.

"Tim. That's it. Tim Colter."

The man withdrew the cigar and exhaled blue smoke toward the ceiling. "The same Tim Colter from Oregon way."

"Yes. I think so. Yes."

The man nodded, but breathed in deeply, held it, and slowly exhaled. "I've read about him." He gestured with the cigar, and said, "Go on," before returning the cigar to his mouth.

Monroe talked more about Mix Range.

"I don't know any Mix Range," the man said.

"He's one of Slade's boys."

"I see."

Monroe finished the story, about how Mix Range had left the corral Colter turned into a jail, hobbled back to Slade's gin mill, and the ambush set up outside the street that left a lot of gunmen dead—and Jed Reno, Mix Range, and Tim Colter without a scratch.

"Who set up that stupid affair?" the man asked.

"Slade, I guess," the mayor answered, "but I sent Eugene Harker running over to the trading post, had him set the building afire. I figured that might give Slade's men an advantage—get rid of that lawman, you see."

The cigar came out again.

"You thought of that yourself?" the man asked.

"Yes, sir," Monroe answered.

The man grinned. The cigar returned to his mouth, and the red tip glowed as he drew in a deep breath, really deep, and then the man walked forward until he stood right in front of Jasper Monroe. The cigar came out of the man's mouth. He stared at the tip, blew on it, sending ashes into the air like dust motes, and made the tip a deeper orange. Next, the man pressed the tip of the cigar onto Jasper Monroe's neck.

"*Aiiiiiiyyyyyyyyy!*" Monroe staggered back, pressing his still-wet right hand against the welt already forming, but the man grabbed his shirtfront, jerked him forward, and spoke a hoarse whisper.

"Who the hell are you to think?"

The man shoved the mayor backward, and Jasper Monroe toppled into the soapy bathtub.

"Don't . . . ," Monroe cried out as the man stepped toward him.

The man did not stop.

"The marshal . . . he's set up shop . . . right next door!"

That stopped the man. He looked at the Navajo rug, and he pressed his lips together, listening.

The wind blew. Music played in the saloons and gambling halls. Coyotes yipped.

Nothing came from next door. The man picked up the cigar he had dropped onto the wet floor. He started to return it to his mouth, but then tossed it into the washtub, between Jasper Monroe's legs that hung out of the tub.

"So how many men did Slade lose?"

Monroe answered.

The man's head shook. "Worthless bunch. They can't even wound one lawdog and a one-eyed old coot who's forty years past his prime?"

"Jed Reno's tougher than a cob." Monroe thought about trying to climb out of the tub, but decided against it. "And you ought to see that cannon this marshal wears on his hip."

The man's head shook. "No, it's a good thing Slade's boys didn't finish the job. You kill a dumb oaf like B.B. Cutter, and no one gives a hoot or a holler. He's buried. He's forgotten a day later. But you shoot down a federal lawman, and we start getting pestered by the big boys in Boise City, and maybe as far away as Washington City."

Monroe did manage to pull his feet inside the empty tub. He knew he looked stupid, sitting in a washtub that held only suds, some water, a smoldering cigar, and a coward named Jasper Monroe.

"The U.P. is backing him, too," Monroe said.

"That figures." The man found another cigar in a pocket on the inside of his coat. He bit off the end, spit to the floor, and fetched another lucifer. Within a few moments, the cigar was lighted, the match pitched into the tub at Monroe's feet, and he walked to the wall and leaned against it.

"I made him the town marshal," Monroe said weakly.

"How come?"

"He asked me to."

The man snorted.

"Well, he didn't really ask. More like . . ."

"Demanded," the man said.

Monroe could only nod an answer.

"That doesn't matter," the man said. "He's still got his deputy's commission from the big cheese in the territorial capital. And we all know what the U.P. thinks about this town. The brass in Council Bluffs will rest a little easier knowing that there's a local lawdog in this town. That'll help. And they'll probably be jumping with joy because our lawman happens to be a famous Oregon pistol-fighter who gets his name written up with pretty drawings of him killing folks in *Frank Leslie's Illustrated Newspaper*."

"*Harper's Weekly,*" Monroe corrected.

The man did not listen. Which, Monroe decided, might be a good thing. After all, the man was smoking another cigar, and Monroe's neck still burned.

"And the *National Police Gazette,*" the man said. He dragged on the cigar, thinking.

"What made you want to torch Reno's post?" he asked after a long while.

"Well. I thought it would have helped Slade. Thought if we got rid of the marshal . . ."

The man nodded. "Maybe. Let Slade hang for killing a federal lawman. Problem is, all that did was kill a bunch of Slade's gunnies. Which is not a bad thing, I reckon."

The man smoked again. Jasper Monroe's butt was getting cold from the water and soap in the tubs, and his muscles were stiffening. And sitting in a tub that was not full of hot water was not very comfortable.

"He wrote a letter," Monroe said.

The man who ran Violence turned to stare. "To whom?"

"His girl, I guess. In Oregon."

The man smoked, thought, and smoked some more. "Has the mail gone out?"

"Not yet."

"Then I'll wander by the post office and read the letter. And any more letters your new lawdog writes, you'll read them. And report back to me."

Monroe managed to nod.

"We don't want any more federal deputies coming here, but we don't want a lawman we can't control sticking his nose into my business—your business, too. Making him town marshal wasn't a good idea, though."

"Well . . . we can revoke it. . . . I mean–"

"No. No. Don't worry about it." He kept smoking,

thinking, smoking and thinking, thinking and smoking, while Jasper Monroe just got wetter, colder, and ached a lot more. Both feet had fallen asleep.

"But we'll have to kill Tim Colter. There's just no way around that. Colter must die."

The cigar came out of the man's mouth, and this time the mouth turned into a smile. "He just can't be killed over some town matter. Has to be federal. Federal . . . or . . . personal."

"Personal?" Monroe asked.

The man who ran the town that was known as Violence did not answer.

Slowly he turned and walked toward the back door. That made Jasper Monroe breathe a little easier. The last words the man who ran Violence said to Monroe:

"Personal. Personal's better. Federal will work. But personal comes first."

The Violet Committee of Aldermen met the next morning in the land office.

"What did . . ." Duncan Gates lowered his voice. ". . . *he* say?" The land speculator began wiping his glasses with a handkerchief he fetched from his pocket.

"Not much." Without thinking, Jasper Monroe touched the round burn mark on his neck. Then the mayor told the gathered men all that the man who ran the town of Violence had said last night.

"Killing a lawman is bad business," Henry Yost said.

Spitting into the spittoon, Paddy O'Rourke laughed. "You did not seem to have any reservations. But . . ." He wiped his mouth with the back of his hand. "I guess, the marshal being your business partner, that made it a wee bit better business for you. In your mind."

Yost swallowed, and looked away. His fists tightened

into hard balls, but a man like Henry Yost knew he was no match for a man like Paddy O'Rourke. Besides, Henry Yost also knew that he was nothing but a gutless coward.

"Listen," said Aloysius Murden, who was already sweating. "I don't think this lawman is what we need to fear. Just let him alone. What we have to do is do something about those farmers. I thought they'd be gone after winter, but not a one has left. And more are on their way. Our Clear Creek Emigration Company could doom us all. If those farmers stick . . ."

"They can't stick," Monroe said. "This land can't be farmed. It's cattle country or wild country."

"But more are coming," Murden cried out.

"We need more, damn it," Gates said. "The more farmers we have, the more homesteads, the better off he will be."

"But . . ." Murden could not finish. He had to mop his brow.

"He did not say what he had in mind?" Yost asked.

"No," Monroe replied. "He just said—as I've already told you—something about personal or federal. Then he walked out."

They thought this over in silence. O'Rourke frowned, and said, "He still isn't interested in getting rid of that lousy ex-Reb Slade?"

"He has other plans for Slade, Paddy," Gates said. "You know that."

"Slade will likely wind up hanging for what we do," Murden said.

"What I do, you mean," O'Rourke corrected. "Because all of you know that's why you invited me into your sorry little plan."

Another few minutes of quiet passed before Monroe tried to convince the other aldermen of his bravery. "I got the trading post burned."

Again, O'Rourke spit. "You mean you sent your darky to burn it down."

"Where is Harker anyway?" Gates asked.

"He's not privy to this," O'Rourke said.

"It'll get us more business," Monroe said, trying to explain another one of his reasons for burning down Reno's trading post. "With him out of the picture."

"Out of the picture." O'Rourke's head bobbed. "Yes, that brings up another question. What is to become of that one-eyed old reprobate?"

Monroe wet his lips, and touched the burn mark on his neck again. "Well, it means that Jed Reno will have to die, too. I guess."

CHAPTER 24

"What do you think?" Colter asked.

Jed Reno stood in the edge of the burned-over range, closer to the town of Violence than the ruins of the old trapper's trading post.

The big man fingered some ash, and then crept out of the blackened earth to the grass that waved in the wind.

"One fellow," Reno finally answered. "Looks like."

Tim Colter had to smile in amazement. "You can tell . . . after a day . . . and after all those railroaders came to help put out that fire. You can tell this is the trail made by the man who set your building on fire."

Glaring, the one-eyed trapper turned on his moccasins. "You questioning my talents?"

"That wasn't a question, pard. Just a statement."

"Most of the railroaders come by one of them little cars that they have to pump to make go." He crouched again, fingering the grass. "Seems like a lot of work to get someplace." He moved forward. "Yeah, only one." He stood again and pointed southward. "Swung wide. That way. On the way back to town."

"So he wouldn't be spotted," Colter said. That, too, was not a question.

They had started that morning at the ruins, seeing if

they might have missed anything right after the fire. Not looking for sign of the person who set the fire, but for any valuables, or a blanket, anything, that they could use. This was the West, and people recycled anything they could. Even some of the rafters and logs, charred and ruined and practically worthless, would come in handy for some-one—somehow, sometime—most likely. Yet, the fire had been brutal, fueled by coal oil and whiskey.

"You lost everything, didn't you?" Colter had asked.

Jed Reno shook his head. "Got my Colt. Better yet, got my Hawken. Got my horse and saddle." Then he pointed to the dirt beyond the house. "And my bank."

"Bank?"

"Money, boy. Put coins and bank notes and script and gold and silver in jars. You wouldn't notice it by looking at me, but I'm a wealthy man. By Violence's standards."

Then Jed Reno's one eye had found something. Some-thing anyone else would have dismissed—even if they had noticed it. That came with living in the mountains long be-fore anyone ever dreamed of a Pony Express company, or telegraphs that could bring news from San Francisco to New York City, or a railroad track that would link the Pa-cific with the Atlantic. It came because mountain men knew to pay close attention to every single detail. If some-thing looked out of place, that could mean death. Jed Reno had survived close to fifty years in this country by observing things. Ordinary things that were not so ordi-nary, but aroused one's suspicions.

"What is it?" Colter had asked.

The old man pointed at a heel print in the sand. Just a heel print. Even Tim Colter would have shrugged it off.

"A boot?" Colter had asked.

Reno's head had moved sideways, and he had started following the trail.

"Can you follow it?" Colter now asked. "All the way to wherever he came from?"

Reno chuckled. "Well, not to his mama's place, where the son of a bitch was born. No. I can't follow the trail that far. But I can find out where he went to."

The track had been from a shoe. Not a boot. The railroad workers wore work boots. Colter wore riding boots. Jed Reno wore moccasins. And the print had been fresh, left the day of the fire. Reno could tell. He could tell that the man was small, fast on his feet, and probably left-handed.

"His tracks will get mixed up, once he hits town," Colter said. "A shoe worn by a city man won't be so rare, once you reach town."

"Rare enough." The mountain man's head shook. "Every track's different. Just like every man's different. Besides, Violence ain't Louisville, boy. Ain't even Bowling Green. And this boy, him running off that way, so he wouldn't be seen. That's all right for some eyewitness. But he was going where there won't be too many folks moving about. So, yeah, I can find out where he went to. Exactly. Iffen that's what you want me to do."

"I do."

"Then should I kill the . . . what's that you called him?"

"An arsonist."

"Yeah. Want me to kill him?"

Colter shook his head. "Don't even knock on the door, Jed. All we need right now is to find out who torched your place. Just find that out. Then meet me back at the jail."

Colter walked back toward his horse. "We'll kill him later. But only if we have to."

When Colter walked back to the unfinished building that would serve as his office, he found a young man with long brown hair standing by the hitching rail, holding the reins to the horse, watching Mix Range sweep the dirt, grass, sawdust, and spiders from the unfinished building. He was a lean, leathery man, probably still in his twenties, dressed in well-worn riding boots with big Mexican spurs, woolen pants with the seats and inside of the thighs reinforced with dark leather, a bib-front shirt of red and black checks, a yellow neckerchief, and a high-crowned brown hat.

He wet his cracked lips with his tongue. He had a few patches of stubble on his chin and cheeks, but Colter doubted if the boy could have grown a beard, or even a mustache, in two or three years.

The youth was probably staring at the Oregon Boot that the prisoner turned carpenter still wore, but Colter walked to him warily. He had never seen this kid before, and even boys who couldn't grow beards could kill a man.

"Help you?" Colter asked. His right hand stayed near the LeMat, even if the boy wore no gun. A Spencer carbine was sheathed in the saddle scabbard, and just because Colter spotted no six-shooter on the kid's hip did not mean the boy didn't have a hideaway pistol somewhere.

"What's on that fella's ankle?" the kid said in a thick Texas twang.

"A Gardner Shackle," Colter answered. "Sometimes called an Oregon Boot."

"Strangest thing I ever seen on a man before." The kid led the horse, a small brown mare, to the rail, wrapping the reins around the end, and stepping onto the boardwalk. Colter was heading to the door, figuring that the kid had learned all he needed to know and was about to find a saloon.

"You're the new marshal, ain't you?" the kid asked.

Colter looked at him. The boy seemed harmless enough. "Yeah."

He never saw the punch that knocked him a good two feet backward.

Colter came up, reaching for the LeMat, but the boy just stood there, sucking on his skinned knuckles. Colter shook some senses back into his head. Mix Range had stopped sweeping, and stuck his head between the studs. The long-haired point lowered both hands, spreading them away from his hips.

"Now, Marshal," he said in that slow drawl. "You see here that I ain't packin' no hogleg. This is what we call a friendly fight."

"Don't think I've ever been in one of those." Colter pulled himself to his feet. How could a thin whippersnapper like the boy punch like a sledgehammer?

"Well . . . it's just my way of introducin' myself to the new lawman. Let him see who's boss." He grinned. For a fighter, he had all of his teeth. Stained by tobacco juice. Not straight. But all there.

"Did you introduce yourself to B.B. Cutter?" Colter unbuckled his gunbelt, shot a glance at Mix Range, but decided the big shackle would stop him from staggering out of the building and running for the LeMat. He laid it on a cracker barrel in front of Jasper Monroe's barbershop/ undertaking parlor.

"No, suh. My pa raised me better than go assaultin' women, or fellas who don't know how to defend 'emselves. You ready, Marshal? Or you need another minute or two to collect yerself."

"I'm ready," Colter said.

The kid's face turned into a blank. "Huh?" he said—a second before Tim Colter's right slammed into the boy's jaw.

The punch flipped the kid over the hitching rail, causing his horse to snort, pull away, and snap the reins. The boy was pushing himself to his knees when Colter leaped, slamming his shoulder into the kid's chest. By then, the horse had galloped down Union Street, heading for the corral.

Colter rolled over, came up, sensing the boy more than seeing him, leaping over the boy's boots as he drew back and kicked with both legs. Colter landed, turned, saw the boy launching himself from his back, into the air, landing on his feet, bending at the knees, then coming up in a charge.

The right Colter managed to deflect with his forearm. The left counter grazed over Colter's shoulder when he ducked and threw a short uppercut that missed. That left him open, but Colter absorbed two quick but harmless punches into his upper arm. He backed up. Blinked sweat.

The kid turned, punched, leaving his left side open. Colter slammed hard. One-two-three. One-two. Fake. Jab. Haymaker that knocked the boy's hat off. But Colter didn't stop. He spun, bringing up his leg, knocking into the boy's side, and slamming him toward the hitching rail. Colter took a moment to find Mix Range. And the LeMat. Both remained where he had last seen them, and the only difference was that Range's mouth hung open in amazement.

Colter looked back, almost too late. The punch caught him right against the ear as he turned his head. Colter grunted, fell back, but faked a spin to his right, and turned left instead. The boy shot past him. By the time the kid had recovered, Colter was in a defensive stance, waiting, hands up, elbows down, rocking the arms like the pistons on one of those steam-powered engines.

The kid wiped blood off his nose. He grinned.

Colter smiled back. He had done more damage than he thought. The kid's smile now revealed a missing tooth.

Both charged at the same time, but Colter lowered his head, then jerked it up, and caught the kid in the jaw. The boy's head snapped back, hard, ugly—almost knotting Colter's stomach with fear that he had broken the boy's neck. A quick punch that split Colter's lips told him that was not the case.

Now it was Tim Colter moving backward, driven across Union Street by the boy's wicked blows. Colter fell to his knees and hands, and let the boy carry himself over with momentum. The kid hit with a grunt, and then Colter was on top of him. Now Colter had an advantage. He outweighed the boy. He slammed a right into the boy's nose, felt the cartilage give way, felt the warm blood. He sank his buttocks deep against the kid's stomach. He hit again. Again. Again. The boy turned limp. Colter pushed himself up, staggered toward the nearest watering trough, and dipped his head in the water. Once. Twice. Three times.

When he turned around, his chest was heaving; pain was shooting throughout his body; he tasted blood with salty sweat, the dirt of the street, the filth of a horse's watering trough in a town like Violence.

Colter managed to blink until his vision finally focused. The LeMat and the holster remained on the cracker barrel. Mix Range still stared through the two-by-four studs. The boy still lay in the center of Union Street.

Only now, the kid had company. Two men, who looked a lot like the boy, stood at the boy's boots and long hair. Another older man knelt beside the kid, calling out his name.

"Levi. You all right, boy? Can you hear me, Levi?" The old man also spoke with that twang.

The two younger men aimed six-shooters at Colter's belly.

CHAPTER 25

Slowly the old man pushed himself to his feet, while the young boy in the dirt managed to mumble something before he came up on his hands and knees, and vomited. The man backed away from the mess, looked at Colter, and, to Colter's astonishment, laughed.

"First time Levi's ever been whupped, Marshal. How'd you manage that?"

Colter shook the water out of his hair. Wet his lips. Tested his teeth with his tongue. To his surprise, his seemed to still be in their proper place.

"I cheated." Colter tried to surmise what chance he would have at dashing across the street, diving over the hitching rail, snatching the LeMat out of the holster, and shooting the three newcomers. And maybe Levi if he had to.

Zero.

But maybe he wouldn't have to.

"Don't blame you." The man laughed again. He had covered the distance between Levi and Colter now and held out his right hand. "Would've done the same myself. Name's Warren, Marshal. Clint Warren. Got a spread a ways south of this town." He tilted his head. "These are my sons. Brod—short for Broderick—and Tyrone, short for nothin'. You've already made the acquaintance of my youngest, Levi. Pleased to know you."

Colter accepted the handshake, firm, solid, hard as the iron rails of the U.P. line. The old man turned around, and snapped, "Brod. Put that Colt away, boy. You, too, Tyrone. Tyrone, you help your kid brother over here. Get him washed up. And you, Brod, get mounted and go fetch your brother's horse. While the marshal and me get acquainted our ownselves."

"Like Levi and I got acquainted?" Colter asked.

The old man laughed. "Shucks, no, Marshal. I do my meetin's and gettin's-to-knows-yous with whiskey. Rye whiskey. And not what they call rye in one of those god-awful saloons in this town. Carry a good bottle with me. Brod, when you've got that horse, bring the marshal and me my rye. Would you do that fer me, son?"

Clint Warren stood about six-four, maybe 220 pounds without his boots on. Or his pistols. Although he hailed from Texas, he had fought for the Union. Colter had heard of such men, and that Texas, like Tennessee and other states that withdrew from the Union, had pockets where most of the citizens remained staunch Unionists. By Jupiter, that's why there was a new state of West Virginia. Before the war, that part of the Old Dominion had been within the boundaries of Virginia. But the residents petitioned for admittance into the Union. Virginia, and the Confederacy, had lost a sizable chunk of land—and some citizens who could have been conscripted into the Confederate Army. Not that the boys in gray would have wanted those Unionists fighting alongside them.

Colter had already sized up the youngest of Warren's sons. After all, for such a slender sort, Levi Warren packed quite the wallop. Colter had not run into many cowboys. Sure, there were ranches in Oregon, but most of those lay east of the Willamette Valley, where he had first settled. He had read some wild and woolly tales in newspapers and magazines about Abilene, Kansas, and those Texas cowboys. He wondered if all cowhands were like Levi Warren.

Brod, the oldest, looked more like a prizefighter, or wannabe pugilist, than Levi. He was big, even taller than his old man, in tall boots with 2½-inch heels. He wore chaps, and a pistol stuck in his waistband—no holster. His shirt was collarless, his vest frayed, stained, and torn, with the string from a sack of Bull Durham hanging out of the one pocket that hadn't been ripped off his vest. Broderick also had a thick mustache, and his nose seemed crooked from so many fistfights. Maybe Colter was lucky. He could have had to tangle with Brod Warren.

Tyrone seemed the odd man out among the Warrens. Both the old man and two of the sons looked like the drawings of cowboys that Colter had seen in *Frank Leslie's Illustrated Newspaper, Saturday Evening Post,* and *Harper's Weekly.* Tyrone looked more like a man who belonged behind the faro layouts at Paddy O'Rourke's Blarney Stone. He wore black-striped britches that stuck inside shiny black boots, and the rowels of the spurs on his heels were tiny compared to the big stars on the other Warren men. He also wore a bright blue shirt, a silk material, with mother-of-pearl buttons, a fancy brocade vest of red, black, and green. His shirt had a paper collar, and a long string tie, also black, hung down to the buttons of his vest. His hat, however, was white, wide-brimmed with a low crown. His pistols were what struck Colter most about Tyrone Warren. Two nickel-plated guns, with ivory grips, holstered butt forward for cross-draws.

That told Colter that Tyrone Warren would be the one to watch. Levi and Brod used their fists when they tangled with a man. Tyrone must have preferred the two Remington .44s he carried.

Yet, Colter also understood something else about this clan of Texas Unionists. They would not fight . . . without their father's blessing. So the old man was the one to pay attention to . . . and the old man must have known that Levi was coming to town to tangle with the new lawman.

So Clint Warren and Tim Colter sat in chairs on the boardwalk in front of the unfinished building, talking about this and that. More of a getting-to-know-you kind of talk. The old Texan sipped rye. Colter thought it too early in the day to be partaking of intoxicating spirits, so he merely applied the whiskey on his cuts and bruises. It burned like the hinges of Hell, but it would help Colter more than whiskey in his belly.

"My boys are a bit on the wild side," Clint Warren said, "but they're good boys. You gonna charge Levi for that little row y'all had?"

Colter's head shook. He could tell that the rancher seemed worried, and maybe he had good reason. Assaulting a federal peace officer could send young Levi Warren to the federal pen at Fort Leavenworth for at least a year.

"Well, it was a bit harmless," Warren said with relief.

Colter turned and gave the old man a hard stare. "Not sure I'd call it harmless."

The two men smiled.

"Marshal, I might as well let you know something right now." Warren's tone turned serious, and even the drawl almost disappeared. "I've got two thousand head of Texas longhorns trailing up here. Mixed stock. Some bulls. Mostly heifers and steers."

"That's a lot of beef."

The rancher nodded. "Well, this is a big country."

"Where do you plan on grazing your herd?" Colter asked.

"This land's open range, suh. That's the way of things in cattle country."

He went on to talk about the changes going on down in

Texas and Kansas. The Civil War had given Easterners and Northerners a taste for beef. Cattle had been practically worthless down in Texas, but ranchers and plenty of out-of-work ex-Rebels, not to mention recently freed slaves, found jobs pushing cattle to Kansas or Missouri. Towns like Sedalia, Baxter Springs, and Abilene boomed. A steer worth three dollars in Texas could fetch upward of forty bucks in Abilene. The West had suddenly found a new form of business. Ranching. And it was becoming big business.

"We're a long way from Kansas, though," Colter pointed out.

"Well, it's not just Kansas these days," Clint Warren explained. "Back in '66, a cattleman I know, just a bit, named Charles Goodnight and another man named Oliver Loving took a herd west. For the most part, they followed the old Butterfield line from around Fort Belknap in Texas to Horsehead Crossin' on the Pecos River. Then took the herd up the Pecos all the way to Fort Sumner and the Bosque Redondo. You've heard of it?"

"Just what I've read," Colter explained. "Reservation for the Navajo down in New Mexico Territory, or something like that. Right?"

Warren nodded. "And Mescalero Apache."

After dabbing the last cut with whiskey, Colter again pointed out that New Mexico Territory might be as far away as Abilene, Kansas, from the town of Violence.

"But they pushed up farther north. Past Raton Pass and into the Colorado country. They did that just last year. This year, Goodnight, or maybe it was Loving, decided to get going. Signed a contract with a guy named Iliff, to bring beef to the U.P. boys in Cheyenne, Wyoming."

Colter nodded. "A steak . . . a real beefsteak . . . would hit the spot, I guess, after nothing but antelope and jackrabbit."

"You come to my home, ol' hoss. . . ." The drawl had returned. "You come with me, anytime, and my boys—their wives, I mean—will fry you up a steak three inches thick that weighs five pounds."

"I'd be at your place a week trying to finish it."

The rancher laughed. "I'll put you up in the bunkhouse till you've cleaned off the bone, son."

He cleared his throat and explained. "I got a crew followin' Goodnight's trail to Cheyenne. Then they'll cut over, or maybe before, and head to Violence." He lowered his voice. "I'd like to give you fair warnin', hoss. Cowboys . . . after three or four months herdin' cattle, when they hit town, they can be cantankerous. They be doin' it just for fun, you see. Not tryin' to hurt nobody, but you mix whiskey with young kids, and them kids are carryin' Colt's six-shooters, and, well, things can get wild and woolly. That's something you might ought to remember, Marshal."

"I'll remember."

"Good." The rancher sipped more whiskey, and then corked the bottle. The conversation was over. He started to rise, but Tim Colter stopped him with a look.

"Two thousand head of cattle, Mr. Warren. That's a lot of beef."

"It ain't nothin'. Not really. Not yet." He gestured toward the ranges that swept all across Clear Creek and the territory. "Good grass. Sweet water. The Union Pacific did me a good favor, though. Hirin' hunters to feed all them workers layin' track. Shootin' of the buffalo. And sendin' the game north and south, away from the rails. Yes, sir. They've helped turn this land into cattle country. And that's what it's gonna be. Cattle. Open range. So, yeah, I'm bringin' in two thousand cattle, but I won't be done. Not by a damned sight. Next year, I'll bring in more. And the year after, more. My claims will grow. Because I was the one who got here first. You just wait and see, Marshal. And don't worry. You'll be eatin' beefsteaks free. That I'll promise you. On account that you deserve it. Because you're clean-in' up this town. Which is what we need."

"Well, there is just one thing, Mr. Warren–"

"Call me Clint, boy. Call me Clint."

"Well . . ." Colter breathed in deeply, and slowly ex-haled. He looked the old man squarely in his eyes. "You've got the claims for some land. You . . . and your three sons. But others have claims here, too. I'm talking about the farmers. They've filed their claims, paid their fees, started their homesteads. Legal claims. Not open range. I don't want any trouble between you and those farmers."

Colter grinned. He decided any chance he had of eating steaks for free for the rest of his life had just ended. Clint Warren was a man who was used to getting his way. And now the rancher had just learned that Tim Colter, with a federal commission for the territory and a town job as lawman, stood in his way.

CHAPTER 26

Clint Warren's face hardened. He sank back onto the chair, but leaned forward. Now he whispered. Now he did not force the drawl that made him sound so friendly.

"Those sodbusters won't last, Marshal. This is cattle country. You know that. I know that. And after a drought or a hard winter or a Cheyenne raid, them foreigners will be hightailin' it back all the way to Belgium."

"When they do," Colter pointed out, "you'll have the opportunity to buy their claims. Until then, I don't think your cattle should be straying onto their wheat fields."

"Which they will never make," Warren snapped.

"And you know that. And I know that. But until those families from Belgium know that, I have to follow the law. And the law's with them."

Warren started talking, but Colter had found something that interested him more. Jed Reno was walking around the corner, coming from the north side. He saw Warren and paused, then studied the bruises and cuts on Colter's face. His hard eye turned sharply to Clint Warren, but the mountain man found no signs of injuries on the old man's face.

"It was Levi," Colter said.

Reno nodded.

"Any luck?" Colter asked.

The old trapper shook his head. "Lost the trail. Boy got smart. Come to the U.P. line and walked along the rails and crossties. Not much of a chance for me to pick it up after that."

"Trail?" Warren asked.

"Looking for the man who torched Jed's trading post," Colter said. And he said nothing else.

"Yeah," Warren said, turning to study Jed Reno. "Heard what happened. Sorry to hear that, ol' hoss. You gonna rebuild?"

"We'll see. For now, I'll just keep my traps clean. And my Hawken loaded."

With a grunt, Clint Warren pushed himself to his feet. "I'll keep my cattle on grazing land that ain't bein' claimed by any ignorant sodbuster who can't even speak good English. Till they flee for their grandmammies and grandpappies and hurry back to where they belong. That suit you?"

Colter nodded.

"You see where my boys went?" the old man asked.

Mix Range replied, "To The Cheyenne Saloon."

The rancher chuckled. "Well, I'd better cut them off before Tyrone or Brod decide they'd like to see if they can tackle the man who killed Stewart Rose. I wish you good luck, Marshal. I'll keep my boys in line. My sons, I mean. Might not have no control when those waddies of mine come in from Texas."

"I'll take care of your waddies, Mr. Warren." Colter shook the old man's hand, and watched him walk to his horse, tethered to the hitching rail. He swung into the saddle like a man thirty years younger, and started walking the animal east toward the saloon.

"But, Mr. Warren," Colter called out.

The man stopped his horse. The leather of the saddle squeaked as he turned to face the marshal.

"When do you expect those men to be here?"

"July be my guess," Warren answered. "You take care of yourself. You, too, Reno."

They watched him go, and then Reno squatted in the dirt in front of Colter.

"Must've been a good fight," Reno said with a wicked grin. "Plumb sorry I missed it. He whup you?"

"Would have. But I sort of . . . cheated."

The grin turned more wicked. "I taught you well."

"He beat the tar out of young Levi," Mix Range said. "I thought you was gonna kill him, sure as shootin'."

"It wasn't that bad," Colter said.

"Your face," Reno said, "begs to differ from that statement."

When he could speak without hurting too much, Tim Colter talked more with Jed Reno about the trail. The man who set the fire had been fairly smart. Swung wide around the south edge of town, then cut down Third Street all the way to the railroad tracks north of Union Street. That's where Reno lost the trail.

"It could've been anybody."

Reno and Colter turned to stare at Mix Range, who had joined in on the conversation without an invitation.

"Not anybody. City gent. That leaves out most of the gamblers at The Blarney Stone and the barkeeps and gunmen at Slade's Saloon."

"And the whores," Mix Range said.

"Leaves out Murden," Colter said. "He's too fat."

"And his pard, Gates." Reno pointed at his eye patch.

"Them spectacles he wears. Couldn't see. And he ain't got the sand."

"Nor would the guy from the hotel, Yost," Colter said.

"So that leaves . . . ?" Reno turned to stare at the building next door. "The mayor?"

"Nah." Again, Mix Range answered. "I seen him. He was runnin' to The Blarney Stone when all that was goin' on. Besides, he wears boots." Range picked up the broom and limped back inside the building, to start sweeping again.

"Well," Reno said. "You got a lot of folks to keep an eye on. Could be the man who done it just sent some ol' boy to burn my place down. And I'd pay more attention to them boys who come here with guns than them with matches."

"What do you think of Clint Warren?" Colter asked.

"One of his boys bought a calendar from my place. Paid a whole dime for it. That's about all I know of him. You think he's a friend?"

Colter, to his surprise, found his head shaking. "I don't think a father, any father, would befriend the man who just whipped his son in a fistfight. And he and those farmers will be fighting over land before long."

His lips started hurting again.

"There's one thing he said that troubles me, though."

"What's that?"

Colter didn't get a chance to answer. Some drunk was shooting out the windows at The Railroaders Lounge.

It had not been like this in Oregon, even when Colter had taken the lawman's job in the mining camps. Even as a federal lawman for the entire district, Tim Colter had been able to sleep. Relax. Sometimes during those times off, far west of Violence, Tim Colter had even walked around without his six-shooter strapped on his hip.

The drunk was easy enough. Tim Colter came into the saloon with his LeMat in his hand. The drunk turned, dropped the empty Remington on the floor, and charged, swinging punches blindly, yelling that he would rip off the badge—which Colter was not wearing—and make him eat it. Colter swung the revolver, and down went the drunk.

Maybe a five-pound Oregon Boot. And a week in the corral, doing odd jobs. After all, the windows in The Railroaders Lounge would have to be replaced. To keep the dust out. Before winter returned.

Mix Range had been such a good hand with the fire, and that broom, that Tim Colter, Deputy U.S. Marshal and Marshal of Violet, Idaho Territory, rewarded the Alamo gunman. He left the thirty-pound Gardner Shackle in the canvas sack, then put one on Range that weighed only fifteen pounds. Range, showing ever the Southern graciousness, even thanked him.

The town of Violence wasn't populated with only thugs and heartless souls. The baker and his wife brought a tarp, which they nailed up on the studs to make a wall that would stop most of the west wind. A few other merchants came with blankets; one brought a chair; and before two more days had passed, there was a traveling table, one used by officers during the late War to Preserve the Union, and a gun case. Everyone seemed to come to bring something. Even the waitress from the café brought food and coffee over, after the rush for breakfast, the rush for dinner, and any leftovers that wouldn't keep till morning, after supper. Everyone dropped by.

"Everyone," Colter corrected when Jed Reno was looking to find a likely spot to place a spittoon the owner of Jake's Place had donated. "Except the carpenters."

Reno sat down. He scratched his beard.

"Who owns this place?" Colter asked.

Reno could only shrug.

"We could go over to the land office, ask Mr. Yost. But I'd bet he'd tell us it was owned by one Jasper Monroe."

"You reckon?"

"I reckon."

Colter wiped his mouth. Breakfast was passable this morning. He listened. Sure enough, even though the sun was barely up, the saw was whirring at what passed for a sawmill in this part of the country. Hammers struck nails. Other handsaws—like the one Colter had left with Micah Slade—cut two-by-four studs or wooden planks. Violence was still growing. But no carpenters were working on this building.

"When's the last time you saw someone working on this place?" Colter asked Jed Reno.

But it was Mix Range who answered. "Day before you put that boot on me. The real big, heavy one."

Colter and Reno both turned to look at the killer, who sopped up the gravy with his fingers, and stuck those fingers in his mouth to suck. Finished, he wiped his hands on his trousers and looked at the walls, which were studs—unless you counted the canvas tarp.

"You're starting to grow on me, Mix," Colter said. "That worries me."

"Well," the outlaw said, "you're growin' on me, too. Maybe it's on account that I respect men who beats me. And you's beat me."

"How did you turn out so bad, son?" Jed Reno asked.

"Things happen. They just happen."

Tim Colter could relate to that. He was destined to be a gentleman farmer, married with a brood of kids, growing crops in Oregon's Willamette Valley. Just one of a myriad farmers who came, settled the country, made the country grow. A man who would do his job, and do it well, but never be known for anything, or as anything, outside of his farm and his church and maybe the county that he called home.

But things happen. Maybe for a reason. Maybe because of fate. Maybe . . . just maybe . . . things just happened. Tim Colter had survived a wagon train massacre—by luck or by God's intervention. Stubbornly he had set out to do something that should have left him dead. He had met Jed Reno. He had learned to survive. And that experience, more than twenty years ago, had changed Tim Colter. Changed his life. Changed the path he thought he was supposed to take.

Instead, he had become a lawman. And he had set off after an outlaw named Stewart Rose, who had come into the state of Oregon for some crazy reason that only Stewart Rose had known. A vacation, perhaps? To get away from the heat down in Texas and Kansas and a few other places. Tim Colter had found the outlaw and his gang. Or maybe Stewart Rose had found Tim Colter. No matter. Once again, Tim Colter had survived. He had killed. That's one thing Tim Colter had become good at. Surviving. Killing.

His legend had grown. And now he was in a town known as Violence. With a one-eyed mountain man who had trained him, taught him, and mentored him. And with an uneducated Southern killer and thief whom, for some crazy reason, Tim Colter had started to like.

"You know," Mix Range said, "my daddy built houses and stores back in Alabama. I helped him for a couple of years. Afore I decided that a six-shooter fit my hand better than a ball-peen hammer. But I was a fair to middlin' carpenter, I think. Get some wood. Some nails. A saw. I bet I could finish this here office for you." He nodded at his assessment, before another thought struck him. "Reckon I'd need a ladder, too. And a level. Some pencils. Miter box if you can find one. I don't know. You reckon you want windows in this place?"

He gestured toward a room in the back, like the rest of the building, set off by two-by-four studs. "And that there place. I bet it would make a fine jail cell. But you'd need some iron cages for it, Marshal."

CHAPTER 27

Peace came, ever so briefly, to Violence, Idaho Territory. Oh, the corral always had at least a half-dozen drunks lying on the grass or the mud, but usually Tim Colter didn't even have to put an Oregon Boot on those old railroad boys or carpenters. Usually, he just escorted them to the pen, opened the gate, and watched them stagger inside. Sometimes he had fun with them, telling them to go to the corner. The corral was round. But they'd give up quickly, sit down, fall down, and start snoring. A few others he had to drag to the corral, and a couple he had to crack over the head with the LeMat's barrel or butt. He didn't bother fining them. Just let them sleep it off in the corral, and then they would wake up—eventually—although they might not quite have sobered up, but they could walk, or stagger, back to their homes, tents, or jobs. Or take the trail they'd been traveling before stopping off for whiskey, poker, and women.

One big gent who worked at the sawmill did get a shackle on his left ankle, but that was because he had been so drunk, he took a crowbar and tried to tear up the tracks laid by the U.P. workers last fall. That one had to pay a fine and spend six weeks in jail. Or get off on good behavior and no fine if he helped Mix Range finish the carpentry work when he knocked off work at his regular job, and on his one day off, a Sunday. It wasn't like he would be spending that day in church. There was no church in Violence.

"Is that how all deputy marshals do things?" Jed Reno asked.

"What's that?" Colter said.

"I don't know. Law and all that stuff I never paid much mind to. Just seemed to recall that a lawman like yourself did the peacekeeping, but it was some hifalutin judge who handed down the sentences, told folks how much they'd have to pay, or how many nights they'd have to spend in the calaboose, or when they'd be going to prison for so long, or what day they'd be hanged by the neck till they was dead, dead, dead."

Colter shrugged. "Let him appeal."

Reno scratched his beard. "Huh?"

The U.P. trains brought more settlers, and more railroad men, more iron rails and wooden beams and everything else men needed for this massive venture. Express riders, however, brought most of the mail.

This wasn't the Pony Express, that short-lived venture that had ceased running in the autumn of 1861 with the completion of the telegraph lines. No, other companies had formed, but running shorter routes. The Wells, Fargo & Company, "carriers of the Overland Mail," had taken over the business founded by Russell, Majors, and Waddell, and Ben Holladay was the king of the company, getting passengers, mail, and money delivered from Missouri and as far west as Sacramento, California, with stops in Omaha and Denver and to Salt Lake City, Utah. Other lines ran from Salt Lake or Denver or Sacramento to Virginia City and Helena in Montana, to Boise City in Idaho

Territory. Then express riders would carry mail to other places, such as Cheyenne or Laramie City or even Violence, Idaho Territory. The letters from Boise were addressed to Deputy Marshal Tim Colter, but those were just wanted dodgers and other information, and a paycheck for his monthly services. Of course, while there was a bank in Violence, Custer could count to ten. And since no one was dumb enough to cash a check, Colter merely put the checks in the jar that Jed Colter brought in and kept buried, somewhere, behind the ruins of his trading post and dugout.

There were other letters, too, and those Tim read often. Somehow Betsy McDonnell had forgiven him. They had called off their wedding. She said she would wait till he finished the job. He wrote her back. She wrote him. He wrote. She wrote. It was a nice break from the violence in Violence.

June came and went. Tim Colter thought about that wedding date that also came, and passed, with no wedding, with no Betsy McDonnell; yet her letters came, and she sounded happy, content, and still willing to wait. July came. Clint Warren's cattle, however, did not come yet. Neither Tim Colter nor Jed Reno was saddened by that. Cowboys . . . railroaders . . . and the bloodsuckers who feasted on a town like Violence—that could be a lethal gathering.

Violence and the Union Pacific celebrated Independence Day. Colter wasn't sure what the Flemish farmers and their families thought about the fireworks and the horse races and all the food, but they seemed to accept it. They loved the fireworks, and, in a rare moment in this town, the fireworks were actual skyrockets and Roman candles and firecrackers. No one drew a revolver or pulled a trigger that day—at least not inside the limits of the town

Murden and Gates had platted. It turned out to be one of
the most peaceful days in the city's history.

Which had to be one for the history books.

The wind blew hot. Peace came to Violence, more or
less. Even the corral held only one or two drunks each
night. Sodbusters came to see Jed Reno, shocked and saddened that his trading post was no longer anything but a
place for pack rats and spiders. They asked about the
money they owed the one-eyed ex–fur trapper.

"Them records burned in that fire. Don't know how
much you owe. So I reckon that means you don't owe me
a thing."

But you could not tell that to a person who had left Belgium with his family, or come alone, to start a new life in
America. To farm. To build this country. They replaced the
café that had no name—nor much in the way of good
cooking—and brought dumplings and apple fritters and
good coffee and fine bread. They almost tried to make Tim
Colter fat.

"This could be a nice place to live," Mix Range said as
he shoved the last fritter into his mouth.

Colter stared. The walls were up; the drunken carpenter
had long since finished his obligation, and had gone back
to work at the sawmill. Mix Range no longer wore the fifteen-
pound Oregon Boot, but a ten-pounder, and half the time
Tim Colter forgot to lock that on the killer's ankle after he
climbed down off the roof. The original roof leaked, but
Mix Range had patched that up. The door often dragged
on the floor, but Range swore he would get around to finishing it. But first he wanted to get the jail set, but the iron
bars and the heavy jail door had yet to make it on the train
from Omaha. So Mix Range busied himself with minor
things. He didn't sleep in the corral at nights. As always,
he sat in the room that, eventually, would be the jail.

The express rider brought more letters, and Tim Colter was reading the latest from Betsy McDonnell when the farmers came into town. This wasn't the usual delegation. Women only came on the last Saturday of the month, and when they came, they did their shopping while the men gathered around and drank coffee and pointed to the sky and asked about the weather. Or so Tim Colter thought. He didn't understand most of what they said.

On this afternoon, the women gathered in front of the lawman's office. One of them had been appointed to speak, since she had some grasp of the English tongue. So Tim Colter, Jed Reno, and Mix Range stood on the boardwalk and listened.

"A schoolteacher?" Colter asked when the woman had finished her talk and stepped back into the sea of brown poplin dresses and bunned hair.

"*Ja.*" The heads of the ladies bobbed in unison.

"Well, I don't know," Colter said. This wasn't what he had expected. The woman told to speak spoke again, and Colter managed to grasp that the sodbusters had maybe two dozen kids who needed to learn how to talk in English, to do math in English, to read in English, to count in English, and to be regular Americans.

"I see." Colter looked at Jed Reno and Mix Range for help, but realized that was pointless.

One woman pushed her way from the back of the crowd until she appeared through an opening. Most of the farmwives were dressed in brown poplin dresses, but she wore black: a black dress, black boots, a black veil, which she lifted with rough hands. Her face was gaunt, and her eyes, bloodshot from tears, were sunk deep in her head. Most of the women's faces had been burned by sun and rain, but this woman seemed pale. Her eyes sought out Tim Colter, but did not register, and they finally locked on Jed Reno.

The woman started out from the designated speakers. One woman reached for her, but the lady in black brushed the hand aside, then spoke something sharply in a language that Colter could not understand.

"Mr. Reno," she said when she stopped a few feet in front of the old fur trapper.

CHAPTER 28

"Mrs. Slootmaekers." Jed Reno's head bowed, and the tough old bird stared down at his moccasins, unable to hold the old woman's gaze.

Old? Colter looked again. No, she wasn't old. By Jupiter, she might even be younger than Tim Colter himself. She looked ancient, but Mrs. Slootmaekers must have lived one hard life.

"Our children . . . should learn . . ." She stopped, turned to face her own people, and spoke in their language. A few heads bobbed in agreement; and motivated by this, Mrs. Slootmaekers again looked at Jed Reno. "Should learn," she repeated, her accent hard, but the English words understandable, "the ways . . . of America."

A murmur rose among the farming delegation.

"We . . . ," the woman continued, "all of us . . . should know . . . this."

Heads nodded in agreement again.

"Yes'm," Jed Reno agreed. "It's a good thing to know, I reckon."

"There is . . . no one . . ." She spoke something in what Tim Colter guessed to be Flemish, before continuing on in English. "Nobody . . . will teach . . . can teach . . . in this town."

"I reckon that's true, Mrs. Slootmaekers."

"For us . . . to make this . . . our . . . home . . ." Mrs. Slootmaekers suddenly wailed, and almost collapsed. Reno's lips flattened, but he could not reach out, for some reason that Colter couldn't quite grasp. The leaders of the delegation ran and grabbed her arms, supporting her. Tim Colter could only blink.

"My . . . Ferre . . . he . . . he so wanted to learn. . . . He . . . was . . . a good . . . boy."

"Yes'm," Reno said.

"You know . . . ," the woman cried out. "He . . . wanted . . . to be . . . American."

"Yes'm."

She found some inner strength deep within, and she pulled away from the arms and hands and friends supporting her. Her thin arm raised, and she pointed a bony, callused finger at Jed Reno. "I have . . . no . . ." She had to look away, and regain her composure. "Ferre is . . . gone . . . to God," Mrs. Slootmaekers said. "We do not . . . want . . . others . . . their sons . . . or daughters . . . to . . . It should not . . . happen."

"No, ma'am," Jed Reno said. "It never should've happened."

"*Ja,*" came the echo of the women calling on Marshal Tim Colter. "*Ja. Ja. Ja.*"

"School . . . teacher," Mrs. Slootmaekers said. "We must . . . have one."

"*Ja. Ja. Ja. Ja.*"

Jed Reno nodded, and now his lone eye locked hard on Tim Colter. In fact, Colter tried to remember if he had ever seen that look on the mountain man's face. Determined, but deeply saddened . . . and filled with a hurt.

Colter cleared his throat.

"I tell you what," he said, when he realized everyone in the party—including Mrs. Slootmaekers—had turned to stare him down. "I'll write the marshal in Boise. And I'll send a letter to the newspaper in Council Bluffs or Omaha. Ask them if they might post an item in the paper, a news story, not an advertisement, where you'd have to pay. See if that gets you any interest. That sound all right?"

"*Ja.*" Again the bunned heads nodded as one.

Colter smiled as he watched them go. Then he and Jed Reno disappeared into his office, the one with the old Civil War table, and now a gun case, and two chairs, and a trash can.

"What was that about, Jed?" Colter asked.

Reno decided to brace himself with a snort from the jug he and Mix Range tried to keep hidden from Tim Colter. He wiped his lips, corked the jug, and tossed the stoneware container to Mix Range.

"That was Mrs. Slootmaekers," Reno said.

"I gathered that much."

"Her boy was Ferre. Ferre Slootmaekers."

Colter waited.

"He was a good boy," Reno said.

Colter remembered then. "The boy," he said. "The boy who worked for you. The one who everyone said killed Marshal Cutter."

Reno sighed, and took back the jug Mix Range had returned to him. The old man started to drink, but shook his head, and slid the jug onto Tim Colter's desk.

"He's also the reason I up and wrote you that letter. Good kid, Ferre was. Good family, I reckon. His death broke that woman's heart, it did."

"I know," Colter said, and this time the words took some effort. "I know what it's like, Jed . . . to lose . . . a son."

Reno nodded. "I know that. Blue-eyed boy. Spoke pretty good English. Hard worker, he was. Sixteen, I reckon. Yeah, sixteen years old. Gangly kid, but didn't have no trouble lifting crates and boxes and kegs. He could probably have

toted your sack of Oregon Boots and never complained or broke out in a hard, stinky sweat. Hailed from someplace they called Mechelen sometimes, and *Dijlestad* other times. So I paid him, sent him on his way home, but they say he went into The Blarney Stone. Got drunk. Killed Cutter, and Cutter killed him. I saw him. Well, I saw the both of them, cut down dead, but it's Ferre—the one who I still see at nights. In my dreams. Shot in his belly, and shot in his throat. So it's 'cause of young Ferre that I wrote you."

"It's all right, Jed," Tim Colter said. "I'm glad you wrote me. I'm glad I'm here. And I will write the marshal in Boise City. You'll get a schoolteacher here. That I promise you and all those sodbusters."

He wrote, of course, the letter that day. Telling the Idaho territorial marshal what he wanted, and he also wrote a letter to the U.P. brass in Council Bluffs, Iowa. Then he found another piece of paper and an envelope.

First, Tim Colter read the letter from Betsy and wrote her back. He told her about this day's visit, and how things had changed for the better in Violet. He even called the town by its right name, not Violence. He told her that maybe peace was finally coming to the town, and that he might be coming home soon. They could be married—if she still wanted that. He rushed through the letter, wanting to get it to the post office before the express rider rode back out with the mail for Denver. The mail did not come to Violet often.

The man who ran the town of Violence came into the office of Mayor Jasper Monroe for a shave and haircut. And he fished a silver coin from his vest pocket to send Eugene Harker on his way to buy a whiskey from Jake's Place.

Mayor Jasper Monroe stopped sharpening the razor on

the leather strop, and secured the barber's cloth over the chest and shoulders of the man who ran the town of Violence. He handed the letters that Marshal Tim Colter had dropped off at the post office, which, technically, was not a post office at all, since the city of Violet had yet to apply for one. The mail came, general delivery, to the mercantile. The man who ran the mercantile, and served as the one in charge of the mail, had given the letters to Jasper Monroe without question.

A leathery hand came out of the cotton covering. "The razor," the man said.

Jasper Monroe placed the ivory handle of the straight razor in the man's hand. He used the blade to slice open the first envelope. Once the letter was out, the man read, pursed his lips, refolded the piece of stationery—the U.P.'s letterhead—and returned it to the envelope. The next envelope and correspondence were treated the same way. The man read, nodded as if in thought, and again returned the letter into the envelope.

"So the sodbusters want a teacher," the man said. He looked at the other envelope, and studied it longer before opening it.

"Won't the people getting these letters be suspicious?" Mayor Jasper Monroe said. "Opened mail and all."

"Glue the envelope. Crumple it. Hell, just gettin' a letter out of this territory and into the hands of the person it was written to takes a damned miracle. They'll be happy to have gotten it. Besides, I ain't begrudgin' even no foreign-speakin' crazy farmer the chance of gettin' an education. Good thing to have, don't you reckon?"

"Yes, sir." The man withdrew the letter, and handed the razor back to Monroe.

"Sharpen it. Cuttin' papers dulls a blade."

He read. He chuckled. "Well, this is rather interestin'," he said, and re-read the letter. "Fetch me a pencil and

paper." Jasper Monroe quickly obeyed, and the man who ran the town of Violence copied the address of one Betsy McDonnell, Bullfrog Café, General Delivery, Salem, Oregon, onto the paper, which he folded and returned to some pocket hidden underneath the cotton covering to protect Monroe's customers from being covered with hair clippings.

"I don't think we'll need this," said the man, "but I like to have all of my options covered." His hand returned to stuff the letter back into the envelope addressed to Betsy McDonnell. "Lather me up, barber. And don't even think about tryin' to cut my throat."

"I w-wouldn't do that," Jasper Monroe stammered.

"The hell you wouldn't. You think about it every day."

Certainly, Jasper Monroe thought about it, but he also could guess that the man who ran the town of Violence had a pistol underneath that protective sheet of cotton, and would kill Jasper Monroe if his razor nicked cheek or chin. He shaved closely, but carefully, and managed to survive the shaving.

The man who ran the town of Violence dried off his face himself, thanked Monroe, and tossed him a nickel. Then Clint Warren, the man who ran the town of Violence, walked outside. He felt pretty damned good, and very confident.

Meanwhile, Tim Colter remained in fine spirits. Until the train arrived one morning, for on it was a passenger, a man with the last name Rose.

Stewart Rose's brother. And he wore a brace of Navy Colts.

CHAPTER 29

Rancher Clint Warren, the man who ran the town of Violence, met Chet Rose in the livery stable that had just opened on Fifth Street. He tossed the brother of Stewart Rose a leather pouch that jingled with coins. Then he handed the gunfighter a cigar.

"Make it personal," said the man.

"He killed my kid brother," Chet Rose said. "It is personal." Then Chet Rose stuck the cigar into the top pocket of his vest. "I'll smoke this after that man-killin' bastard lies dead on the street." His other hand held the pouch, which he tossed up and caught, smiling at the sound the coins made. "Sounds just 'bout right."

"Enjoy your stay in Violence," said the man who ran the town. "Then get out. You don't know me. So don't come asking for more money when Colter's dead." He spun on his heel, and walked out, through the door that led to the corral and not Union Street, so as not to be seen by passersby. The man who ran the town of Violence, after all, was a careful man.

Chet Rose watched him leave. He thought about killing the man who had sent for him. After all, the man had just paid him a good sum of money—more than his stupid brother was worth—and he doubted if the man had enough money on his person to make murder worthwhile. He slipped the coin bag into the pocket of his linen duster, and walked out of the livery. Only he took the front entrance. The coins still jingled. The wind blew. The locomotive that had brought him all the way from Omaha, Nebraska, chugged and coughed and groaned. Smoke shot out of the stack in short heaves. Few people moved about the street at this time of day, just past dawn. Still asleep, Chet Rose thought. That was a good thing. For Chet, loaded up on coffee served on the train, was wide awake. He had never been able to sleep on trains anyway. Mostly, because he had been robbing them.

He wore tan trousers, brown boots, and one gaudy pullover, collarless shirt with prints of small flowers, yellow and pink roses, green leaves against a navy blue background. His bandanna was crimson. His hat black. He pushed back the duster, revealing the Navy Colt on his right hip, and walked across the dirt until he stepped onto the boardwalk in front of a vacant building.

Chet Rose decided that the best spot, for the best show, would be between two places he figured quite popular in a town like this one. Walking down the south side of the street, he came to a place called The Blarney Stone. Across from it was Slade's Saloon. Not that anyone was drinking, gambling, or whoring at this hour in the morning, but it would have to do. Someone whistled behind him, and Chet Rose stepped aside, until the whistling man walked past him.

"Hey, boy," Chet Rose called out to the Negro.

The black man stopped "Camptown Races" and turned. "Yes, sir," he said.

"You know where the marshal's office is, boy?"

"Yes, sir." The black man pointed across and down the street. "It's right—"

"I don't care where it's at, boy. I asked you if you knowed

where it was. Now I'm gonna tell you what you're gonna do for me."

The man swallowed down his fear. That made Chet Rose smile.

"You go fetch the marshal. Tell him that Chet Rose is waitin' for him right here on Union Street. Tell him Chet Rose is Stewart Rose's brother. You got that, boy?"

"Yes, sir."

"Repeat it."

The black man did, almost verbatim. Chet Rose smiled, and told the Negro to run along. He leaned against a wooden column, and tugged on the gun in his holster. He had slicked down the insides of the holster with grease from a hog, and the Navy Colt came out smoothly. He checked the percussion caps as he spun the cylinder on his hand, and watched as the black man crossed the street, and began knocking on the door of a frame building. The door opened. The black man disappeared inside. The door closed.

Chet Rose grinned. He slipped the .36-caliber revolver back into the holster, then looked across at the other column. He counted seven bullet holes that had splintered the wood, which told him that he had made a wise choice when he picked this spot for a showdown with Marshal Tim Colter. This would work out just fine, just fine, he told himself. Plenty of shootings had happened in this little burg's brief history. Men had been shot and killed right here. But on this morning, on this day, Chet Rose would give the townspeople something that they would be talking about for years to come. Their grandkids would be telling their own young'uns about the fine summer morning when Chet Rose gunned down Deputy U.S. Marshal Tim Colter on the streets of Violence, Idaho Territory.

*   *   *

After a big yawn, Tim Colter poured black coffee into a tin cup on his desk. The coffee was cold, and from the previous day, and did little to wake him up. Jed Reno busied himself trying to get a fire lighted in the potbelly stove. Eugene Harker stood by the window, staring down the street. From inside the jail room, still unfinished, Mix Range snored.

"What did this gent say his name was?" Colter didn't think he had heard correctly.

"Chet Rose, Marshal, sir." The black man stepped away from the window. "He's still just standing there, sir, in front of The Blarney Stone, leaning against one of them wooden posts."

"Rose." Colter stepped back and opened one of the drawers of his desk. Since setting up shop here, the U.P. had been quite thorough in delivering the latest wanted dodgers. It took Colter less than a minute to pull one out. He held up the poster for Eugene Harker to study. "This the gent?"

"I reckon. Same beady eyes and a nose that got busted a few times."

Colter laid the poster on the desk. Reno rose, looked at the paper, and then his one eye locked on Tim Colter.

"Brother of the gent you killed in Oregon?"

Colter nodded.

Reno tapped the poster. "Their mama and daddy must be real proud of 'em two sons they raised." Reno read. "Train robbery. Bank robbery. Murder." Reno closed the grate to the stove, now that a fire was going, and moved to the window. Next he glanced at the Hawken rifle in the gun case.

"I can kill him real easy, boy. From right here. He'd never knowed what killed him till his brother told him in Hell."

After finishing the cold coffee, Tim Colter laughed and

walked to the case. "Thank you, no, Jed. I'll do this my way." He buckled on the gunbelt and checked the loads on the LeMat.

"Don't be a fool, boy," Reno said. "You know better than that. You didn't give that Warren boy a fair chance when you tussled with him. Ain't that how I taught you?"

The LeMat fell into the holster. Tim Colter found his hat and set it on his head. "That was payback. Levi Warren sucker-punched me. This fellow wants revenge. Family honor. That's a big deal with boys from Texas, I hear."

"The Warrens hail from Texas," Reno said.

"Don't worry, Jed." Colter moved to the door and pulled it open.

"I'll be seeing you, Marshal, sir," Eugene Harker said. Instead of running into Jasper Monroe's office next door, though, the freedman crossed the street, moving as fast as a pronghorn antelope, went down the alley between two buildings facing the marshal's office, and disappeared.

Colter stepped outside. Reno followed him.

"Stay here, Jed," Colter said. "I'll see you in a few minutes."

"I hope so," Jed Reno called to Colter's back as the lawman stepped off the boardwalk and moved to the center of the street. Then Tim Colter began walking down Union Street toward the gunman in the linen duster, who kept leaning against a wooden column in front of Paddy O'Rourke's gambling hall.

As Colter walked, he noticed a few curtains moving from other businesses along Union Street, and more than a few doors closing. People either wanted to see what was about to happen, or they wanted not to get killed by a stray bullet. A few courageous souls even stepped out onto the boardwalk, but none of those stood anywhere near The Blarney Stone or Slade's Saloon. Slowly, with the ease of a man sure of himself, his ability, and his revolver, Chet

Rose stepped off the boardwalk and moved to the center of the street.

When forty feet of Union Street dust separated the two men, Tim Colter stopped walking.

"Chet Rose," he called out, "you're under arrest."

The gunman laughed. Something jingled in the duster he wore. "I ain't wanted for nothin' in Violence, mister. Or anywhere in Idaho Territory."

"Train robbery's a federal offense."

"Yeah. Well. I didn't come here to get arrested, you yellow-livered lawdog. I come on account of what you done to Stewart. Stewart was a good boy. So this here ain't legal. Ain't got nothin' to do with no laws or such. This here's personal. Family honor. So I'm callin' you out."

"How did you know I was here?" Colter asked.

"Word gets around, boy. I got friends."

"You don't have any friends, Stewart. Neither did your brother."

The gunfighter's eyes blazed with anger, and he was cursing savagely as he moved to his left, drawing the Colt from its holster.

Tim Colter did not move. He had learned that moving made it hard to get a good aim. He had also learned another thing about gunfighting, something that, apparently, Chet Rose had not comprehended.

The trail-robbing murderer from Texas fired from his hip, and then dropped to a knee. The .36-caliber Colt belched flame and smoke as Chet Rose, his face a mask of anger and hatred, fanned back the hammer of the revolver with his left palm. His right finger stayed on the trigger. The Colt sprayed lead balls down Union Street.

One bullet clipped a lock of Tim Colter's hair. Another dug up dirt between the lawman's legs.

Colter drew deliberately. Some might even have called his draw slow. Jed Reno thought it to be eternally slow.

The heavy LeMat came up in Colter's right hand. Only then did Tim Colter move. He swung his left leg behind his right, bracing his weight, and making himself a smaller target as the right arm extended, the big revolver now an extension of his right hand.

Chet Rose's last of six shots punched nothing but air a few yards to Colter's right.

Now the man was standing, still cursing, chucking the empty, smoking Navy into the dust, and reaching behind him for his backup pistol, a .30-caliber Sharps derringer. Rose had no chance of making that shot at this range, so Colter didn't squeeze the trigger.

From the boardwalk in front of the marshal's office, Jed Reno screamed, "Shoot that cur, boy! Don't give him no chance!"

Tim Colter, however, wanted to take Chet Rose alive. The Sharps spat four times, and then Rose was running toward The Blarney Stone, reaching for yet another pistol. This one was a Harper's Ferry, looked to be bigger than a .50-caliber weapon. A single-shot pistol, with a percussion cap, with a ten-inch barrel. A gun like that was one Jed Reno could appreciate. Tim Colter appreciated it, too. Because that gun could blow a hole through Tim's belly that one of the U.P.'s handcars could fit through.

Besides, this time, Chet Rose stopped running. He stood at the edge of the boardwalk in front of O'Rourke's building; he was panting. But as he raised his right hand, which held the big pistol, he turned steady.

"I'm killin' you, Colter. And you know that this here's not for Stewart. It's for me!"

Reno screamed, again, "Shoot that cur dog, boy!"

The gunman's finger began to tighten on the pistol's trigger. But Tim Colter touched the LeMat's trigger first.

The LeMat roared, and one shot drilled Chet Rose in the center of his chest. He fell backward, against one of the wooden columns. That shot should have killed the murdering scoundrel instantly. But Rose remained standing, and kept a good grip on the Harper's Ferry pistol, although the barrel was pointed skyward. Somehow, Chet Rose managed to stagger a few feet back into the street. Colter waited for the killer to fall.

Instead, Rose stopped, spit out bloody phlegm. His hat fell off his head, and the wind blew it toward the water trough in front of Slade's Saloon. Rose lowered the Harper's Ferry .54, and aimed again at Tim Colter.

Once more, the LeMat spoke, but this time Tim Colter took no unnecessary chances. He touched the trigger, thumbed back the hammer, shot again. Two more bullets drilled Chet Rose in the chest. The gun in the killer's right hand roared, but the bullet slammed into the dirt only a few feet in front of Rose's feet. Colter shot again, and that bullet put Chet Rose on the ground.

Chet Rose still sat up. Blood spilled from one corner of his lips. He supported himself with his left hand, which was pressed hard into the dirt.

Colter moved forward, holding the big LeMat, which he had cocked again, just to be safe. When he was just a couple of yards from the gunman, Colter stopped. Now he lowered the revolver's hammer, and let the heavy cannon fall into the holster.

The dying killer's mouth opened. He coughed, spit, and shook his head.

"You . . ." That was all he could manage. Death began to glaze over his eyes.

"Say hello to your brother for me," Tim Colter said.

The gunman's lips curled into a snarl, and froze, like his eyes, as he fell onto his side, shuddered once, and died.

Colter looked around, studying the rooftops and the alleys, and any windows from The Blarney Stone and Slade's Saloon. The last time he had been in a gunfight on Union

Street, there had been more than one assassin. He wet his lips. A few people began to emerge from the buildings, but all were smart enough to keep their hands far from their hips, even if their hips supported no pistols.

Satisfied at last, Tim Colter put his boot under the outlaw's chest and turned him over. Chet Rose was dead as he was ever going to be, his shirtfront stained crimson, and a hateful expression on his stiffening face.

When he turned back to walk to his office, Mayor Jasper Monroe had opened the door and stepped onto the boardwalk. The man was shaking in his boots, and he hadn't even been shot at.

"More business for you, Mayor," Colter said as he walked back. "And I don't mean a haircut and shave."

The mayor's head bobbed, and he timidly walked to the corpse in the street.

Tim Colter stopped in front of the office. Jed Reno was squatting in the street just past the boardwalk. He was fingering a print in the dirt. Colter stopped, saw the print, and his two eyes locked onto Jed Reno's one when the mountain man lifted his head.

CHAPTER 30

Tim Colter put the key in the lock on the Oregon Boot and carefully removed the shackle from the left ankle of his prisoner. "Now," he told the railroader, "be a good boy and stay out of Jake's Place." The Irishman, who looked like a few hours short of death, nodded with his bloodshot eyes squeezed tight, and then staggered out of the door and onto Union Street.

The door did not close, for Jed Reno was walking inside.

These days, of course, warm as July had become, the door stayed open. So did the window, which Mix Range had put in, just to keep a breeze in the marshal's hot office. Even in July, there was always a breeze blowing. It might be hot, but at least it blew.

Colter dropped the shackle into the sack on the chair. On the roof, Mix Range was hammering away. Little wonder that the railroader, who had gotten drunk and tried to tear apart Jake's Place, looked so lousy, and in such a hurry—or as big of a hurry as a man who had consumed enough of Jake's rotgut to kill most men could muster up at this time of day.

"He's back," Reno said. "At his little shack."

Colter filled two mugs with coffee, keeping one for himself and handing the other to the one-eyed mountain man.

"When he comes to work at Monroe's," Colter said, "we'll invite him in for a little talk."

Reno did not drink the coffee. "Ain't altogether certain he'll be coming to work."

That caused Colter to lower his tin cup, even before he had tasted it. He waited.

"He was packing a trunk," Reno said. Now he sipped the coffee.

As if on cue, the whistle of the train, at what passed for Violence's depot, shrieked.

"East or west?" Colter asked.

"East."

Colter nodded. West would mean that Eugene Harker had grown fed up of city life in Violence and was returning to his previous job of laying track for the Union Pacific. East meant he wanted to get out of the territory.

"All right," Colter said. "Let's go pay—"

He stopped as a big figure filled the open doorway. The big figure belonged to Clint Warren, who was the man who ran the town of Violence—only neither Reno nor Colter knew that.

"Mornin', gents." Warren smiled.

Both men returned the greeting, and Colter gestured toward the coffeepot.

"Thank you kindly, but I'll pass. Drunk about a gallon at the bunkhouse before we rode into town. Got some business to square away, and then we'll be ridin' out to meet the herd. Thought I ought to give you fair warnin'."

Colter let out a breath. "Well, I appreciate that, Clint. When do you expect them to hit town?"

"Two days, I'd guess," he answered. "That give you long enough to settle your affairs?" He grinned to let them know he was joking. "The both of you?" Now he laughed.

"I suppose so." Colter drew the LeMat from his holster and checked the caps on the cylinder. To let Clint Warren know that he wasn't joking.

"Well," the big man turned to go, "I'll be seein' you around, gents. I'll do my best, you know, to keep the lid on 'em boys. But like I done told you, after all them weeks in the saddle, eatin' dust, and starin' at nothin' but the hindquarters of a bunch of stinkin' longhorn cattle . . . well . . ." He left the rest unsaid, and his spurs jingled as he walked down the boardwalk, past the barbershop and undertaking parlor.

The train whistle blew again. Colter holstered the big LeMat, and picked up his hat off the desk. "Let's go pay Mr. Harker a visit before he flees the coop," he said.

They were walking out the door when a man's body crashed through the big plate-glass window at The Blarney Stone.

"Gentlemen," Clint Warren said as he entered the office at the Yost Hotel. "Sorry I'm late." He wasn't. "Some things came up that I just had to attend to." Which was definitely true.

"O'Rourke ain't here yet," Mayor Jasper Monroe said.

"He won't be here." Warren pulled up a chair and found a cigar in his vest pocket.

A gun fired along Union Street. Bottles broke. Women screamed.

"What the hell is all that commotion?" Duncan Gates asked.

"That's why Mr. O'Rourke won't be here." Clint Warren struck a match against his thumbnail and fired up the stogie. He blew a perfect ring toward the office's tin-punched ceiling. "Let's get started. I'll be busy in probably ten or twenty minutes."

* * *

It was Paddy O'Rourke himself who had flown out of his own window, landed on the boardwalk, and rolled into the dust and dung on Union Street. As Tim Colter and Jed Reno hurried across the street, the Irishman pushed himself up, groggily, and made a wild turn to head back into his gambling parlor. Instead, his boot found some horse apples, and down he went again. This time, it took him longer to get up.

He was bleeding from his face and hands, and his green jacket had been torn by shards of glass. His nose had been busted, too, and a fog coated his eyes. Yet, like most Irishmen, he remained game, and hard to put down. He pushed himself to his feet again, only to be shoved back onto Union Street sod.

"What's happening?" Tim Colter asked, removing his hand from the gambler's shoulder. Jed Reno stood at the entrance, aiming his Hawken through the batwing doors, but looking into the opening of what had been the finest window in all of Violence, and perhaps all of this massive territory.

O'Rourke shook the cobwebs out of his head. "I do me own fightin', laddie. And I'll . . ."

He tried to stand, and Colter let him, because the lawman had heard the squeaking of the batwing doors and a grunt from Jed Reno.

Massive Brod Warren stood behind the doors to the gambling joint, a cigarette dangling from his lips, which grinned a wild smile. The tip of the smoke glowed, and the big man—still wearing that same collarless shirt and the frayed tan vest that he had worn the last time Colter had seen him—stepped out of The Blarney Stone, and let the doors slam behind him.

He removed the cigarette and exhaled smoke.

"How 'bout lettin' me finish this fight, Marshal," Brod said, and it was not a request or a question, but a demand.

"Let me at that no-good—"

Colter turned, saw the derringer in O'Rourke's hand, and clubbed the gambler with the barrel of the LeMat. The Irishman dropped into the dust without another word, and Colter kicked the derringer into the middle of Union Street.

Big Brod Warren said, "Marshal, you spoilt my fun."

Just then a bottle of beer busted out the pane of another window, and someone inside The Blarney Stone cut loose with a yell. More glass broke. Women screamed. Men hooted, cursed, or fled through the open window or the back doors. No one dared to come through the front entrance—not with Brod Warren standing there.

"Hell," Jed Reno said with a sigh.

"Yeah," Tim Colter agreed, and watched Brod Warren coming right at him.

"My cattle will be here in two days," Clint Warren told his silent partners. "Three at the most. But we have a problem. Those sodbusters are still here—and those plows will ruin my pastures."

"You have the marshal, too," Mayor Monroe pointed out.

Warren lowered the cigar.

" 'You'?" he said. "The correct word is 'we.' " He wasn't smiling now.

He pointed at the land speculators. "You platted this town knowing if I could get a ranch started here, we would be set, and Violence—or whatever the hell you want to call it—would wipe out Cheyenne, wipe out Laramie City, and be the king of this territory. And you— and all of you—would make out like bandits, once we bought out those claims from those stupid farmers from where the hell off in Europe."

He pointed at Yost. "You made out pretty good, once we got rid of that holier-than-thou partner of yours, didn't you? Isn't that what you wanted? Isn't that what we agreed on?"

Yost hung his head.

"And you, Mr. Mayor, you figured this would be your start. From cutting hair to cutting ends to shaving off a few extra dollars. Be governor one day. King of the territory. You put up money with all these other gentlemen. And it was you, if I remember correctly, who brought Paddy O'Rourke into our fold."

"Where is O'Rourke?" Murden asked.

"My boy Brod is kicking him into oblivion. Just to save us some time. Keep the law occupied."

"But the law . . . Colter . . . ," Mayor Monroe started.

"Don't worry. I told Brod not to win this fight. Keep it friendly. Right now Colter and the U.P. think that Micah Slade is fighting Paddy O'Rourke for control of this city. And that's what we want them to think. Keep their eyes on those two buckets of blood. But we'll have to get rid of Colter. He's too bullheaded, and too smart for his own good."

"He's also fast," Gates noted. "Faster than at least your gunman."

"Like I said, we try personal first. Rose lost. So what? But I have something else in mind now, and I like it." He stopped, puffed more on the cigar, and listened to the racket outside. That was shaping up to be one heck of a fight. He wondered how Brod was faring? Maybe he shouldn't have told his son to hold those punches. Maybe Brod could have done what Stewart Rose's brother couldn't do. Kill Tim Colter. Maybe kill Jed Reno, too. But then the federal authorities would be coming down, and coming down like a ton of bricks, on Violence, Idaho Territory, and would leave Clint Warren with a bunch of cattle, an army of Flemish sodbusters, and a son facing a legal hanging for killing a federal deputy.

Yet, folks in Violence would be talking about this fight for many years to come. And here he was, Clint Warren, the man who ran this town, talking to a bunch of yellow-livered, money-grabbing idiots.

"I have my own plans for Marshal Colter, boys. Good ones. I've got some boys who plan to rob a train, and that's a federal job. And if that don't work, well, a while back I sent me off a letter. Out of my public duty. For those sodbusters who want a school for their young'uns. Well, they're gonna get one. She should arrive sometime soon."

"Hey," Murden asked. "Where's Eugene Harker?"

Clint Warren grinned. "Mr. Harker won't be joinin' us, gents. Another reason for that little ruckus outside. No, sir, Mr. Harker won't be joinin' us ever again."

CHAPTER 31

Out of the corner of his eye, Tim Colter saw Jed Reno shifting the Hawken and drawing the Colt revolver. The old trapper braced the stock of the long gun against his left thigh, while his right hand held the Colt and the thumb eared back the hammer. The rifle pointed at a few faces gathering in front of the busted window. The revolver aimed at Brod Warren's two brothers as they came through the batwing doors.

"Easy, boys," Reno said.

The two brothers frowned.

Big Brod, of course, kept right on smiling, and that grin stretched across his face when Tim Colter, sighing heavily, holstered the big LeMat. Brod swung a haymaker, but Colter ducked underneath it and came up with two quick punches in the cowhand's stomach. Brod grunted, and Colter quickly shot backward, avoiding another wild punch. That one left Clint Warren's behemoth son off-balance, so Colter fired three quick jabs into Brod's face. Blood spurted. Nose cartilage gave way, and Brod backed away, raising his arms to protect his face while shaking his head and wailing out a stream of profanity.

Colter stopped, glanced again at Reno and the saloon, and afterward turned toward Brod, who was speaking.

"You ain't that big . . . but you sure is quick."

"Why don't we quit this foolishness," Colter suggested. His jaw tilted toward the still unconscious Paddy O'Rourke. "You tell me what this was all about."

Brod's hands were clenched again. His face remained bloody, but he kept right on smiling.

"Just havin' some fun."

And he came again, swinging those powerful arms like the blades on a windmill.

Colter backed away, into the middle of the street, giving him more room. He was smaller than Brod, and that gave him an advantage, especially out here in the open. But those fists kept coming; Brod Warren kept laughing, while blood spilled off his chin; and the arms, those muscular, intimidating arms, kept swinging.

One of them clipped Colter's left ear, just a glancing blow, but it sent the deputy marshal spinning into the wooden column across the street at Slade's Saloon. If Brod had caught him full, Colter figured, his head would now be rolling down Union Street. He had no time to shake his head, or even clear his thoughts, because Colter knew the big man was coming to finish him.

"C'mon, you big waddy. Stomp that lawdog all the way to China."

The words came from Micah Slade. A crowd had gathered in front of Slade's Saloon, too. And, now that Colter had a fairly clear view of Union Street, they were outside of practically every store, gin joint—even the hotel—at any place open for business.

Brod Warren let loose with a powerful punch.

Colter ducked, dived left, his right hand splashing in the water trough. Wood cracked. Brod Warren screamed. Colter came up to his knees, splashed the water on his face, and sprang to his feet.

To Colter's astonishment, Brod Warren was backing

away from him, away from Slade's Saloon, and away from the column he had just cracked. Yes, the cowboy's punch had knocked the wooden stud off-kilter, separating the top from the awning. The big man's right hand already began swelling, and those giant knuckles, which had looked like hills, were beginning to resemble mountains. Practically every bone in his hand had been busted by that brutal punch.

It did not stop Brod Warren, however. It merely made him mad.

He let out a primeval roar, those eyes filling with hatred, and the cowhand charged to the hoots and hollers of those gathered in front of Slade's Saloon and The Blarney Stone. Brod Warren no longer smiled. Hate filled his face.

Colter brought up his right arm to deflect the big man's punch. And Brod, so angered, had punched with his right hand. The busted bones slammed into Colter's forearm, hurting Colter like blazes, but sending spasms of pain shooting through Brod's hand down his arm, into his shoulders, and down his spine. The big man backed up, tears filling his eyes, and he lowered his right hand, now useless.

Of course, Brod Warren still had a rock-hard left hand, which was about the size of a mountain and hit like a freight train. Colter decided he should take care of business now, before the shock wore off and the big bully remembered he had another fist, which was not broken and swollen.

So Tim Colter stepped in, letting loose with a left uppercut that caught the cowboy's jaw. The head snapped back, and the battered cowboy hat fell off. Colter drove a fist into the stomach; and as Brod doubled over, Colter caught the man with another driving punch, which came up to slam into the already-busted, bleeding nose. Colter didn't stop. Indeed, he knew he could not stop. The next jab glanced off Brod's shoulder, but Colter recovered and sent two more to the man's face. Colter blinked. He could see the fog and the haze beginning to cloud Brod's eyes. The cowhand was finished. Should be finished. Yet, Tim Colter knew he could not quit. Those Warren boys were tough as cobs, and if Brod snapped out of that daze, he might break Tim Colter into ten thousand little pieces.

Another jab into the stomach. Two more. The man doubled over, and Colter had to finish it. Now. Both hands shot up, grabbed fistfuls of Brod's hair, and he brought the head down while bringing his knee up. But this was Violence. Where anything was fair in any kind of fight.

He felt the jaw break, and heard a muffled whine. Colter stepped back, to let Brod drop to his knees. The man was still up—if only on his knees—and started shaking his head, and his busted hand, trying to shake some sense into his being.

Tim Colter swore.

So did several others watching.

One prostitute let out a whistle.

Colter stepped up, then swung a haymaker into the man's temple. That almost broke Tim Colter's hand.

As he stepped back, trying to shake some feeling into his fingers and swollen, scarred knuckles, Tim Colter blinked. The big cowhand was trying to keep from falling face-first into the dust, but his arms trembled, and he moaned as he fell like some giant redwood tree crashing to the earth.

Colter weaved his way back to the water trough in front of Slade's Saloon, sucking on his bleeding knuckles before cupping his hands and filling them with water. The water revived him. When he turned back, he saw the two other Warren boys standing over their unconscious brother. Jed Reno was at their side, still holding the Colt loosely in one hand, while butting the stock of the Hawken on the dirt. The old man grinned widely.

When he made his way back to the center of the street, Tyrone Warren, still looking like he should be dealing faro, looked up. "You've whipped both of my brothers, Marshal." He said it as though he were impressed.

"He gonna get one of 'em iron boots?" Levi Warren asked.

Colter shook his head. He looked over at Paddy O'Rourke, who was just now coming around. "Get him home, boys." He grinned, which hurt. "I don't think I've got a shackle big enough for him. But . . ." Colter tilted his hat at the Irishman, who was being helped to his feet by a couple of his tinhorn gamblers and gunmen. ". . . O'Rourke might hit you up for damages."

"Pa'll take it out of Brod's pay," Tyrone said. "Here he comes now."

Colter turned, instinctively putting his hand on the butt of the LeMat. The rancher puffed on a cigar, glanced at O'Rourke, at the busted window, and at his big son, still facedown in the dirt.

"You done that, Marshal," the old rancher said as he withdrew the cigar from his mouth, "all by your lonesome?"

"Tell your cowboys that," Colter answered. He was in no mood for jokes. "When they come to Violence."

Warren's eyes hardened into iron. "I'll remember that. And I'll give 'em fair warnin'." He looked down at the crumpled mass of Brod Warren, and then the face rose to meet the stares of his two other sons. "Get your brother back home, you dumb oafs." He spun around, fished out a coin purse, and tossed some twenty-dollar pieces at Paddy O'Rourke's feet.

"Let's go," Colter said, nodding at Jed Reno.

The mountain man put away the Colt, hoisted the heavy Hawken to his shoulder, and nodded. They crossed Union Street, picked up the boardwalk past Slade's Saloon, and moved east. At the edge of town, they found Eugene

Harker's home. You might have called it better than a sod
hut, or a tent, and for a former slave, Eugene Harker
might have considered it a mansion. He had taken parts of
a weathered, abandoned, half-burned boxcar and pieced
together a home. Many places in town had dirt floors, but
Harker's home was wood—the wooden floor of the old
railroad car. He had wooden walls, too, and a pretty de-
cent roof. A stove to keep him warm in the cruelest of windows. A canvas covering for a door, which he could pull
up or off to the side to allow light or a breeze in the summer. The canvas was closed.

Tim Colter knocked on the U.P. wood near the canvas.
He called out Harker's name.

No answer came.

"It's Tim Colter, Mr. Harker," Colter said. "And Jed
Reno."

Which was met with silence.

"Might have gone to work," Reno said.

"Yeah," Colter agreed. He had not seen the freedman in
the crowd during or after the big set-to with Brod Warren,
but Tim Colter's vision had been clouded by a few blows
delivered by that big brute. He hadn't seen a lot of people,
he figured.

"Talk to him at work, you could," Reno said. "Or bring
him to the office."

"I'd rather do it here," Colter said. "Away from eyes."

"And ears." Reno nodded.

Colter shrugged. If Harker wasn't home, there was no
point in . . . He dropped to a knee, and stuck a finger at
the floorboard near the canvas. Reno came quickly, flat-
tening his lips when Colter raised his pointer finger.

Blood.

Both men drew their revolvers, with Reno pushing the
barrel of the Colt between canvas and the frame. Slowly
he used the case-hardened barrel to push the canvas open.

It was pitch dark inside. No candle. No lantern. Just a few threads of sunlight shining through the opening. The fur trapper looked at Colter, who nodded.

Both men stepped inside, covering the darkness with their guns. Satisfied that no one, no threat, faced them, Colter pulled back the canvas covering all the way, letting more light inside. They didn't have to look far. Just a few feet from the door, Eugene Harker lay in a crumpled heap, blood running from underneath his body to the opening.

A lot of blood, though most of it had begun to dry.

With a savage curse, Tim Colter holstered the LeMat and hurried to the freedman. Reno knelt beside him, and both men gently rolled the man over. Their heads came back, and they wet their lips.

"By Jupiter . . ." Reno shook his head. "Who'd do that to a man?"

Colter put his finger on the black man's cold throat, frowned, and next lifted the left wrist. Nothing. With a heavy sigh, he shook his head.

They stared into the face of Eugene Harker. Or what had been his face. One eye stared blankly, never to see again. The other had been knocked out of its socket. His nose and lips were mashed into bloody pulp. His teeth broken into shards, but not before he had bit off part of his tongue.

"I've seen some beatings in my day," Reno said, pushing himself up, then stepping out of the foul-smelling home of Eugene Harker, to breathe fresh air, to get the sour taste out of his mouth, to get far away from what once had been a good man. "Indians would mutilate a white man, or another Indian, but that was their way. So the enemy wouldn't come after them in the Happy Hunting Ground. But those were Indians. No Indian done this."

"No man did this, either," Colter said. "It was a monster. A damned monster."

Colter rose. "I'll let our fair mayor know that he has more business. But that he'll have to do the burying and the singing himself."

"You best let me do that, boy," Reno said, and the firmness of that one-eyed stare told Colter that the mountain man would brook no argument. "You're a mite riled, and one funeral's enough for one day." He looked back toward the ramshackle home. "He wasn't a bad man, I reckon. Just got mixed up with some wrong boys."

"Like Monroe."

"The tracks match. The one Harker left by our office. The one I found leading away from my old post. But that don't actually mean that it was Harker that set fire to my place."

Colter remained firm. "Yes," he said, "it does."

"Maybe. But it don't mean Monroe sent him to burn my place down."

"Yes," Colter said, and he began walking away. "It does. I just can't prove it—especially now that Harker can't talk."

CHAPTER 32

After a while, Tim Colter did let it go. That was one thing he had learned about being a lawman. If you followed the law—really followed it, and not went off on your own trail for justice, as some men with badges tended to do—then you had to come to terms that, well, sometimes, justice did not prevail. Crimes went unpunished. Guilty men went free. Dead men, and women, and children—as he remembered Ferre Slootmaekers and his poor mother, Sien—were, sometimes, not avenged.

Besides, two days later, the cowboys from Texas arrived. Clint Warren, however, came first. And he came with a cigar.

"For you, Marshal," he said with a little smile.

Colter took the cigar, studying it, rolling it in his fingers. It was a fine cigar. Havana. Smelled great. Colter laid it on his desk and looked up at the old rancher, waiting.

"I figure any man who whips two of my sons deserves a cigar." He nodded and his smile widened. "Most folks will tell you that takes some doin'."

Colter showed the rancher a few knuckles that had yet to heal, and some bruises on his face, and that ear that seemed as though it would never return to its normal shape.

That made the rancher laugh.

"You might want to enjoy that cigar now, though, Mr. Colter," Clint Warren said. "Because I got cattle in the valley and a lot of Texas cowpunchers who want to see the elephant and tree this town."

"Thanks for the warning," Colter said.

"Just bein' a good citizen." And Clint Warren was gone, spurs jingling to his musical laughter as he walked down the boardwalk toward Slade's Saloon.

Well, Warren had warned Tim Colter, and the old rancher must have warned his hired hands. Because to the surprise of Tim Colter, Jed Reno, Mayor Jasper Monroe, and practically every business owner in Violence, those Texas waddies seemed to be on their best behavior. Oh, they got a little wild every now and then, shot up one of the new stores, and ripped down some buildings that were being put up. And there were quite a few fistfights among the railroad crews. Yet, most of them were easy to corral after too much whiskey, cards, and women at Slade's, O'Rourke's, Jake's, and the other rough-and-tumble businesses that continued to grow along Union Street.

Until, that is, the stagecoach from Salt Lake City arrived four days later.

Jed Reno and Tim Colter were in the corral, releasing the Oregon Boots on a couple of waddies, two railroaders, and one gambler, who had shot a man dead at Jake's Place and refused to pay for the dead man's burial. Self-defense, of course. Everybody who ever killed a man in Violence had pleaded self-defense, and since there was still no judge in this town—except when Tim Colter passed a sentence, which he knew would never be upheld by a higher court, or even the U.S. marshal in Boise City—usually, a fine was all the killer had to pay.

That didn't settle well in Tim Colter's stomach, but he

was savvy enough—and so was Jed Reno—not to buck the tiger too much in a place like Violence.

They heard the catcalls and whistles as they left the corral, carrying the heavy sack of shackles that would soon be put on other drunks and hard cases.

"Must be a new soiled dove," Reno said. The old mountain man yawned and nodded at a woman who was standing atop a hitching rail, waving an umbrella at two cowboys and three railroaders who had, well, sort of treed the newcomer.

Colter sighed. "Wrong side of the street for a hurdy-gurdy girl," he said.

Because the woman stood in front of Jasper Monroe's office, which was on the same side of Union Street as Slade's Saloon and the other watering holes. The gambling dens and the brothels and cribs were on the south side of Union Street. That was how Violence separated decency, with decency being loosely defined.

They walked. They stared.

The woman did a pretty good job of keeping the hands of her admirers at bay. She even pelted one railroader so hard with the umbrella, he staggered back and yelped like a schoolboy, holding his head and cursing at the men laughing at him.

"Good balance," Reno said.

Colter stared at him.

"Keeping her feet and all," Reno explained. "Most folks would've fallen off that rail, swinging that . . . Colter, what did you call it?"

"Umbrella."

"Yeah. She's still up there. Hell, she just belted another one but good. That's some strumpet."

Tim Colter stopped. He stared. He dropped the sack of shackles into the street. He cursed.

"That's no strumpet, Jed," he said, and swore again.

The gunshot ripped through the morning air, and the railroaders and cowboys and admirers turned at the sound of Colter's LeMat. The woman lost her footing and fell, but did not tumble because Jasper Monroe and Aloysius Murden caught her, and pulled her off the dirt of Union Street and onto the dirt that covered the boardwalk in front of Monroe's barbershop and undertaking parlor.

"Back off, boys." There was an edge to Colter's voice, and the cowboys and railroaders and admirers understood that well enough. They helped the one with the bleeding head to his feet, and they shuffled off across the street toward The Blarney Stone.

Colter came to the boardwalk. He blinked, wet his lips, and holstered the heavy pistol. Slowly he removed his hat. The woman nodded. He returned the greeting.

Behind him came the clanging of the iron boots in the sack Jed Reno had picked up. "Ma'am," Jed Reno said, for he was the only one who had found his voice, "welcome to Violence."

The woman's mouth opened, but she had no voice. Not from the shock she had just been given.

"Miss . . . ," Jasper Monroe tried.

"Betsy," Colter said at last, "what in Heaven's name are you doing here?"

"Teaching school?" Colter asked in disbelief.

He poured a cup of coffee, and set it in front of Betsy McDonnell. They were in his office, her luggage on the floor, Jed Reno filling his pipe bowl with his blend of tobacco, and Mix Range using a screwdriver to secure some shelves on a bookcase he was finishing. Colter blinked.

"I got a letter," she said, and she pulled out her purse. She was still shaken, and her face had just begun to return to its normal color. Her breaths came out quickly. Her chest still heaved as her heart hammered against the ribs.

Salem, Oregon, and the Bullfrog Café were a long, long way from Union Street, Violence, Idaho Territory.

She found the letter, opened it with trembling hands, and slid it across the table. Colter picked it up, read it, and frowned.

"Why didn't you tell me about this?" he asked.

"I did," she said. "In two letters I wrote. I wrote you that I was coming. Twice. They asked me to come. They said you wanted me to come. I wrote twice. You never answered. I . . ."

Colter shook his head dumbly. He looked at Jed Reno. Hell, he even looked at Mix Range, who had lowered his screwdriver, glanced at Betsy, and said, "I wish my schoolmistress looked like you, ma'am. I might have turned out all right."

Betsy studied Mix Range. Her lips parted, but she did not speak.

"I never got any letters, Betsy," Tim said as if apologizing. "And I sure didn't want you here."

That, he immediately regretted. It wasn't what he meant to say, but he had said it, and she wasn't waiting to hear his explanation.

Mix Range went back to turning screws through wood. Jed Reno studied the pipe he lighted, and stared out the window at the bustling activity on Union Street. Betsy McDonnell gave Tim Colter a lesson in language, in manners, in words Mix Range could not comprehend, but some that would have made even Mix Range blush. She forgot about the rough treatment she had received just a few minutes earlier, forgot that Tim Colter had saved her from even more embarrassment. She did not stop her tirade until she had pretty much finished using words one might not find in a *Common School Dictionary*. She only paused to catch her breath, but it was Jed Reno who came to Colter's defense.

"He don't mean that, ma'am." Reno pointed the stem of the pipe out the window. "Just that this ain't no fit place for a proper lady. The mayor . . . you met him . . . and some other muckety-mucks in this burg sent for their wives last November. Maybe December. They come by January. They was gone by March. Back east. This just ain't a fit place for a good woman. And you're a good woman. Finest I've ever laid eyes on. And I sure appreciate your coming here to help them Flemish children."

Betsy McDonnell blinked, and then bowed slightly at the one-eyed trapper. "Thank you," she said at last.

"No, ma'am," Jed Reno said. "It's us who should be thanking you."

"Thank you," Mix Range said, as if taking his cue.

"Betsy." Now it was Tim Colter who could talk.

She turned. She even smiled. He smiled back, but only briefly.

"Not getting a letter or two from you is one thing," he said. He had been doing a lot of thinking during Betsy's monologue. "The express riders, the trains, the stages, the distance. You know how slow the mail can be. But . . ." He pointed at the letter she had received. "There is no Violet School Board in this town. . . . I doubt if there's a school in this whole territory, and certainly no school board." He shook his head. "Mrs. Dorothy Greer? There's no Dorothy Greer that I know of in this town, and she certainly doesn't represent any school board."

"But . . ."

They fell silent.

"Someone wanted you to come here," Colter said.

"To get to you," Reno said, nodding at Colter.

"What do you mean?" Betsy asked.

Colter had no time to answer. Because as he was preparing his statement, the door swung open, and several women barged in. None was a Mrs. Dorothy Greer, but one was Mrs. Sien Slootmaekers, mother of the late Ferre Slootmaekers. And while they were hugging and kissing Betsy McDonnell, an Irish railroad worker came in, screaming:

"Marshal . . . some sons-a-bitchin' cowpokes be robbing the train!"

CHAPTER 33

Who, Tim Colter thought as he ran onto Front Street, would rob a train? In 1868? In Idaho Territory?

Well, he had read about train robbers before. For a few years, reports had landed in the offices of U.S. marshals across the continent about a gang known as the Reno Brothers. Back in the fall of 1866, they had robbed an Ohio and Mississippi Railway train and made off with sixteen thousand dollars. The three robbers had been arrested when a passenger identified them as the bandits, but they all posted bail, and then the witness got himself gunned down. Charges had been dismissed, the Renos and the other gang members were released, but the Pinkertons were after them now. Especially since they had not stopped robbing trains. But the Renos were running around in Indiana and the Midwest—a long way from Violence, Idaho Territory.

Footsteps sounded behind him, but Colter did not have to look back. He knew that would be Jed Reno, armed with that Colt and his big flintlock. He ran down the boardwalk as people gave him a wide berth, moving toward the black smoke puffing from the stack of a Union Pacific engine. When he reached the depot, the U.P. man, in striped trousers and a shirt with a paper collar, pointed down the railroad with his left hand. His right held a handkerchief tightly against his bald head, which was bleeding a considerable amount.

"They took off," he said. Tears of pain filled his eyes. "On a . . . handcar."

Holstering his LeMat, Colter stared down the tracks. In the distance, he could see a rail car moving west. Jed Reno stepped past him, and brought the Hawken to his shoulder. After steadying the barrel, the old man drew a breath, held it, but then exhaled and brought the big rifle down, shaking his head.

"Out of range," he said. "No need to waste lead."

"A handcar?" Colter shook his head, and looked around while the Union Pacific stationmaster said that four men—four cowboys—had walked inside the depot shortly after the train arrived. When two U.P. workers came out with the strongbox to pay the workers, the cowboys pulled their six-shooters.

"Nobody robs trains," another U.P. man said.

Apparently, he had not heard about the hell the Reno boys had been raising over in Indiana.

"Took our watches, too," said the U.P. man. "And our wallets."

"We're wastin' time," said another voice, and Colter blinked as he turned around to see Mix Range hurrying past him toward the rails. Another handcar was on a sidetrack. "Let's go get 'em."

Colter did not hesitate. Nor did Jed Reno. Both men jumped off the platform. "Get that switch turned," Colter shouted back at the U.P. men. He climbed on the cart as Mix Range started pushing down on the iron bar. The cart was rolling as Jed Reno tossed his Hawken onto the car and then leaped on, with Colter pulling him up.

A few U.P. men worked the switch, moving the rails, which set in place just a few seconds before the cart rolled onto the main tracks. They rode west, the sun on their backs, chasing the other U.P. handcar, with four men and a strongbox.

Colter had done some fast thinking. He had no time to saddle any horses. They might lose the robbers, and—Violence being a railroad town—he had found few horses on the hitching posts at this time of day. The cowboys—those that were not robbing trains—were sleeping off their hangovers back at the cow camp at Clint Warren's ranch.

The rails led west. There was no way to go, except to Laramie City and wherever the rails reached by now. If they kept going west—and they certainly would not start back east—they would run into more U.P. workers, who would not treat them kindly when they realized those Texas waddies had stolen money meant for track layers, surveyors, foremen, and everyone else on the railroad's payroll. Those cowboys could be stupid, but Tim Colter didn't think so.

He moved around to the front of the cart and began helping Mix Range work the pump. Instantly they picked up more speed.

"Why would cowboys rob a train?" Jed Reno asked.

"Out of money," Mix Range answered. "That's why I robbed banks and stores and saloons and . . ." He shut up, and then offered Colter a wan smile.

"But why take one of these contraptions?" Reno asked. He moved toward the front of the cart, dangled his legs over the side, and kept the Hawken over his thighs, waiting for the thieves to come into range. Wind roared as the cart's speed increased.

Colter and Range had already worked up a good sweat. Making one of these handcars go took a lot more effort than one would think. Colter wished he had thought to bring gloves. The iron bars he pushed down and let up, over and over again, rubbed his hands raw.

"I'm betting they have horses hobbled somewhere," Colter said.

"One more man then," Reno said. "Holding the horses."

"One." Colter pumped down, then let his arms come up as Mix Range pushed. "Maybe more."

Reno looked back at Mix Range. "You got a gun?"

The Alabama boy's face went blank. He blinked, bit his lip as he worked the pump, and shook his head. "I'm a prisoner," he said. "Remember?"

"Yeah." Reno drew the Colt, found a capper in a leather pouch, which hung from his shoulder, and fitted a percussion cap onto the sixth nipple on the cylinder of the .44-caliber pistol.

They went down a short hill, picking up speed, and the momentum carried them back up the next hill and across the flats again. Colter kept at the pump, but his back was to the men they chased, and he didn't like that at all. When a man wore a tin star, he wanted to see the men he was chasing—especially when those men packed guns.

"Are we closer?" Colter called out above the roar of the wind in his ears.

"Yeah," Reno answered. "Two of them are cranking on the handle. They's cowboys, all right. I can see their hats and their leggings. Guess that's the strongbox in front of their cart. Then there's them two cowboys."

"What are they doing?" Colter asked.

"Aiming their guns at us, boy. What else?"

The iron handle went down, came up, went down, came up.

"Still out of range, I think," Reno said.

Five pumps on that handle later, and a shot rang out. It whined off the iron handle, inches from Colter's blistered hands, sending a spark flying as the bullet ricocheted off into the pale blue sky, leaving a white mark on the iron bar.

Colter let go of the bar and dropped to the floor of the

cart. Drawing his revolver, he spun around, but barked an order to Mix Range. "Keep us moving, Mix. Don't slow down."

In the corner of his eye, he caught sight of Jed Reno as the one-eyed trapper brought the Hawken to his shoulder. "Reckon they're in range after all."

Now, only one of the cowboys worked the pump, which kept the handcar rolling down the U.P. rails. The one who had been helping, had turned, and aimed a revolver. He stood facing east. The man working the cart had his back to Colter, Reno, and Range. Another lay on the ground on the south side of the cart. The last man was beside the strongbox, on a knee, at the front of the cart, near the man aiming the revolver, which belched smoke.

Colter didn't hear the shot, not with the wind roaring in his ears, and he did not feel any lead sing past him.

They were too far away for an accurate pistol shot.

Yet, the man lying on his belly had a rifle, and it rang out. That slug tore through the air, buzzing past Colter's right ear like a bumblebee. Colter sighed, then lowered the LeMat. A shot from that revolver would be as useless as the one the cowboy had fired at them.

The rifle from the man on his belly spat out another shot, which dug into the dirt on the south side of the tracks about ten yards in front of the cart. A second later, the rifle fired again. This one thudded into the floor of the cart, leaving a trail of splinters inches from the rear of the machine.

"Boy got himself a repeating rifle," Reno said. The old man pulled back the hammer on the Hawken.

"Can you get him—" Colter couldn't finish. Another shot from the handcar in front of them sent a slug that whined off the front wheel. "From here?" Colter finished.

"Risky," Reno said. "Him on the floor like that and all. But that don't make . . ." Another shot from the man with the repeating rifle went wide and high. ". . . make no never mind to me."

Reno fired the big Hawken, and the smoke was past the cart so quickly, Colter did not even catch the scent of gunpowder. He heard, instead, the report of the rifle from the cart ahead of them. That told Colter that Reno had missed his shot, but then he saw something that changed his mind.

The cowboy pumping the cart bent low with the handle, and when the pump came up, the cowboy went flying backward, off the cart, landing on the tracks, and, thankfully, rolling off to the side. . . .

As he pulled out his bullet pouch and powder horn, Reno had swung his legs back onto the cart's floor. The old man grinned at Colter as he began to reload the Hawken, even as another bullet tore through the air.

"That old cuss was a bigger target," Reno said.

The cart flew past the body on the side of the tracks. One quick glance—which was all Colter could see with the handcar speeding west—told him that the man was dead. Maybe two hundred yards separated the two carts now. The repeating rifle barked twice, but then the cowboy had to sit up to reload. Their cart was slowing down, so the one with the Colt went back to pumping the handle.

Colter, along with Reno and Range, had one advantage. They were looking at where they were going, but the train robbers kept their eyes east, at Colter, Range, and Reno.

"What the hell?" As he brought the handle up, Range jutted his chin off toward the west. "What's that there?"

Colter saw the men on the side of the tracks. Indians? No, these were white men. At first, he thought they might be the robbers' accomplices, the ones left here with the horses the men would use to make their getaway. But . . . no . . . those men did not wear cowboy hats. And, from what Colter could see, they didn't carry guns. One was running forward along the south side of the tracks, waving a red bandanna over his head. Colter couldn't hear him because of the roar of wind.

And the gunshot. The cowboy with the repeating rifle had finished reloading, and the Henry rifle—Colter assumed it was a Henry—rang out twice more. One of those shots ricocheted off the handle in front of Mix Range.

Range sang out with a curse. "That would've blowed my head off if I hadn't been a-pumpin'," he said.

The man started to fire again, but stopped, as the car sped past the man waving the red bandanna. Other men stood alongside the tracks, waving arms, shouting.

Colter took a chance. He stood, careful to avoid the iron bar that kept moving up and down. Reno had finished reloading the Hawken, and so he brought the stock to his shoulder. The other cowhand, the one closest to the strongbox who was not working the handle, fired his revolver.

Now their cart passed the man waving the red bandanna. Reno was closest, but he was aiming at the man with the .44-caliber Henry. Colter wet his lips. Leaned over. He tried to hear what the man was yelling as the car raced past him.

"Fools . . ." That was about all Colter could catch. No. It had been "damned fools." And then he looked back at the man, who had turned, and kept pointing. Pointing west.

Tim Colter understood one more word.

"Bridge."

A bullet tore a hole through the brim of his hat, but the hat—a good-fitting hat—remained firm on Colter's head. He turned, focused again on the men they chased. They were close now. Twenty yards. The Colt barked again. Colter shifted the pivot on the LeMat, and braced himself as he aimed. They raced past the other Union Pacific workers on both sides of the tracks, and heard their screams and curses.

The Hawken roared.

The man with the Henry rifle screamed and rolled off the side of the cart, the rifle bounding down the embankment. Colter started to pull the trigger on the LeMat. That's when he saw. That's when he realized. That's when he turned to Jed Reno and shouted.

"JUMP!"

CHAPTER 34

The two cowboys left on the cart managed to turn just before they reached the bridge.

Well, where there would have been a bridge.

They must have screamed. One seemed to try to leap off the cart, while the other just stared in horror at the fate that awaited him. The car left the rails, and for a moment—an incredibly brief moment—the car seemed to be flying like a raven. Then it crashed like a boulder, disappearing as the second cart—the one abandoned by Colter, Reno, and Range—followed, leaving the air, moving down, out of sight, crashing on the rocks below.

Colter managed to lower the hammer on the LeMat before he jumped off the cart. He landed on the sagebrush and sod with a prayer that the powerful revolver would not go off anyway, and blow his head off, or injure or kill one of the railroad workers or Mix Range. Or Jed Reno. The prayer was answered, but he did drop the heavy pistol as he bounced across the plains.

He felt as if he kept rolling, then . . . What was that saying? "A rolling stone gathers no moss." Eventually, as he rolled and bounced and got jarred this way and the other, Colter seemed to understand that he was rolling downhill.

Down the incline. That's why there was a bridge here . . . or was supposed to be a bridge.

Tasting blood on his tongue, and feeling the rough ground and brush rip through his shirt and pants, and skin, he felt himself slowing, then came to a stop. His hat was gone. Even a good-fitting hat could not have withstood that little tumble. His head ached. He turned his head and spit out blood. That was a good sign. Not the blood, though it wasn't much. But the fact that he could turn his head. His neck wasn't broken. Nor was his back. His ears rang, but he had pushed himself up to a seated position when the first railroad man reached him.

The man let loose with a stream of profanity in Gaelic— or what Colter assumed was Gaelic—but he recognized the marshal of Violence, and stopped his profane tirade, and settled on one knee.

"Are ye all right, Marshal?"

Colter nodded, spit out another bit of blood, but ran his tongue around his mouth. He seemed to have all of his tongue. So he had not bit off part, or all, of it. His arms moved. He could wiggle his boots. He stood and looked up the hill he had rolled down. His first thought was to start climbing. The Irish railroader had risen and offered a firm hand to help him up the rise.

Colter shook his head. "I'm halfway down already," he said.

The railroader understood, and walked down the rest of the distance with him. They crossed rocks, went through a few boulders, and made their way down to the streambed. Colter looked up at where a trestle should have held the U.P. rails across the gulley.

His first thought was that rains had washed away the tracks, but no. He shook his aching head. No, there had been little rain this summer. And the creek bed was dry.

Then he noticed the charred pilings that still stood. Most had collapsed in a heap.

"Lightning?" Colter asked.

"Injuns," the railroader answered. "What in bloody hell was this about?"

Colter stopped. He saw the two handcars on the rocks, now reduced to kindling and bent iron.

"Some cowhands robbed the U.P. train when it came to the depot," he said.

"Bloody hell. What?"

"Yeah." Colter kept walking.

From somewhere overhead, another Irish-accented voice called down. "Is everyone all right?"

"No," Colter answered in a whisper as he neared the wreckage. "Not everyone."

The strongbox had busted open, and the workers had filled the script and coin into canvas bags, which they had then toted up the hill to the side of the tracks. The two bodies of the broken remains of the two cowboys had been hauled up in blankets, and were laid beside the bodies of the two men Jed Reno had shot.

Another big man who swung a sledgehammer for a living had found Colter's LeMat, returned it, along with his hat, and now Colter was checking the weapon—the hat back on his head—and blowing dust out of the cylinder and hammer. The barrel somehow remained free of debris. Tim Colter wasn't sure how much of that money would actually get back to the U.P. brass in Violence, but he had done his job. Most of his job.

Mix Range had busted his nose. Jed Reno had a few fresh scratches and a big bruise forming on his right hand. But his Hawken and Colt were ready, loaded, and clean.

"I don't think," Colter explained to the chief of the

crew, "that these four boys planned to push their way to join the Central Pacific."

The Irish leader laughed. "Not this year. Maybe not the next."

"So where were they going?" he asked.

"Laramie City?" one of the workers asked as an answer.

Colter's head shook. "Would you?"

"Horses," Reno prodded them.

One of the men—a lean, thin, redheaded man with a face filled with freckles—stepped forward. "I saw a couple of boys riding that way this morn." He gestured to the southwest. "Figured they was just headin' west. Maybe to Laramie City."

"That don't mean nothin', Timothy," a burly man said with a snort.

"But they was leadin' four saddle mounts. Struck me as odd. And a pack mule."

Colter grinned. The burly man did not, but shuffled back into the army of workers.

"If you were going to stop a cart, probably out of sight, and mount horses . . ." Colter did not have to finish because the redheaded kid answered quickly.

"The hollow," he said. "Three miles west of here."

Colter wet his lips. He pointed at a freight wagon.

"You boys mind renting that wagon to us?"

"Marshal," said the Irish leader, "ye jus' saved us a month's pay. Ye take that with the Union Pacific's blessing. We'll pick it up when we come back to Violence for some drinkin' and gamblin'.."

They rode—Mix Range driving, Tim Colter beside him, Jed Reno kneeling in the back, staring ahead with his one eye, which seldom missed anything—moving across the rolling hills northwest of the U.P.'s rails. The Irish foreman had described the hollow, and Jed Reno knew where it was. He agreed that it would make a likely place to change from handcar to horses. They would probably ride south, toward Virginia Dale, and then maybe into Denver City—if they weren't killed by the owlhoots that populated Virginia Dale. Colter figured the cowboys would least expect a posse to come in from the north. If anyone had trailed them, they'd be riding in from the south.

"You don't reckon they noticed the trestle had been burned up?" Mix Range asked.

"The kid said they'd swung wide south by then," Colter answered. "No. I don't think they'd noticed the bridge was out. If they had, they would have ridden back to warn their boys. Not because they wanted to save their hides, but they would want to save that money from the strongbox."

"Injuns." Range looked across the hills. "I don't want to run into no Sioux warriors."

"Cheyennes," Reno said. "Railroad boys haven't made life easier on that tribe of late. Army sure hasn't helped. And what I hear tell they done at Sand Creek back in '64 . . . well . . ."

"They have a right to be mad," Colter agreed, and he told Jed Reno about Red Prairie, what the railroaders had been about to do to that fine Cheyenne warrior before Colter had intervened.

"I taught you pretty good, boy," Reno said with a grin. "Didn't I?"

Colter grinned back. "You sure did."

They fell silent now as the mules pulled the wagon. Reno pointed north, and Range tugged on the lines, turning the mules in that direction. The grass grew high, even green despite a lack of moisture, and they moved on a mile or two, then moved back along a dry creek bed south. Toward the hollow.

"Way I figure things," Reno said, "is that we stop about a half mile from that meeting place. Leave Mix here with the wagon and mules. You go off west a bit, I come in from the east. Get the drop on the boys. You want them alive, I reckon."

"I would at that," Colter answered. "Just curious why six cowboys would try to rob a train."

"Think they was put up to it?" Reno asked.

"I'd like them to tell me."

A mile south, Mix Range pulled the mules to a halt. Tim Colter was standing now, shielding his eyes from the sun, as he stared off down the creek bed. He wasn't looking at the ground, though, but the sky.

"You might not get an answer, boy," Jed Reno said.

"Yeah." Colter spit the disgust out of his mouth and onto sagebrush. "Got a feeling you're right."

"Let's go back," Mix Range suggested. "Get them railroad boys to come with us." His voice cracked with fear. He sweated more than he had while pushing that handcar after the robbers.

"No." Colter sat down. "Keep the wagon going. We might need these mules."

Reno spit. "A buckboard pulled by mules sure won't outrun no Cheyenne dog soldiers on good, grass-fed war ponies."

Buzzards kept circling in the clear sky.

Thirty minutes later, their nerves taut, their guns ready—for Reno had loaned his Colt to Mix Range—they reached the hollow. The horses and pack mule were gone. The two cowboys remained, but Tim Colter would be getting no answers from those two boys. The two robbers who had broken their bodies among the boulders and smashed handcars, back along the U.P. line, had been much more fortunate than these two poor souls.

Not that Tim Colter felt any sympathy for them. They had been part of the holdup, as much as the other four dead men.

"Well." Jed Reno spit.

Mix Range stood over some sagebrush that he was watering with his vomit.

"Yeah." Tim Colter sighed. "I think there's a shovel in the back of the wagon. We might as well bury them."

Reno snorted. "You mean . . . what the buzzards left behind."

CHAPTER 35

Suppertime had come and gone before Tim Colter had time to breathe again—and continue his questioning of this correspondence with a nonexistent school board in the town of Violet. Train robberies were federal offenses— and Colter had that commission as a deputy United States marshal. Even though all six outlaws were dead, and the money recovered, he had to send telegraphs back to Washington City and a lot of paperwork to Boise City. The money was recovered from the payroll strongbox, and from most of the wallets of the train executives. Their watches, however, had been smashed to oblivion, along with the bodies of the two men who had plummeted over the canyon.

So Colter had sent Jed Reno to look after Betsy McDonnell while he caught up on his duties. He figured she would be at the only hotel in town, and he had other work to do, too. He checked on the prisoners in the corral, released two from their five-pound Oregon Boots, talked to at least five Union Pacific officials, and felt relieved when the foreman of the group repairing the bridge and trestle arrived in town with another wagon, the strongbox, and all of the stolen loot.

The prisoners wanted to eat. Mayor Jasper Monroe wanted ten minutes for a report, and, well, that made Colter tend to regret getting that job as the town marshal. Now he had obligations to Monroe. What he needed was a deputy, but he had already sent Jed Reno on an incredibly important assignment.

"You need anything, Marshal?"

At first, Tim Colter didn't recognize the voice. It was one nasal drawl.

Colter looked up. He sat at the desk in his office on Union Street, chewing on a piece of jerky—the only food he had eaten since breakfast—and sipping on cold coffee that had thickened like molasses. He sighed, and studied the crooked nose on Mix Range.

That gave Colter pause.

Everything had been moving like a locomotive churning across the Northern Plains since Betsy had arrived. Colter had had little time to think about anything . . . until now.

"What the hell got into you, Mix?" he asked.

The killer and two-bit criminal stared. "What you talkin' 'bout?"

"When they said the train had been robbed, why on earth did you follow Jed and me to the depot?"

The gunman stared, blinked, and, after a moment, shrugged.

"And getting on the handcar? What was that about?"

"I don't know. Those boys had taken one. I seen the other one. Wasn't no horses handy. Just come to me . . . of a sudden. Didn't really think nothin' 'bout it."

He considered that for a moment, but did not look down at the paperwork piled on his desk. Instead, he put his elbows on the desktop, locked his fingers together, and placed his chin on the bridge his hands made. He studied Mix Range a little harder.

"You killed a couple of peace officers in Texas," Colter said. "According to the warrants."

The prisoner shrugged.

"Why don't you tell me what happened down there?"

Range's tongue ran underneath the inside of his lip, back and forth, like the pendulum on a clock. A finger on his right hand gently tested his nose. His head weaved a little, and then the right hand rose to scratch his head, then his beard stubble, and then smoothed his mustache.

"Well . . . ," he said, which was as far as he got.

"Go on," Colter said, and he listened.

If Mix Range was telling the truth—and the gunman didn't seem intelligent enough to make anything up—he had drifted west from Horseshoe Bend, Alabama, after the War to Preserve the Union. Made his way to Natchez on the Mississippi River, then worked awhile in Shreveport, Louisiana, finally dealt faro and Spanish monte in the old cotton town and riverboat town of Jefferson in the Piney Woods of eastern Texas, and eventually made it to Dallas.

He had done some carpentry work there, putting together quickly- and crudely-constructed houses, and had met a girl.

"What was her name?" Colter asked.

"Jennie Wyndham."

Not a name someone would likely make up, Colter deduced.

Jennie worked for a dressmaker in town near the Trinity River. Mix Range was paying her a visit—the Presbyterians were having a dance, which was something Mix Range, as a Baptist, and Jennie Wyndham, who grew up in Pennsylvania among the Society of Friends, had never gotten the opportunity to attend. They were going on that Saturday night.

Then a couple of overzealous peace officers stopped Jennie as she was leaving the dressmaker's shop.

Mix Range had come to her rescue.

"One of 'em said he was placin' me under arrest," Range

said. "I told'm that was fine and dandy with me, that I'd let the town's chief of police and maybe even the mayor know what was goin' on. That's when the other feller drawed his Remington. An' Jennie screamed, and the first one, the big one, knocked her down to shut her up."

Range studied his boots as he kept talking.

"Well, Dallas wasn't no friendly town. So it paid to keep a pistol handy. I had one. And I was a much better shot than either of 'em two dandies. Long and short of things, Marshal, is they was lyin' on the streets, one dead, the other dyin', and some other copper was blowin' on his whistle, and I just figured it was time to hightail it out of there. I grabbed Jennie, hurried her to her house about six blocks away. And I thought about goin' to turn myself in, let the chief know what had happened. But damn if whilst I was walkin' to the courthouse to do just that very thing, a couple other policemen started shootin' at me. Stole me the first horse I could grab a rein on, and rode out toward Denton. And kept ridin'."

Colter nodded. "What about Jennie Wilson?"

"Wyndham," Mix Range corrected. Colter said, "Right." But he had been testing the prisoner. "Jennie Wyndham."

"She was a good girl, Marshal. Didn't see no need in bringin' her into my troubles."

"But . . ."

"One of the policemen died right away, but the other lived . . . just long enough to tell some other copper that I'd done the shootin'. He didn't mention Jennie, or if he did, the one who heard what someone read to me in a newspaper was his 'dyin' testimony,' didn't bring her name up. I figured . . . why should I? So I just lit out for parts unknown. Likely, they'd 'ave strung me up in Dallas, had I stuck around for a trial."

"Likely," Colter agreed.

"Well, I reckon I should get back to the corral," Mix Range said. "I mean . . . the jail."

Colter waved him to an empty chair, and the Alabaman sat down, sighing, probably figuring he was about to be forced to put on the thirty-pound shackle.

"How'd you get up here?" Colter asked.

The gunman shrugged. "Heard they was hirin' workers for the U.P. Figured no Texas lawdog would come lookin' for me this far north."

"But you weren't working for the Union Pacific," Colter said.

Range's head shook. "No. I never seemed to fall in with the right folks—except when I met Jennie Wyndham—and that just got her in trouble. When I couldn't get no job, I went into Slade's place, and . . . well . . . I got a bit drunk. Think I got into a fight with one of his bouncers, and I whupped him. And I reckon, drunk as I was, I told Slade a few things 'bout my past."

Colter understood. "So he hired you."

"Yep."

"As an . . . enforcer."

"The way Slade put it, he wanted to take over this town. But so did someone else."

"Paddy O'Rourke," Colter said.

"Slade never said no names. He told me there could be only one king of Violence, and Micah Slade said it was gonna be him. You know the rest of the story, I guess. Is it all right now, Marshal, if I go to the corral? I've had a right awful day." He touched his nose.

Mix Range's sigh filled the room as Colter shook his head. He opened a drawer in the desk and pulled out a badge. It was a deputy's badge, actually, an old U.S. marshal's badge, but there was no designation stamped in the tin. He tossed it to Mix Range, who caught it, and stared. He blinked as he tried to comprehend what Tim Colter meant.

"I got a better job for you, Mix," Colter said. "How'd you like to be on the right side of the law for a change?"

"But I'm a wanted man."

Colter smiled warmly. "This isn't Texas, Mix. It's Idaho Territory. Pays ten dollars a month. And you sleep in here from now on. Not the corral. Hell, you put a roof over this place, and got the walls up, and the window in. You should enjoy what you built."

"I don't know nothin' about bein' no lawman."

"Join the crowd," Colter said. "Half of what I've done in this town wouldn't hold up in an actual court. But we happen to be the law. And we're the good guys in a town that's rotten to the core. That's what makes the difference." Colter pointed at the badge. "You want it?"

Range grinned widely, and pinned the badge on the front of his shirt. "Do I? You bet I do. Always wanted to be a good guy."

Colter told him to raise his right hand. Range lifted his left, corrected himself, and brought the right hand up. He said, "I do." Colter nodded. Everything was official, or as official as anything came in Violence.

"You might regret your first job, though," Colter said.

"What is it?"

He hooked his thumb toward the wall. "See what our neighbor, Mayor Monroe, wants. I need to find my bride-to-be."

Betsy McDonnell wasn't in the hotel. Mr. Yost said she had checked in earlier that day, her luggage had been delivered, but he had not seen her in hours. She wasn't in the café. There was no church in Violence, and Colter didn't think she would be in O'Rourke's or Slade's places of business. He scratched his head as he walked down Union Street, along the south side, and he kept walking, past Second Street, Fourth, to the corral at Sixth. Then he looked beyond, past the edge of Violence, at what once had been Jed Reno's trading post.

The sun was setting, a brilliant orange that turned red and purple and pink and white, shining over the charred ruins. People surrounded the place. A tent had gone up. Wagons—farm wagons—were parked alongside mules, without saddles, and big draft horses. By Jupiter, Tim Colter could even hear music. A fiddle was playing. Voices sang in perfect harmony. Children pitched horseshoes or played some other games.

Colter turned around. He looked down Union Street, and heard the laughter, the curses, and the bad banjo music. Prostitutes sang their calls. Railroaders swore and staggered. This looked like Hell. He turned back toward the ruins of Reno's place. Yet, that sounded like Heaven.

He walked past the snoring of the prisoners, and kept walking, until he reached the outskirts of Reno's place.

He caught a hoop a Flemish girl had been rolling. Smiling, he pushed it back to her. She blinked, curtseyed, and hurried away with the hoop toward some other children.

The song that came from the canvas tent was a familiar tune, but Colter did not understand the words. He moved, as if in a dream, toward the tent, seeing the men and women gathered. Then he saw another tent, filled with children in their clothes of earthen colors. He smelled food, good food, and apple dumplings. It reminded him again that he had not eaten.

His head shook. Finally he saw Jed Reno, standing at the entrance of what once had been the dugout of his post.

He was talking to three men in brown clothes, with dark beards and black hats.

Before he could start toward Reno to ask him what in blazes was going on here, a voice called his name.

He turned around, saw her, and swept Betsy McDonnell into his arms.

CHAPTER 36

"It doesn't matter," she told him.

He shook his head. "You get a letter from a woman no one has ever heard of. From a school board, when there is no school board in this town, maybe not even in this entire territory. And—"

She stepped closer to him, put two fingers on his lips, and then she tilted her head to the children, Flemish children playing and laughing.

"That's what matters," she whispered. "And that we're together."

"I am glad to see you," he said when she lowered her hand. "But something is wrong here. . . ."

"*Ja.*" Both Tim Colter and Betsy McDonnell turned to see a big, black-bearded man who towered over them. He would even have towered over Jed Reno, if Reno wasn't so busy sitting on an overturned bucket, telling a bunch of farm kids and a couple of their fathers, and even one mother, a bunch of lies . . . well, exaggerations . . . about his days trapping beaver and fighting Indians. "Something is wrong."

How word spread to the farming community that a schoolteacher had arrived was easy enough. Betsy Mc-

Donnell had stepped off the stage, been hoo-rawed by some local drunks, and word reached someone that the new lady was here to teach school. Which meant the prayers of the Flemish farmers had been answered. Someone told someone, and that someone told someone else, and one farmer ran to the next homestead, and the cycle kept repeating itself until everyone loaded up, left their plows in the fields, and they arrived in Violence.

Jed Reno then told someone that, well, since his trading post wasn't being used for anything but homes for rats, snakes, and coyotes, if the farmers wanted, they could make that the schoolhouse.

"You, too, Jed?" Colter asked when they were alone later that night.

"Town could use some educating," the one-eyed trapper said.

"What it could use," Colter said, "is a torch."

Reno shrugged.

"Betsy told you that some of the letters she got had been opened before they reached her," Colter said.

Reno's head bobbed.

Mix Range, who had been awakened upon the return, and was stoking the fire in the stove, closed the grate and shook his head. "Ain't that wrong?"

"Wrong." Colter agreed. "Illegal. Unethical."

"And not right." Range rose to slide the pot of coffee onto the burner.

"Well." Reno filled his pipe. "It could be like this. Some fella is taking the mail along his way, and, well, he's an educated gent, but there ain't nothing much to read in this place. Why, I once bunked with a trapper who would read anything. Newspapers that he found that was so wrinkled and dried and faded that it would practically blind a fellow. He even took to going into caves and trying to read them pictures some Indians had drawed on the walls and ceilings, who knows how long ago. Some folks like to read. So he picks a letter, opens it, figures it won't hurt nobody. I wouldn't put it past anyone out here in this wide spot of lonesome."

Colter sighed. "And then someone writes a letter to get Betsy out here."

"All right." Reno lighted his pipe. "So we need to keep a watchful eye on her."

"First thing in the morning," Colter said, "is that we need to talk to the postmaster here."

"He ain't no real postmaster," Reno said. "I was talking to Gates one time, and he was explaining things to me. Duncan just handles the mail that comes this way."

"And opens it," Colter said.

Reno drew in a mouthful of smoke. "Let's find out. Tomorrow."

And maybe they would have. If Duncan Gates wasn't dead in the alley that connected First and Third Streets.

Hal Murdock, the Civil War veteran from Wisconsin who had lost his right leg, right arm, and right eye at Gettysburg, had found him that morning, on his way to Paddy O'Rourke's gambling hall to empty the spittoons, clean up any blood, and sweep out the joint before the patrons started coming in that afternoon.

"Stiff as he is," Reno said after turning the body over with his right foot, "I'd say he got it sometime last night." He looked up and down the alley. "On his way home. Shortcut, I expect."

"Or meeting someone," Colter said.

Reno looked at the body. "Same person who met Eugene Harker would be my guess."

"This close to Slade's and O'Rourke's," Colter said, "nobody would have heard the beating he was being given."

"Not likely. Reckon there's no point in me trying to follow a trail."

Colter said, "Give it a try. It's a forlorn hope, but you
never know. Maybe the man didn't walk on any boardwalks. Let me know if you find anything. I'll go tell Jasper
Monroe he has another customer."

There was another person Tim Colter needed to see that
day. After telling Monroe he had some undertaking business waiting for him in that alley, Colter was walking toward the livery stable—where the horses were kept, not
prisoners—when he saw Clint Warren riding into town
down Union Street. His three sons flanked him. So did six
other riders.

Colter stepped onto the street and waited for them.
That brought a smile to the old rancher's face. He kicked
his horse into a trot. His sons and hired men did the same.
They rode, smiling, right arms hanging near their holstered
revolvers or the stocks of their rifles in the scabbards. A
few passersby on the boardwalks that morning gasped,
wondering if the rancher would trample the lawman.

Colter did not waver. He did not blink. But he did put
his right palm on the butt of the big LeMat.

And that stopped Clint Warren and his sons and men . . .
a few feet in front of the federal deputy.

"Mornin', Marshal." Warren leaned back in the saddle,
which creaked underneath his weight. The big man moved
one leg, hooking it over the horn of his saddle.

"Say hello to the law, boys."

The men obeyed, except Big Brod, who could not speak
with his jaw busted and wrapped shut with crude bandages.

"I was about to ride out to pay you a visit, Clint,"
Colter said.

"Takin' me up on that offer of a thick, burned steak." The man grinned.

"I've got a complaint about you," Colter said.

No one was smiling at that.

"Who's complainin'?" Clint Warren asked after a long pause. He moved his foot back into the stirrup, and leaned low in the saddle, over the brown horse's neck.

"Three of those farmers say you have cattle on their claims."

"Farmers." Warren leaned back sharply, and his face reddened. "You takin' sides with a bunch of ignorant sodbusters who don't know even how to speak good English."

Tim Colter never took his eyes off the big rancher, nor did he move his hand from the LeMat, but he noticed everything—enough to say, in a dry whisper, "Warren, if that cowpoke on the blue roan slides that Winchester one more inch out of the scabbard, I'll start shooting. And won't stop till I'm dead. Which means you'll be dead long before I am."

The rancher wheeled and found the culprit, a young, long-haired boy with a pockmarked face and fuzz for a mustache and goatee. "Witte, you damned fool. Keep your hands on your reins, boy, or I'll shoot you my ownself."

When the cowhand complied with his boss's request, Colter kept talking. "The only side I'm taking, Warren, is the side of the law. Those farmers have filed legal claims for one hundred and sixty acres. Just as you've done. They want to try to turn this country into farmland, that's their choice. Who knows? Maybe they'll make it."

"Like hell. You ain't that dumb, lawman. You know no farmer can grow crops here. This is land for cattle. It's land for me."

"You've got your land. For all I care, you can put your

cattle on land that isn't claimed by anyone—for now. But you need to get your cattle off those farmers' land."

The big man grinned an evil grin. "We gonna quarrel, Marshal?"

Colter changed the subject. "I had a bit of a quarrel with six of your boys yesterday. They robbed the U.P. payroll here."

With a curt nod, the rancher changed his look. "Not my boys, Marshal. That's why I rode into town today. To talk to you 'bout what happened. Heard all about it."

While listening to Clint Warren's explanation, Colter had to wonder why the rancher came to town with more than a handful of his men, all carrying firearms, just to tell the law that he had fired those boys, turned them loose, told them to get back south to Texas, that they'd worn out their welcome in Idaho Territory.

"I told you," Warren said, "that I don't control all them boys. Paid them to make the drive, tend to my beef. They spent or lost all their money, decided to get some free for the takin'." He smiled again, and few men Tim Colter had ever met could make a smile look so damned ugly.

"I hear you killed all six of those . . . um . . . train robbers."

"Is that what you hear?" Colter asked. He didn't bother to correct the rancher, that Jed Reno had killed two, two others had fallen to their deaths after a trestle had been destroyed, and Cheyenne Indians had caught up with the remaining two.

"Also heard that you got a new schoolteacher in town." That ugly smile got uglier.

"Did Mrs. Dorothy Greer tell you that?"

The grin remained. "Don't reckon I know her."

Warren's son, the one who dressed like a cardsharp, leaned back in his saddle, and said, "Maybe she's one of them new hurdy-gurdy girls."

"Who?" Clint Warren laughed. "That Mrs. Greer, or the new schoolmarm?"

"We're done talking, boys." Colter stepped back, spread his legs apart, and moved the hand away from the LeMat. Colter's eyes told the cowhands that if they wanted to make their play, now was the time to make it . . . and die. "Get your cattle off the farmers' land. Or there will be beef for breakfast in Violence for quite a while."

They rode past Tim Colter at a trot, coming close, but careful enough to keep their horses from hitting, even grazing, the lawman. They turned south along the last street, and pushed their horses into gallops. A few minutes later, there was nothing left of Clint Warren except the dust that lingered in the air, and the bitter taste that remained in Tim Colter's mouth.

Not that he had long to think about it, or rinse out his mouth with some of Mix Range's coffee. Some drunk had taken one of Paddy O'Rourke's dealers out onto Union Street, and punches were flying; bets were being made on both sides of the street.

Tim Colter knew Clint Warren was no friend. He even knew the rancher was likely the one who had killed the postmaster and Eugene Harker. With his bare hands. Warren had taught two of his sons how to fight with fists, and, from firsthand experience, Colter knew the old man had taught them well. But the boys hadn't killed those two men. That had been done by someone who enjoyed it, and Clint Warren was the kind of man who would enjoy beating a man to death with bare knuckles.

A man like Clint Warren would give no more thought over killing an innocent man with a brutal beating than most men would have over . . . well . . . over crushing that locust that Colter had just stepped on.

"But," Colter thought aloud, "how can I prove that Warren's a murderer?"

Then he stopped, and turned back along the boardwalk, and he looked closer at the insect he had accidentally stepped on.

"Locust," he said.

CHAPTER 37

The town cemetery, Tim Colter knew, was the most populated acreage in Violence. Colter stood in the wind, hat in his hand, watching the funeral. Well, it wasn't exactly a funeral, just a burial. And a man like Duncan Gates, one of the town's founding fathers, didn't rate an actual mourner. His partner, Aloysius Murden, wasn't there. Just Tim Colter . . . and the town's undertaker, Mayor Jasper Monroe.

"You want some help?" Colter asked.

Monroe, who had tossed his hat, coat, and vest atop one of the crooked crosses, sank the spade deeper into the earth. His hands held the handle, and his right foot remained on the spade. As he looked up, sweat was plastering his thin hair on his head, and was running down his face. His shirt was already drenched.

When the mayor didn't answer, Colter walked over and took the spade. If he didn't help, then an out-of-shape townsman like Jasper Monroe would be digging this grave for the next two days. Or someone might be digging a grave for the mayor after he croaked from a heart attack.

Colter moved the dirt over, and let the blade bite into more sod. "I bet now you miss Eugene Harker," he said, without looking up.

The mayor did not answer.

"You know he's going to kill you, too." Colter did not look up when he spoke those words, but kept right on digging the grave for Duncan Gates.

Finally the mayor said in a frightened voice, "What are you . . . talking about?"

The ground, Colter was pleased to see, was surprisingly soft, once you got through the sod. He dumped more dirt on the side. "You know exactly what I'm talking about. Clint Warren. He wants this town. This land. For his little empire."

More dirt. It felt good, Colter thought, to be working like this, working muscles, sweating, not using his LeMat or his fists.

"No," Monroe sang out. "No . . . it's Slade . . . and O'Rourke. They're the ones fighting for control."

He stopped shoveling to wipe his brow. It was awful hot this day. Now he stared hard at the timid little mayor.

"Yeah. They are. But they are both rank amateurs. All muscle, no brains. And not much money." He returned to digging. "Oh, they make money, all right. A saloon. A gambling parlor. Probably bigger money than you'll make as a barber . . . or an undertaker. But they're not smart. At least, not as smart as Clint Warren." He stopped again. "Not as tough as a rancher, either." He glanced at the covered corpse of Duncan Gates. "You think either O'Rourke or Slade could have done that to a man? It would've sickened the both of them. They would have shot him, maybe stabbed him, or slit his throat. But to beat a man like that." He sighed, shook his head, and went back to digging. Then Colter laughed. "You ever wonder who'll be digging your grave, Jasper?"

When he had the grave deep enough, maybe not quite six feet deep, but Duncan Gates had been a skinny, little man—and not much of a man at that. Five feet, or 4½ feet, seemed plenty. After Colter climbed out of the hole, he dug the spade into the mound of dirt, and walked over to the body of Duncan Gates. He grabbed the head end, Monroe took the feet, and they carried him to the edge, and dropped him in the hole.

"Anything you want to say?" Colter asked. He looked up at the mayor, whose head was bowed, and his hands clasped.

Suddenly the mayor swatted at an insect that had landed on his collar.

"What the hell is going on with all these damned grass-hoppers?"

He dined that night in the little café with Mix Range, Jed Reno, Betsy McDonnell, and Mrs. Sien Slootmaekers, who kept lauding Betsy so much that Colter had to smile at how Betsy's cheeks blushed. After supper, Mrs. Sloot-maekers climbed into the buckboard and headed back to her farm, and Colter escorted Betsy back to the hotel. Then he and his deputies patrolled the streets, doing their rounds, checking the doors of the legitimate businesses that closed by six o'clock—not the saloons, cribs, and gambling parlors that wouldn't close till around dawn.

"You reckon that mayor will come around?" Reno asked.

"I'll keep working on him."

They walked past Paddy O'Rourke's building—the big window still boarded up.

"Kinda quiet tonight," Mix Range said.

Reno pointed the barrel of the Hawken across the street. "So's Slade's place."

Colter walked on, but stopped, turned back, and studied both buildings thoughtfully.

"What you thinking?" Reno asked.

"If O'Rourke was one of the aldermen of this town, why would Warren have his son throw him out the window?"

Reno shrugged. "To get you into a brawl. Figured his boy could whip you."

"Figured wrong, he did," Mix Range said.

Colter shook his head. "Easier ways to draw me into a fight. That might be Warren's way of telling O'Rourke that he's been tossed out . . . of the business . . . the real business of Violence." He looked over at Slade's. "Which would give Slade reason to make a move."

"What kind of move?" Reno asked.

"Take over O'Rourke's," Colter said. "You control the gambling, the prostitution, and the drinking in this town."

"What does Warren get out of that?"

"One less rival. Only one bug he needs to crush under his boot heel."

Mix Range stepped on another locust, which caused Reno and Colter to laugh. Range looked at the bottom of his boot, and then picked up the mashed bug with his fingers, staring at it.

"Good eating," Reno said. "Grasshoppers."

Range made a face.

"Crunchy. Like the skin of fried chicken, fried long and hard and greasy and good. Always liked that when I was a little boy, but can't recollect the last time I ever ate chicken. But grasshopper. Ate that regular when game was scarce."

Range tossed the dead bug's remains onto the street, and wiped his fingers on his pants leg. "You really et bugs?"

"Sure. Injuns taught me how. It's good for you. Not bad tasting, neither, though it takes some getting used to. And I knew some Injuns, and they'd have their boys learn to shoot arrows at grasshoppers. Good practice. Takes a lot of skill with a bow and arrow to hit a grasshopper that's leaping off a leaf."

"There's been a lot of these bugs lately," Range said.

"Yeah," Reno agreed. "More than usual."

"I think," Colter reminded his two deputies, "that we have more pressing concerns than locusts."

They walked down the boardwalk to the eastern edge of town, crossed Union Street, and began working their way west on the north side of the street.

"If Slade's planning on making a play," Reno said, "he'd need to get rid of you."

Colter nodded. "Which would make Clint Warren happy, too."

"But how would he go about doing it?" Mix Range asked.

"We'll find out," Colter answered, and drew the LeMat to check the loads. He kept the gun out as he walked past Slade's Saloon.

Colter was up early the next morning, and busied himself filling out more paperwork while listening for Mayor Jasper Monroe to arrive next door. Nine o'clock came, and still the mayor was not there. Nine-thirty. Ten.

Setting his pencil down on the desktop, he pushed back his chair, grabbed the tin cup of coffee, and sipped while he thought.

Warren would not have killed Monroe. Not yet. A mercantile owner who handled the mail—even if Duncan Gates had a stake with the land office in Violence—and a freedman who helped a barber and undertaker—men like that would not be missed in a town like this. But kill the mayor of a town backed by the Union Pacific? No. Not yet.

"I hope," Colter said aloud.

The train whistle blew. That would be the eastbound,

moving down to Cheyenne. Which gave Tim Colter more pause.

What if I scared Monroe too much? he thought. *Would he pack his bags and hightail it back to civilization? Get out while he was still alive? Run like hell from a crazed butcher like Clint Warren?*

It made more sense, Colter realized, than Clint Warren killing Jasper Monroe.

He heard the bells, whistles, and steam from the locomotive, the creaking of the engine and its rolling stock as it pushed out from the depot, grunting, chugging, building up steam, and speed, a mechanical but oddly musical sound that, to Colter's surprise, he actually enjoyed. A man could get used to working in a railroad town, if that town ever became even moderately civilized. Colter did not think that would ever happen in a town like Violence.

Reports on his desk told him that the U.P. brass in Council Bluffs, Iowa, was already frowning upon this railroad stop of Violet, alias Violence. Cheyenne was booming to the east, and Laramie City kept growing to the west. Violence was caught in the middle, and beginning to feel the squeeze.

It could not survive. It did not need to survive. What it needed, Colter realized, was an Old Testament purging. Let the walls of Violence come tumbling down.

Finishing the coffee, he took up the pencil again, and began sorting through the paperwork, checking off what he needed, scratching through items, making notes, and every now and then replacing pencil with pen, when he needed to write something official or sign his name on a document or writ.

It was pushing noon. Reno would be off on a scout, probably making his way back to Violence. Mix Range should be checking on the prisoners in the corral. Mayor

Jasper Monroe still had not come to work. Colter's stomach growled. He thought maybe he would walk over to the schoolhouse, and share his dinner with Betsy McDonnell. That's where he was going when the door burst in.

"They took her!" cried one of the ragamuffin schoolkids.

"Took who?" Colter asked. Two more children came inside, all red-eyed from crying, and Mrs. Sien Slootmaekers squeezed through them, and starting talking—more like yelling. She had been crying, too, but Mrs. Slootmaekers was so stirred up, so shaken, so desperate, she kept speaking in Flemish.

Colter asked the biggest girl among the children to tell him what had happened.

All the girl did was just wail; and the louder Mrs. Slootmaekers spoke, the more the girl cried.

It was then that Mix Range staggered inside, holding his bleeding head.

"Marshal," he said, his face contorted in pain. "Tried to stop . . . them . . . bas—"

He collapsed in Colter's arms.

Knowing, but dreading, what had happened, Colter eased Range to the chair behind the desk.

"Where's Betsy?" Colter asked.

"They took her," said one of the children. Colter looked at Range, whose head nodded, and then Colter turned toward the girl who could speak English.

"Where?"

"They took her," the girl said. She pointed, but she was pointing toward the school.

"Two . . . men . . ." Mrs. Sien Slootmaekers had stopped yelling, and remembered just enough English. She pointed at Mix Range. "He try . . . help . . . but . . . clonk on head."

He had heard enough. Seeing Jed Reno's Colt in Mix Range's waistband, he pulled it out, checked the loads, and shoved it inside his belt near the small of his back.

Then he moved to the gun case Mix Range had built, and withdrew a Henry rifle, jacking a load into the chamber.

"One man . . . no hair," a new kid said. "But had funny glasses. Dark."

"*Ja,*" agreed Mrs. Sien Slootmaekers, nodding her head.

"Other . . . ," the first girl said. "Two . . ." She pointed at the Colt revolver. "In . . ." She made a motion of tying something around her waist.

"*Ja,*" said the girl who had been crying most of the time.

"I'm comin' with . . ." Mix Range tried to stand, only to fall back heavily into the chair.

"Stay put," Colter ordered. "Mrs. Slootmaekers, you get these kids back to the schoolhouse." Not that it was a schoolhouse, just some tents and the cleaned-out sod part of Reno's old trading post. "Get there. Stay there."

He left the office, and stepped onto the street, looking down at Paddy O'Rourke's Blarney Stone.

A baldheaded man with shaded glasses. And another man with a pair of Colts—Navy Colts, Colter remembered—stuck inside a sash. Those were two of the gamblers who worked for Paddy O'Rourke.

"Saw 'em," Mix Range confirmed, wincing in obvious pain. "Took Miss Betsy through . . . the front door . . . of . . . Blarney Stone."

"Said . . . ," Mrs. Slootmaekers said deliberately, enunciating the few English words she knew, "to come get her yourself."

So it was O'Rourke—and not Micah Slade—who had started the ball.

CHAPTER 38

Keeping the Henry rifle in front of him, finger in the trigger guard, hammer cocked, Tim Colter moved down the boardwalk, keeping an eye on the south side of Front Street. The people on the north boardwalk quickly disappeared. So did a few on the south side.

Not all of them, however. Some seemed not to have noticed him, moving carefully but with an intense purpose. A farmer pointed. A woman shielded her eyes. They stared off to the north and east, focusing on something. A few others farther down the street, well past The Blarney Stone, did the same.

A few words reached Colter, even though the wind was blowing hard from the north.

"What is that?"

"Cloud."

Down the road, behind Colter, a woman screamed. Another person yelled something, but Colter could only catch three words. "End . . . world . . . *Pray!*"

He would have to cross the street. Colter knew that. And if Micah Slade and some of his boys were in Slade's Saloon, they might open fire—if that had been Slade's plan to kill Colter, and wipe out O'Rourke. Now, as he moved closer toward the saloon and the gambling den across the street, more people began to notice him. And those people quickly disappeared. Toward the depot, though, railroaders were pointing north, too, and at the sky.

"Storm," someone said.

"But . . . what . . . kind?"

He had made it to the edge of Slade's Saloon. Colter stared across the street. No lights shone inside the gambling hall, and by this time, the gambling element was getting ready for another long day. They would be shuffling cards, checking their loaded dice, making sure the roulette wheels knew where and when to stop. A few games of faro, keno, or poker would be just getting under way—some of those not to end until twelve to sixteen hours later.

First he checked the roofs of The Blarney Stone and the neighboring buildings, and even down the street toward the livery stable. He focused on the windows and the door. Next, using the wooden support column for cover, he looked at Slade's Saloon. Inside came the clinking of glass, boots on the floor, laughter, conversation, and even the ping of tobacco hitting the insides of a spittoon. Normal noises. Unlike the stillness and quiet from The Blarney Stone. No one could be seen near the windows or batwing doors, but Colter couldn't see the rooftop of the saloon from where he stood. He wet his lips, looked west, then east, and finally stepped off the boardwalk, away from the wooden column, and made his way across Union Street.

His ears strained for any sound behind him: the metallic click of a gun being cocked, the pops of knee joints as a man might rise, or the squeaking of boards or thumping of boots. All he could hear, however, was his own breaths, his own heartbeat, and the dull murmurs of conversation.

Colter came along the side of The Blarney Stone. He braced his back against the plank sides, and now studied the rooftop of Slade's Saloon and the neighboring businesses. His mouth fell open, and he breathed in deeply, staring in amazement.

Dark clouds moved across the horizon with a wild intensity. Tornado? He shook his head. Not here. Not in this country. He had never heard of a twister ripping through here. Now he knew what had drawn the attention of those farmers and others in this town. He realized it was more than just one cloud. He could count six. Brown and large, moving oddly, from the inside.

Others were stepping off the north side of the boardwalk now, standing in the street, pointing at those odd clouds.

Colter understood. Old Testament. All those locusts he had seen. A swarm of locusts was coming to Violence like some plague summoned by the Almighty. But Colter did not care about that right now. Inside The Blarney Stone was Betsy McDonnell.

He moved then, kicked through the batwing doors, and dived to his right.

A gunshot roared. Colter felt the bullet slam into the wooden floor near him. He rolled again, knocking over a circular table that would allow him some protection. Two bullets hit the table, but did not penetrate the thick wood. Colter guessed those shots came from the Navy Colts. A rifle slug would have torn through the wood. His ears rang from the noise.

"Colter!"

He recognized Paddy O'Rourke's nasal brogue. He did not answer.

"I can kill this woman, Colter. Blow her damned brains out."

Holding a deep breath for the longest time, Tim Colter finally exhaled. Now he could hear the screams of people outside as the swarm of locusts descended upon Violence. He was taking a chance, a desperate chance.

"What the hell?" said one of O'Rourke's gunmen.

"It's the end of days, O'Rourke," Colter said. "Go ahead and kill Betsy. Because we're all about to die."

Locusts slammed into the windows that had not been busted during recent gunfights, fistfights, or O'Rourke's brawl with Brod Warren. Some came inside, *clicking, clicking, clicking,* and for a moment, even Tim Colter feared that this, indeed, was the beginning of the end, that God had looked down on Violence and, disgusted with this wickedness, had decided that the walls would come tumbling down.

Footsteps sounded, and Colter watched the baldheaded gambler move to the doorway, holding his revolver in his right hand, the barrel pointed down.

The man's face paled, and he turned around, dropping the gun. "My God," he said—and a second later, a bullet slammed through his body, his chest exploding crimson, and he was hurled fifteen feet before he landed on top of a poker table, which crashed underneath his weight.

This wasn't what Colter had expected. What anyone would have guessed.

Micah Slade and his three gunmen stormed through the batwing doors. Slade either did not care about the swarm of insects terrifying most of the residents of Violence, or he had seen such incidents before. It was not that uncommon. Even Jed Reno had told stories about clouds of insects, devouring anything green. But Slade could not have picked a worse time to attempt to take over the town and kill O'Rourke.

Colter might have talked some sense into O'Rourke, gotten Betsy out of here alive. Now . . . it was a free-for-all.

One of the gunmen saw Colter, and whirled, thumbing back the hammer on his Remington. Colter shot him in the chest, and the man, already dead, fell against Slade's gunman with the shotgun. Lucky? Or God's grace? Colter couldn't tell, but he let out a quick prayer, because the shotgun-toting killer had been pointing the double-barrel cannon at the banister, where O'Rourke stood with Betsy.

Instead, Slade's man touched off the shotgun as he was being pushed aside by the man Colter had just killed—and both barrels of double-ought buckshot ripped through the legs of another one of Slade's men.

The man let out a horrific scream as he fell.

Colter moved now, coming up, looking up toward Betsy and O'Rourke. Betsy was no prim and proper lady, nor was she a defenseless woman. Taking advantage of O'Rourke's shock, she had knocked the Colt from his grip, and now tore at his face with her fingernails. He backed up, and she tripped him. Down he went, tumbling over the stairs.

Micah Slade saw this, and shot once, twice, but locusts buzzed past him, spoiling his aim. He swatted at the bugs, stepping back and cursing.

The two-gunned gambler came up from behind a roulette wheel, and shot once.

The man whose legs had been blown apart by the two barrels of buckshot no longer screamed. The gambler fired the Navy .36 in his left hand at Slade's third killer. The Colt in his right spat a bullet toward Slade himself. Both shots missed.

Slade brought his revolver up, and snapped a shot at the man behind the bar. The mirror behind the back bar and a bottle of bourbon exploded. Slade saw movement, spun, and aimed at the stairs. He saw Betsy racing down the stairs, but the barrel of his revolver followed her anyway. So Tim Colter shot him.

Slade spun around, dropped to his knees, and cursed. He still gripped his revolver, and tried to snap a shot at Colter. But O'Rourke's man at the bar put a .36-caliber slug in Slade's throat, and the man dropped to the floor, with blood pulsing from the wound three or four times before stopping completely.

Micah Slade was dead.

But this gunfight was far from being over.

"Betsy!" Colter yelled. "Get down!"

He had to duck. The O'Rourke man and the last of Slade's killers sent bullets thudding against the table. Colter moved away, rolled over a couple of locusts. Another bullet shattered a window, and that shot came from the outside. Colter wasn't sure what was going on outside, if people were in such a panic that they were shooting at locusts, or if something else was going on.

He didn't care. He had to focus on one thing right now, which was getting Betsy McDonnell out of this firefight alive.

Another man busted through the batwing doors. Colter turned, held his fire, not sure who it was. The O'Rourke gambler with the twin Navies did not, and both of his guns belched fire, lead, smoke, and death. The man fell against the boards that covered what once had been a fine plate-glass window. He held there long enough for the gambler to send another shot into the man's chest. Then he dropped to the floor.

Instantly the Slade man sent two shots toward the bar. The first one splintered the fine mahogany top. The second slammed into a lantern, which sprayed kerosene and fire across the bar. The fire quickly spread, fueled by spilled liquor and kerosene.

Another man yelled something near the batwing door. Colter saw him, working the lever on his Henry rifle, firing quickly, but not at anyone inside The Blarney Stone. He was shooting at some target down the west side of Union Street. Whoever he was shooting at was shooting back. The man was lifted by a bullet in his gut, and he fell through the doors.

With the Henry, Colter shot the O'Rourke man behind the bar. He slammed against the bar, and his clothes erupted in flames. The man screamed once, before the Slade man put a bullet in his forehead. The Slade man turned then, aiming at Colter, but Paddy O'Rourke shot him dead.

O'Rourke came up now. So did Colter. But Tim quickly lowered the Henry.

Paddy O'Rourke was standing at the foot of the stairs. His big right hand held Betsy McDonnell around the waist, while his other hand held a pistol, the barrel pressing deep into the flesh under Betsy's jaw.

"I'll blow her bloody brains out, Colter!" O'Rourke screamed.

Fire spread across the bar, up the wall. Smoke began filling the gambling parlor. Colter glanced upstairs, but heard no noise. Apparently, the prostitutes who worked in those rooms had been told to leave until this little shebang was over.

"Drop that rifle, Colter," O'Rourke barked.

"Don't do—" Betsy started, but the barrel of the pistol pushed her head back, and she stopped.

Flames leaped up curtains, raced toward the second story. This place was like a tinderbox.

"I'm walking out of here, Colter," the gambler said. "You're staying here. If I see you outside, she's dead." He smiled at the inferno, which quickly intensified. "Welcome to Hell, Marshal. Enjoy your stay."

"This is your place, Paddy," Colter tried. "If it—"

"I have Micah's place across the street now," the gambler said.

He moved out. Colter turned to watch, but made no other move. Keeping Betsy McDonnell as his shield in front of him, O'Rourke carefully stepped over the dead man at the entranceway, and pushed through the batwing doors.

Almost immediately the man was screaming, and Betsy was falling to the boardwalk. Colter rushed outside, seeing Paddy O'Rourke dancing some macabre waltz, off the boardwalk, onto the middle of Union Street. Colter came out, the LeMat in his hand, seeing everything in front of him, and Betsy rolling herself up into a ball, her back against The Blarney Stone's wall. Three other men lay dead in the street; and standing at the northwest corner, Hawken rifle in his arms, was Jed Reno. On the southwest side, Mix Range, his head no longer bleeding, stood with a Spencer repeater. Colter spotted another dead man, hanging halfway over the balcony of Slade's Saloon. So Reno and Range had taken care of the other assassins, Slade and O'Rourke men.

Now, in the middle of Union Street, Paddy O'Rourke danced, spinning, screaming. The pistol belched once. The Irishman wore his green coat, and the locusts had attacked it without mercy. The coat appeared alive as the insects ate the green-dyed thread, devouring it.

Violence had indeed turned into some Old Testament Hell.

The gambler finally stopped spinning, and brought the pistol up. That's when Mrs. Sien Slootmaekers shot him in the head with a Mississippi Rifle. The large-caliber ball tore through Paddy O'Rourke's skull, and blew out what remained of his brains. The man fell, instantly dead, and the locusts flocked back onto the green coat.

CHAPTER 39

Some towns, Tim Colter believed, had to be worth saving.

Violence was not one of them.

The locusts moved on, carried by the wind, and by grass and shrubs and anything green that they could eat. Betsy McDonnell had been wearing a green-striped dress that day. By the time she sat in Tim Colter's office, the dress hung in threads, the white remaining, the green gone.

Like most of the hills and all the land surrounding the town of Violence. Until the wind had blown on toward the south, thousands, perhaps millions, of locusts had devoured the grass, leaving the country for greener pastures—as the saying went—and reducing this part of the territory into nothing but dirt and the remnants, the leafless branches of scrub and brush. When the wind blew—and the wind always blew—dust peppered the sky.

A week after, as *Harper's Weekly* eventually would call it, "The Last Fight Of Violence," trains no longer stopped in Violet, Idaho Territory, formerly Dakota Territory, soon-to-be Wyoming Territory. The U.P. supplies had been rerouted to either Cheyenne or Laramie City. Most of the businessmen—those that had not been on the same side of Union Street and on the same block as The Blarney Stone (for the south side of that block was now ashes)—had packed up their valuables and moved on.

By the middle of August, the only buildings left standing—for scrap lumber usually proved hard to find in this country—were Aloysius Murden's land office, the marshal's office (it came in handy to have a solid deputy who knew his way around hammer and nail), and what had been the schoolhouse and before that Jed Reno's trading post, or what remained of that.

On this hot, dry day, a few Union Pacific railroaders had returned to the town of Violence, loading up the remaining supplies at the abandoned depot to deliver them to the points west, where the end of track lay . . . for the time being . . . for the U.P.'s side of the glorious transcontinental railroad.

Mayor Jasper Monroe was gone. Some people said he ran away on an eastbound train. Others claimed to have seen him riding a mule southeast, toward Denver City down in the Colorado country. A few said he had been killed by Indians. Or had fled west. Or had been carried away by millions of locusts.

Jed Reno kept asking Tim Colter why he stayed here. He should be taking his bride-to-be back to Oregon, or at least to Boise City—the territorial capital—but Colter said he knew what he was doing. He was waiting. He had one final job to do in Violence.

And on August 30, 1868, that came to pass.

Clint Warren rode down empty Union Street, and stopped in front of the marshal's office. Grinning widely, he swung down from the saddle and walked to what remained of the boardwalk. Deputy United States Marshal Tim Colter sat outside, leaning back in his chair, whittling.

"Afternoon, Colter," the rancher said.

"Howdy." Colter focused on trimming that little piece of pine into a toothpick.

"Town sure has changed, hasn't it?" the rancher said.

"It's quiet now," Colter said. "Peaceful."

"Where's your posse, boy?"

Colter folded the knife blade, and stuck the Barlow knife into his vest pocket. He examined his toothpick, seemed satisfied, and stuck it in his mouth, moving it from the left side to the right.

"Reno took Betsy to Clear Creek," Colter answered.

"And that man-killer you pinned a badge on?"

Colter studied the rancher. "Oh, you mean Mix Range? Well, I heard Texas had sent a peace officer up here looking for him. So I sent Mix to the territorial capital."

The big rancher leaned against the column. "I won, boy. This'll be the biggest shipping yard in Idaho Territory, come next year. I'll make that Abilene town look like nothin'. Cattle will be shippin' east with my brand. An' I'll be richer than God."

Dust blew, turning the blue sky into an ugly beige.

"Last I heard, Clint," Colter said, "even Texas longhorns need to eat." He pointed at the barren land.

But Clint Warren only laughed. "I had my three boys drive the herd south. North of Denver City. Grass'll return next spring, Colter, and you know that. Maybe even richer than it is now. And when it's back, all this land—all of it—will be mine."

"What about the farmers?" Colter asked.

The big rancher turned around to spit in the dirt. After wiping his mouth, he stepped off the boardwalk, went to his horse, and opened one of the saddlebags. He pulled out a handful of papers and stepped back onto the boardwalk. He held out his booty toward Colter, who again shifted the toothpick, and plucked out one paper.

"See for yerself, Marshal," the rancher said.

Oh, Tim Colter knew what he held. He had been waiting for days for Warren to ride in. Aloysius Murden had

met with all of those poor Flemish farmers, and had settled their affairs. Beaten by the land—or a plague of grass-
hoppers and locusts and the brutality of nature in this wild
country—the farmers had loaded their wagons with what
remained of their fortunes. Some had boarded eastbound
trains, before the trains stopped their regular stops in Violence. Most had driven off to the east, to Nebraska or
Kansas. A few had pushed south toward the Purgatoire
River in the Colorado country. Many had decided to try
Oregon, maybe Washington, or maybe California to the
west. And several had said they would go back to Boston,
Massachusetts, and then maybe see about finding a way
back home.

Even Mrs. Sien Slootmaekers was gone, with her husband and her late son's baby sister, back east. Exactly
where, Tim Colter did not know. But he wished the family
peace, and the best of luck.

"You can read, boy," Clint Warren said. "All this land is
mine now. All of it. I bought out them dumb-oaf foreigners,
the idiot plow-pushers. I told you I'd win. And I won."

Colter looked at the big man's hands. He wore no
gloves on this day, and scars covered those hands, the misshapen knuckles, the bent joints, and stiff fingers.

Colter looked at the document he held, and then, with a
wry grin, he returned the piece of paper to Clint Warren.

"You and Aloysius Murden make a fine pair," Colter
said. After a short whistle, he rocked again on his chair. "I
thought Jasper Monroe was your main man, till he ran out
of here. So it was that fat man from Boston all this time."
Colter's head shook. "Never really considered him for
that."

"For what?" Warren demanded.

"For being that smart."

Actually, Tim Colter had pegged Murden for the rancher's
primary partner after Mr. Yost fled town after the locust dis-

aster and started a boarding house in Laramie City. Murden was the only one left, and Colter had arrested him two days ago.

Warren lurched forward, and his hands clenched into massive fists. "What you talkin' 'bout, boy. I'm the smart one. I got all them claims. All that land . . . it's mine . . . now."

Now was the time. Tim Colter stopped rocking. He let the legs of the chair rest on the wooden planks, and his head tilted up at the big brute of a rancher.

"Clint," he said easily, "I'm going to give you a lesson. About the Homestead Act of 1862."

Now the rancher looked like the imbecile he was.

"Any citizen of the United States of America," Colter said, "or even an intended citizen can get for his own one hundred and sixty acres."

"That's right." The big man's head bobbed. "And there was a passel of them foreign-tongued sodbusters."

Tim Colter gave the rancher that much with an agreeable nod. "All the man has to do is live on the land, make a few improvements—like building a twelve-by-fourteen home . . . and grow some crops." Colter waited. Warren just grinned. "There seems to be some oversight in that department, by the way."

Now Warren's eyes narrowed, as did that smile.

"Twelve by fourteen, I mean," Colter said. "Is that feet? Inches? Yards? Miles wouldn't make sense. Anyway." Colter waved his left hand in a dismissive gesture. "That part doesn't really matter."

Warren wet his lips.

"The big part is this," Colter said. "Then in five years, the homesteader can file for his patent—basically, that's what you'd call a deed, or a deed of title—show his proof of residency, the improvements that are required by President Abraham Lincoln's law to the local land office. That would be Mr. Murden's land office."

"Yeah," Warren said.

"All the claimant has to do is," Colter said, "once the land agent . . . or the investigator for the General Land Office . . . has signed off on everything . . . is pay a small fee to record everything. Or he could do that after . . . hmmmm . . . I think only six months, but he'd have to pay a dollar and twenty-five cents per acre. That's two hundred bucks. Pretty good chunk of money for most farmers. After that, the land's all his. Free for him to keep farming. Or sell. Pretty good deal. Wasn't anything like that when my folks left Danville, Pennsylvania."

Clint Warren laughed. "And that's what I'm doin', Marshal. I'm takin' over them dumb-arse foreigners' claims. So all this land . . . well . . . it's mine. I told you I'd win, Colter. And I've won. I told you this wasn't farm country. It's cattle country. And next spring, that's all you're gonna see around here. Cattle. Longhorn cattle. Wearin' my brand."

Colter pushed himself out of the chair.

"That's where you're wrong, Clint." Now it was Tim Colter's turn to smile. "You overlooked two critical items about the late president's Act of 1862. First, the farmers have to stay on this land for five years. You're probably four, maybe four and a half, short. After all, those 'sodbusters,' as you call them, weren't even here for six months."

Clint Warren ground his teeth.

"And there's one other thing. You're from Texas, right?"

"Damn right I am," Warren snapped.

"Bet you fought for the Union during the Rebellion?"

"You are damned right. I was—but then I switched to the gray, bucko."

"Well, there's one other thing about the Homestead Act, Clint," Colter said, staying calm. "It stipulates that it's open to anyone who has *never raised arms against the U.S. government.* That's why you see freedmen and foreigners—those who intend to become citizens of the United States of America—applying for homesteads. And not a bunch of Rebels like you."

Colter waited until the big man's weak brain could comprehend what he had just been told.

Shaking his head with a wry laugh, Colter brought his hands to his hips. "I swear, Clint, this caught me by surprise, too. I never figured . . . of all people, you . . . you would be played for a fool—hook, line, and sinker—the way that fat Yankee, Aloysius Murden, just played you."

Colter pointed at the papers still clutched in Warren's massive hands.

"How much did you pay Murden for those papers, Clint? Papers that are utterly worthless to you?"

The big man roared with rage, and stormed onto what had once been Union Street. He moved quickly for such a big man, making a beeline for the land agent's office. Tim Colter wore no gun that day, but now he darted inside his office, found the gun rig, and buckled it across his waist. He came out of his office, stepped onto Union Street, and walked toward the land office.

In front of the office, in the center of the deserted street, stood Clint Warren. One hand rested on the grip of the Army Colt in the holster on his hip. The other hand pointed at the door, with one crooked, massive finger extended.

"Murden, you miserable damned Yankee. Come out here, you gutless wonder, and I'll give you the same thing I gave to your stupid partner. Come out here, boy, and I'll stomp you into oblivion . . . just like I done to Gates."

"And Eugene Harker?" Colter called out behind him.

The rancher's rage was so intense, the damned fool answered.

"Just like that uppity Negro."

The door opened, but the man who stepped outside was

not fat, foolish Aloysius Murden. In fact, two men stepped out. One was Jed Reno. The other was Mix Range.

The rancher stepped back, turning in surprise toward a smiling Tim Colter.

"Witnesses for your confession, Clint," Tim Colter said. "Not that we needed it. Murden already confessed. We were just waiting for you to come to town. So that you could talk yourself onto the gallows."

Clint Warren took two steps back. He looked at Colter, then back at Reno and Range. Then he ran.

CHAPTER 40

For such a big, brutal man, the man who ran the town of Violence moved like the wind. Maybe it was fear that drove him, but Clint Warren had a healthy head start. He bolted across the street, and angled toward the depot. Tim Colter, leaving his LeMat holstered, went after him, and did not look back toward Reno or Range.

Warren drew his revolver, barking out orders. Most of the railroaders merely raised their hands. Two leaped off a handcar, and Warren showed some amazing prowess when he leaped onto the cart. Rolling over, he snapped off one shot at Tim Colter, but the bullet spanged harmlessly off a pile of ruined rails.

The big rancher came up, fired again—this bullet sailed well over Colter's head—and then the man reached for the pump, pushing the handle down, then letting it rise upward, to push it again. The cart moved, westward, toward Laramie City. Clint Warren was a big man, and soon he had the cart moving at a pretty good clip. By then, Tim Colter stood on the rails, watching the fast-moving cart move away, far away, from the long arm of the law.

Cursing, Colter looked behind him as Jed Reno and Mix Range ran toward him. Then an Irish voice sang out, "Here, Marshal . . . with our compliments."

The railroaders pushed another cart down the rails, the hand-pump moving up and down at a fast rate, and Colter moved alongside the track, picking up his pace, shoving the LeMat into its holster. He had barely enough time to glance back at Reno and Range. The distance was too far, Colter thought. They would never catch up with him in time, so he had to leave them behind. He ran closer to the rails, reached up, and leaped, grabbing hold of an iron tie-down, and pulled himself onto the cart.

Turning back toward his deputies, he shouted, "Get your horses! Get your horses!" Seconds later, he was at the pump, working the heavy iron bar, up and down.

Up and down.

Up and down.

Up and down.

Violence was soon behind him. A wild killer who needed to hang was in front of him.

They sped across the locust-devoured landscape. Moving west. Moving fast. Moving far past what once had been a town.

Ahead of him, Clint Warren turned, letting the pump move up and down. The big man drew his pistol, eared back the hammer, and squeezed the trigger. The bullet did not come close.

Tim Colter drew the LeMat, but he knew better than to waste lead. Jed Reno had taught him better than that, so he shoved the big revolver back inside the leather, and kept working the lever.

Down and up.

Down and up.

Down and up.

He wondered about the odds. A lawman, pursuing a felon, on a railroad handcar—for the second time in weeks. How often could that happen? Had it ever happened? He might make the *National Police Gazette*.

Wind . . . that omnipresent wind . . . whipped his face. He kept moving, working the lever, looking ahead of him. Warren snapped another shot. This time, Colter heard the bullet whine off a boulder to his left. That's when Clint Warren understood that the lawman was gaining on him. He shoved the pistol inside his waistband, and returned to work the iron contraption that made the handcar roll.

They crossed the first trestle, a small one.

Colter felt the rough iron bar bite into his palms, his fingers, putting calluses atop his calluses. He looked back toward the town that had once been Violence. He couldn't see either Jed Reno or Mix Range, and he wondered how long it would take them to saddle their mounts. Then he focused on the man running from him. He worked the iron bars, up and down, down and up. His muscles ached. He strained, gritting his teeth, pushing the heavy bar.

The cart picked up speed. But so did the one Clint Warren drove.

Colter remembered. The last time he had chased an outlaw with a handcar, he had lucked out because Indians had destroyed a bridge. But they had crossed the one trestle, and Colter knew the U.P. crews had quickly repaired that burned bridge. Yet, now he noticed something off to the north and south. White puffs of smoke. Indian signs. But what could that mean? Again, he took a brief moment to look behind him, searching for dust that meant horses galloping after him, horses that would be ridden by Jed Reno and Mix Range.

A gunshot exploded, and the bullet whirred past Colter's left ear. Closer than he would have guessed. He ducked, worked the bar, and saw that only fifty or sixty yards separated him from the crazed, brutal killer named Clint Warren. Colter drew the big LeMat from its holster. He stepped away from the pumping lever, dropped to a knee to steady himself, and squeezed the trigger.

The bullet might have missed, but it sure drew the attention of Clint Warren. He spun around, and snapped a shot from his own pistol. And then the handcar disappeared in a cloud of dust—dust because the swarm of locusts had reduced this country into a bowl of nothing but earth, without any grass or anything that could nourish a locust.

Colter blinked, trying to comprehend. Quickly he realized that the heavy iron rails had been pulled apart, as though someone had decided that this was the best way to stop a train. He saw the handcar he had been chasing, laying on its side, maybe a quarter buried underneath the dirt. That made him smile—at least, until another thought struck him.

His handcar was following that same path.

He stepped back from the pump, desperately looking for some brake. Something that might stop the cart he was on from leaving the rails and crashing into the earth. He had yet to figure that part out. The last time he had ridden a handcar, it, too, had flown into oblivion, descending to crash upon boulders and earth and two would-be train robbers.

There was no time to find a brake, a lever, or some damned parachute. So Tim Colter leaped off the side of the handcar just a few moments before it left the rails and slammed into bare earth.

He hit hard, rolled over, and felt the soil rip through his shirt, tearing his skin, leaving him dizzy and aching as he rolled and rolled and rolled. Then he was up, on his knees, and grasping for the LeMat.

Only the big revolver was no longer there. He must have lost it during his rolling and tumbling. Through the dust, through the blurring of his vision, he could just make out the big man. Colter tried for the Barlow knife in the pocket of his pants, but he knew he would be too late. He knew he could not stop Clint Warren.

The big man no longer had a revolver, either, and his nose was busted, and a big gash stretched across his forehead. The right sleeve of his shirt hung in tatters, and his knee was bleeding. Blood spilled from his mangled lips. Yet, the man's face remained intense, and intimidating.

"I'll kill you . . . ," Warren began. "I'll tear you from limb to limb."

And Clint Warren might have done just that. Except an arrow suddenly appeared in his stomach, quivering from the force of impact, buried almost to the feathers on the shaft. The big man stopped, and looked down at the slim piece of ash. His eyes began to glaze. Still, he took another step.

That's when an arrow hit him just above the knee. Another arrow caught his left leg. And two more arrows hit the backs of both legs.

Clint Warren fell to his knees.

He looked to his left, and then his right, and then his eyes found an equally stunned Tim Colter.

"What?" the crazed rancher asked.

Seven more arrows riddled his body. And Clint Warren fell onto his back.

Rough hands instantly jerked Tim Colter to his feet. A knife blade bit into his throat. His nose caught the scent of pemmican and sweat and dye and grease and buffalo.

A voice barked. The knife withdrew from his throat, and Colter felt himself pushed back onto the sod. His eyes opened. He brushed the dirt and grime off his lips, and he stared into a pair of black eyes.

"We are even, white man," the Cheyenne warrior Red Prairie barked in English.

And the Indians, maybe a dozen of them, were gone, just two or three minutes before Jed Reno and Mix Range galloped up.

CHAPTER 41

"Well?" Jed Reno asked. "It sure ain't much to look at."

Tim Colter looked down Union Street. He brought the bottle of white wine—rescued from Paddy O'Rourke's place—and passed the wine to Betsy McDonnell. She didn't even wipe off the mouth of the bottle before she drank. Nor did Jed Reno when Betsy passed the bottle to him.

"But I do like the view." Reno tossed the bottle to Mix Range. "No people to spoil this country," the old mountain man said. "And once all that wood is burned this winter, and the grass grows up again next spring, it'll be prime country."

"There's still the railroad," Mix Range said.

Reno shrugged. "Can't have everything, I guess." He turned toward Betsy. "What do you think, ma'am? Looking better. I mean, I figure you miss them kids, but they never would have made a home in this land. Just ain't farming country."

"Maybe," Betsy said. "But it might be a home . . . for us." She leaned against Tim Colter's shoulder, and Colter kissed her head.

Mix Range burped. "Sure is quiet," he said.

Tim Colter laughed. "Well," he said, "I've always wanted to live in a nice, quiet town."